SUBSPACES

Peter A. Luber

Sageous
New York
2017

Sageous
Amsterdam, NY 12010

First published in 2017
By Sageous

Copyright © Peter A. Luber, 2017
All rights reserved

Subspaces / Peter A. Luber
ISBN: 978-0-692-76412-1

Cover art by Lisa M. Luber
Illustrations by Lisa M. Luber

For Lisa:

Without whose unfailing support, this book, and the others, would not exist.

CONTENTS

No Trees

Joe kicked the pebble that lay in his path with unusual vigor. He was pissed. Who wouldn't be? There were no trees. None.

They weren't dead: this isn't some environmental Lorax bullshit saga. No, they weren't dead; just missing. Joe caught up to the hapless rock, kicked it again, hard. It sailed upward, arced off the driveway and onto the unkempt lawn to his right. His eyes followed the rock, causing an unwanted glance beyond the vicinity of his toes. The rolling Hudson Valley hills filled his raised horizon. Those hills had been carpeted in lush green life, the tall kind, as recently as the day before. Tuesday, he recalled. He allowed his gaze to linger long enough to confirm that the hills were carpeted in green life, only the short kind. Grass covered the hills. Hell, it might have always been there, but you couldn't see it for the trees. Now it was obvious, and nicely trimmed. A million acres of fresh cut lawn. He looked to his left. Nope. No trees there either. They were gone. Not even a stump. And damn it they were there the day before.

They were still there the night before, when Joe got home from work with his wife, Gloria. He distinctly remembered admiring the starry night through the rustling shadows of the old pear tree behind the garage. However, when he walked out to the car with Gloria that morning to wish her a good day (the trees would have to vacate on his day off), they noticed that something had changed. He had dismissed it as a sleep induced illusion by the time he went back to bed, but when he opened the heavy bedroom drapes at about noon, far too much light entered the room.

He reached the end of his formerly tree-lined driveway. His great grandfather apparently did not lovingly plant two carefully spaced rows of oaks 80 years before. He opened his mailbox, pulled out the day's bills. Hmm, he thought, trees're gone, but the bills still come. He wondered briefly where the paper came from, how it managed to survive, but really didn't care. Answers wouldn't bring back the trees. Seeds might, but he never could get a tree to grow from a seed. He spotted his neighbor and occasional friend Al. Al was, as always, meticulously caring for his lawn. Joe lifted a hand in mild greeting. Al spotted the gesture, shut off his weed-whacker. He didn't walk over.

"Afternoon, Joe," Al rumbled. Al didn't mean to rumble -- he was severely overweight, and he smoked three packs a day. But his yard was perfect.

"Hey," Joe managed, turning back toward his house.

"How 'bout those trees?" Al asked, looking at the hills, not Joe, when he casually phrased the question.

"Yeah Al. I noticed it too."

"It really sucks," Al said, shaking his head. He turned his back on the hills, flipped his weed whacker back on, continued over its incredibly annoying buzz, "Figures. Trees are gone, but there're still friggin weeds to whack. Really sucks."

"Sure does," Joe mumbled. He walked back into his house. The dark living room was cool, comforting. He tossed the mail on the coffee table with the rest, dropped into his recliner. He flipped open the arm, pulled out the controller. He turned on the TV, which was already tuned to CNN. Valerie Voss was on, predicting the weather. Valerie Voss was always on, predicting the weather. He had been witnessing her bright-eyed forecasts almost every day for a decade. They were growing old together.

Valerie finished up, cheerfully turning his set over to the co-anchors du jour. She outlived all the co-anchors, yet never got their job. Joe believed, because he had to, that her longevity was probably a sign of Valerie's virtue.

"Or talent," he said aloud while he waited for the segue banter to end and that (and every other) hour's headlines to be read. Surely they would cover the tree incident. The slightly cross-eyed female anchor spoke first, became the living caption of a picture behind her shoulder. Another candidate, she said, but he wouldn't last too long because of the hooker scandal a minor paper in the south had unearthed that morning. Oh well. They still hadn't found the truth behind that damn plane crash from last March, but something new was sure to come up soon.

She had nothing to say about the trees. The male anchor, who looked exactly like the rest of the male anchors (who all resembled Tom Brokaw), was looking at the wrong camera. His ear had nothing to say about the trees, either. His picture was an airplane crash in an Asian country Joe was sure had been absorbed by Russia in the 50's.

"Hmm," he said aloud, "maybe no one has called in about it yet."

He muted the TV -- no sense turning it off, he'd be back in a minute. He sat for a moment before summoning the energy to raise himself from the recliner. That was never easy. He crossed the carpeted living room to the kitchen. He paid a moment's respect to the sink full of dishes, then took the phone off the wall and activated it. He listened passively to the dial tone for a minute, and then pulled the phone away from his ear, looked at it.

"So who the hell do you call about this?" he asked aloud. In response the phone announced that he should hang up and try again. He agreed, set the phone back in its base. He pulled the phone book from its spot between two rarely touched cookbooks, sat on a kitchen chair and set about leafing.

He found the blue government pages, figuring to start at the Department of Agriculture and work his way backwards to the Four-H Club. He dialed the Department of Agriculture. It was busy. Well, that's a good sign, he thought. He grabbed a beer and chips from the refrigerator, clamped the phone book under his arm, and headed to the living room. Might as well be comfortable while I'm trying to get through, he thought.

Joe flopped into his chair. He shifted his weight backward to raise the footrest, and unconsciously smiled when the padded bar slid into place under his calves. He found the controller, turned up the volume on CNN. Noticing the time, he switched immediately to A&E. Columbo. It was one he had seen before, but he didn't care. After all he had a thing to do, didn't he? He set the controller on the arm of the chair, shaking his head as it dutifully slid away, clattering onto the hardwood floor (it never broke). Joe opened his beer and flicked the twist-off lid into the dining room with a snap of his fingers. Gloria hates it when I do that, he thought. Oh well, she won't be home for hours; I can pick it up later. Pick them up -- he could feel it was going to be another multiple-beer day. He took a long first swig, then hit redial. The other end began ringing immediately.

"Shit," Joe mumbled. He leaned forward to grab the controller. In the process he slammed the footrest home and launched several sips of beer from the bottle. He set the bottle on its coaster, dropped to the floor on his knees and scrabbled around for the controller, all without removing the phone from his ear. An old hand at this sport, he managed to find the controller and mute the TV before the third ring. He sat back again, drew his breath, and waited.

After 27 more rings, someone picked up.

"'Lo?" a baritone male voice inquired.

"Is this the Department of Agriculture?"

"Is."

"I was wondering if you could help me. You see, something seems to have happened to --"

"This regarding trees?"

"Yes. Yes it is." Joe was relieved; other people must be calling in too. He was also happy to have gotten his message across before the fellow on the other side fell asleep.

"Trees?" the voice asked again, more slowly.

"Yes, trees. You see --"

"Like forests?"

"Yeah," Joe said slowly, growing suspicious, "Like forests."

"Sorry. Can't help. Try Forestry." Click.

"Wait you don't--" Joe snapped before he heard the dial tone, "Understand. Fine." He took another sip of beer, found the listing for the Department of Forestry.

"Forestry. Duh," he said as he dialed the phone, "I should have thought of that. Hell, they're probably out looking for new jobs at this point." He finished dialing, was met with a busy signal. Good, he thought, back to Columbo. It was one of his favorites, the one where William Shatner was the murderer, and had picked excellent hair for the show. Joe had missed the murder again. He always missed the murder, and was equally pissed every time. He didn't bother trying to remember, happily opting instead to watch Columbo agitate the hell out of Captain Kirk. Joe didn't let the show overshadow his purpose: he hit redial with the next commercial break.

The phone at Forestry was still busy, but he could be persistent for at least another two minutes -- A&E ran a lot of commercials -- so he began turning the phone off and on, then poking the redial button with each new busy signal. This went on for the full two minutes, when he nearly hung up on a ring. He caught his finger in time, muted the TV, and waited for an answer. He sat up and glanced through a window to see if the trees were back yet. They were not. Someone picked up right when Columbo came back on. Well, something, he thought, as he recognized the telltale saccharine of a recorded voice:

"Hello," the female voice chirped, "And thank you for calling the New York State department of Forestry and Recreation. If you're calling from a touch-tone phone, please press `1' now. If you are not, please hold for the next available operator"

Joe pressed "1."

"If you'd like travel or tourism information, please press '1' now; if you'd like to report a fire, please press `2' now; if you need further information, please press `3' now."

Joe pressed `3.'

"Thank you. Please hold while we connect you with next available operator."

"And thank you for the chase," Joe said to Musak. He turned the volume on the TV back up, considered hanging up the phone instead of enduring an instrumental rendition of "Monday Monday", but the music stopped before he gave in.

"Park Service," a cheery young voice greeted him, "May I help you?"

"I sure hope so," Joe said, muting the TV just in time.

"Is there a problem sir? A fire? You could have pressed `2' to report a fire."

"Nope. There's no fire. Wouldn't matter if there was one anyway."

"Why sir?"

"You didn't notice the trees?"

"What trees?"

"That's what I said."

"Sir. You're going to have to be a bit more helpful. Is there a problem with the trees where you live?"

"There are no trees where I live."

"Then why are you calling me, sir?"

"Because there are no trees where I live," Joe said. He heard her sigh, perhaps preparing to hang up.

"There were yesterday, though," he added.

"Huh?" she asked, her attention piqued, "So then you are reporting a fire?"

"Nope."

"An aftermath?"

"Of sorts, I guess. There're just no trees."

"Where do you live, sir?"

"Cold Spring."

"Sir, there are plenty of trees in Cold Spring, and plenty of people. I think the fire would have been reported by now."

"What fire?"

"The one that took the trees."

"There was no fire. The trees are just gone."

Click.

Joe sighed, hung up the phone. He hoped the kids at the 4-H club would be friendly when he got to them. He checked the horizon once more, then grimly shut off the TV and settled down to dialing.

"There must be someone that would want to know about this," he said aloud, "Maybe I should just call the police and have them tell me who, or who not, to call." He almost dialed "911", but he figured it wasn't an emergency anymore, so he located and dialed the seven digit number. It rang immediately. Well, that's a relief, he thought.

It didn't stop ringing for five minutes. Finally it stopped.

"Police, can I help you?" a gruff cop voice snapped.

"God I hope so. Have you seen the trees?" Joe asked.

"What trees?" Oh, God, not again, Joe thought, slapping his palm against his forehead.

"The ones that aren't there anymore," he offered.

"Oh. Those trees. Yeah. We noticed. Is there something we can do for you sir?"

"What about the trees? Is anyone checking into their abduction?"

"Sorry sir. No one here is. I think it's the FBI's responsibility."

"The FBI?"

"Yessir."

"So you guys aren't looking into it all?'

"No sir."

"Did you alert anyone?"

"No sir; figure they'll catch on soon enough."

"Am I the only one who gives a shit about this?"

"Apparently sir, and please control your language. Now, if you'll please give me your name --"

My turn, Joe thought, as he pushed the phone's power button. It wasn't as much fun as slamming a receiver, but at least it was the police. He sat back in the recliner, deciding that if the police weren't interested, then he wouldn't be either. Jeez, he thought, I hope the cops don't have one of those electronic things that identify callers.

His community spirit driven from him, he grabbed the remote and clicked the TV back on. Who needs trees anyway, he thought, they just make fresh air and provide homes for birds, for God's sake. He hated birds. Flying rats, he had heard them called; really noisy flying rats, especially at dawn. He would be content to never experience the ubiquitous crows' screech every Saturday morning. It was the only sound more able to penetrate closed windows and the white noise of fans and air conditioners than the neighbor across the street's weed whacker. Columbo was over, and he absently surfed his 50 channels while he sipped his current beer and worried about the cops calling him back about his attitude. My attitude, he thought. Imagine.

He was prepared to surf the rest of the afternoon, nursing his annoyance at the bureaucratic world until Gloria got home from work. He probably should focus some annoyance at her as well. His wife of ten years had noticed the trees before she started her pre-dawn trudge, without him, to the train station. Her response to the climactic natural disaster was a sleepy shrug while she pecked Joe on the cheek and wished him a happy day off. Joe hadn't questioned her lackadaisical response to the arboreal terrorism. He noticed when she did, but there is nothing, nothing that should be discussed at that hour -- unless of course you were still up from the night before. Had that been the case, they would have been exchanging all manner of physical and biological theory to explain or dismiss the phenomenon. But they had been sleeping, so the missing trees rated about the same attention as the dripping faucet Joe was supposed to fix that day.

"Shit," Joe said, rolling his eyes, "I knew I forgot something. Oh well, I couldn't have been expected to remember such a small thing on such a momentous day." Moments after his discussion, the phone rang. A shiver traversed Joe's entire spine. He knew who it was, and it wasn't the cops. He considered letting it go through to the machine, but reluctantly turned on the phone. Gotta pick it up, he thought.

"Hullo?" he said, thinking he sounded sleepy.

"Hello, dear," Gloria greeted him cheerfully.

"Hi hon. I knew it would be you."

"You did? Why?"

"No reason. Just knew."

"Well then, I guess it's a good thing you picked up. Did you fix the faucet?"

"Um," think fast, rabbit, Joe thought, "No." Smooth!

"No?" Gloria said, sounding disappointed, "How come?"

Joe paused before he answered. He wanted to be careful with his response, because he knew how important repairing that faucet was. It was driving Gloria nuts. He had made the decision finally to fix it the weekend before, and interrupted the high-volume vitriolic monologue she was directing at the poor valve to tell her so. Now, on the day off he had taken partially to attend to it, he had forgotten. He knew Gloria wouldn't be angry, but that only made it worse. He smiled, though, because he had an excuse that might cool her emotions.

"Why, the trees, of course," he proposed.

"What trees?" Had she forgotten?

"You know, the ones that are missing. I was trying to do something about it."

"God," she said -- Joe could almost hear her run her hand through her long hair, "I forgot. No, I didn't forget, really. I just thought it was a dream, you know? And of course I fell asleep almost as soon as I sat down on the train, so I didn't get a chance to be reminded of it."

"Not even when you woke up?"

"Silly," she laughed. Thank God, he thought. She continued, "It would be a little hard to notice the trees are missing from Broadway."

"I guess there is that, but didn't you hear anyone discussing it?"

"Come to think of it, there was some talk on the train, but who listens? Plus, everyone I work with lives here. I doubt they'd know a tree if it fell on them."

"Look out your window," Joe suggested.

"Okay. I haven't done that yet anyway. Am I checking to see if our woods migrated to the city?"

"Nope. Just the opposite. Look down at the street. See any trees? There should be a few planted in the sidewalks in your neighborhood."

"Nope. Not a one. And you're right. I'm sure they used to be there. But..."

"But what?"

"But there're no big holes where they were; just smooth sidewalk. Like they were never there. This is too weird."

"Too," Joe agreed, "What about the gardens on the roofs around you?"

"Still plenty of gardens, but I'm sure there were trees there before. In fact, I know there were, because just the other day I was..."

"And you haven't heard anything on the news about them?" Joe interrupted. He sensed a story, so he changed the subject.

"No, I work for a living," she said, "And don't think I didn't notice what you just did!" Her tone wasn't harsh, but, snagged, he found a response.

"Notice what? You told me about that roof the other day."

"I did? Oh yeah, I remember. But it was cool, you know, the way they had those trees set up like a little forest, you know, with the dirt paths and all, on the --"

"Twentieth floor," Joe finished for her, "I know."

"You're so mean!" Gloria snapped playfully, "Anyway, you won't believe what the idiots in charge of this place did today..."

While they talked for the next twenty minutes, Joe sipped his beer and puttered around the house. He sometimes liked to wander the museum, as they called a small back room downstairs in which most people would park a playroom. Their spare room was wall-to-wall stuff. Good stuff: antiques, knickknacks, small sculptures, models. For a few years it had been a measure of their shared love of creativity and the unusual. Now it was just their stuff. He was absently noticing that the tree branch racing the cage of Rex, their iguana, was gone too, when Gloria noticed she was losing him.

"So. What are you doing right now?"

"Nothing. Just looking at our stuff."

"Well stop looking for a second and pay attention to me."

"Fine," Joe said sarcastically, "I suppose I could."

"So anyway," she said, non-plused by the break, "Back to the woods. What did you say you did about the trees?"

"Nothing."

"Yeah you did, right when you called."

"No. I mean I didn't do anything. I called around, but nobody gave a shit. It was really depressing."

"You don't suppose we're imagining all this, do you?"

"No way. Al saw it too."

"Oh, that helps."

"It's for real. I wish I could have dreams this vivid. You coming home early?"

"Why? You have a plan?"

"Nope. Just curious."

"I know I know. You want to get the babes out of the house before I show up. Right."

"Yeah. Babes. That's the ticket."

"Listen, I gotta get going, especially if I want to make the dash for the train. You gonna keep trying?"

"Trying what?"

"To do something about the trees. I think it's really cool that you wanted to raise the alarm. You're just so darn civic-minded."

"No. I've had enough. I think instead I'll sit out on the porch and admire the river, now that I can see it."

"Sounds good to me," Gloria said, "Anyway, I'll get home when I can."

"Cool."

"You think the trees'll be back, Joe?"

"I don't know, but I haven't tossed my chainsaw yet."

"You wouldn't anyway. I'll see you later."

"Bye," Joe said.

"Bye," Gloria said. Joe stayed on, listened to the phone go dead. This time he didn't mind. They never managed to resolve anything on the phone, but somehow midday conversations with Gloria lifted him. He smiled, shut off the phone, and returned it to its base. He glanced at the kitchen clock, noted that it was too late to start a new project. He cursed his lack of self-control as he reached into the fridge for another beer and headed for the recliner.

He had settled into the chair, twisted the top off his beer, and already had a hand in the chips when the phone rang. Rang? he thought; sounds more like twittering to me. He hauled himself to his feet once more, and returned to the kitchen with his open beer. He picked up the phone, still slightly nervous that an angry police officer was searching for just the right berating language on the other end.

"Hello?"

"Hi. It's me again. Sorry to pull you out of your chair. Oh wait, you were on the porch. Right?"

"Hah hah. What did you forget?"

"I was wondering. Do you think we should sell our ADM stock? I mean, what with the trees and all."

"That's agricultural. This is trees. I've been told they have nothing to do with each other."

"I see," Gloria said. He knew she didn't see, but wasn't going to bite.

"Besides," Joe concluded, "Somebody might want to plant something in all the space. Then--"

"It's agriculture. Got it. Even so, you ought to watch CNBC and check out the price."

"No way. You know I hate staring at the ticker while those talking heads try to get you to sell so they can buy. I'm going outside to watch the grass grow."

"Okay okay, " Gloria said cheerfully, "I just thought I'd ask. Anyway, I really gotta go now. Good luck getting to the porch, and I'll see you soon."

"Thanks, and bye."

"Bye." Joe shut off the phone and, without putting it down, walked straight through the house and out the front door onto his porch. He sat in the Kmart glider and honestly did admire the clear view of the Hudson the missing trees afforded him. Beautiful country, he thought, even without trees.

He rocked gently, squinting slightly at the encroaching sun. It was three o'clock already, and the porch faced west. That meant that the sun would be flashing in his eyes in less than an hour. Hell, he thought, it'll probably be even sooner without any shade. Deciding to take the good with the bad, he sat back and admired the river once more. He figured it was worth it; the hallucination would surely end by tomorrow, and the trees would be back. Then he would once more have to peer between invasive branches to enjoy the distant waves of the river and the banana boats that plied them. He rested his hand behind his head and rocked some more, feeling oddly content. Before he was three rocks into his euphoria, the phone rang.

Relieved that he had the sense to bring it out with him, he picked up the phone that he had set beside him on the glider. It must be Gloria, he thought, rolling his eyes. She always managed to remember something else five minutes after they hung up. He liked to believe it was an excuse to take another moment to say good-bye.

"Yes honey," he said, "What did you forget?"

"Nothing dear," a decidedly male voice answered, "Except to confirm that I'm speaking to Joseph Smith."

"Ugh," was all Joe could manage.

"Is it?"

"Yes. Yes it is. Can I help you?"

"I imagine. This is Sergeant Wolenski, town police."

"Is something wrong?" Joe asked, hoping to sound ignorant.

"You tell me, sir. Did you call earlier in reference to trees, or lack thereof?"

"Maybe."

"You did, and I'm calling to advise you that it is best not to hang up on a police officer, especially after using profanity."

"Well, I wouldn't exactly call it -- "

"Profanity sir. There's only one name for it."

"How did you get mine?"

"Your what, Mr. Smith?"

"That. My name. I didn't give it when I called."

"No, Mr. Smith, you certainly didn't. We have a machine."

"A machine?"

"Yes. A machine."

"Am I in trouble?"

"No Mr. Smith, not currently."

"Then why -- "

"Because of your complaint, sir. We're following up."

"I thought the trees were the FBI's problem?"

"It is sir, but local panic is ours."

"Panic? Did I do that?"

"Not yet, sir."

"When will I?"

"Mr. Smith, please don't piss me off."

"Hey now, watch the profanity sergeant," Joe couldn't believe he said that.

"Sorry sir."

"S'OK."

"Anyway sir, we would like to recommend that you keep the tree incident to yourself."

"Why is that?"

"Don't know sir. They gave me your name and number and told me to say that."

"That's it?"

"Yes Mr. Smith. That's it. Please keep the tree thing to yourself."

"That way no on will notice?"

"I suppose, sir."

"Good plan, Sarge."

"We thought so."

"So does this mean you're not going to arrest me?"

"As long as you keep out of trouble, Mr. Smith."

"I'll do just that, officer."

"That's 'sergeant', Mr. Smith. Now please say good-bye before you hang up this time."

"I'll do my best. Good-bye."

Click.

It didn't feel as good that time, but Joe was happy to be off the phone. Hell, the officer probably was too. The sergeant. Joe sighed, tilting his head away from the sunlight that had begun to invade his porch. He was right; it was much worse without the trees. Fine, he thought as he hauled himself to his feet and headed back inside. He stopped at the door to admire the glider, still swinging from the force of his rising. It was one of his better purchases, that glider. A pressed steel wonder that was already three years old and still in great shape.

He reentered the cool dark house, stepped across the living room. He stopped at his chair but paused before he fell into it. He felt a momentary flash of guilt, stared at the chair for a moment, then fell into it. Momentary guilt is the best kind.

He pulled back the chair, feeling oddly satisfied that the tree incident had torn him from the chores he would otherwise have suffered. If not the chores, then at least the guilt he would have otherwise felt after he passed the day without doing a single domestic assignment. He closed his eyes, nestled his head in his palms, and smiled. He figured he would probably still be in the same position when Gloria came home from work in a couple of hours.

"Maybe," he said aloud, "They'll be back tomorrow."

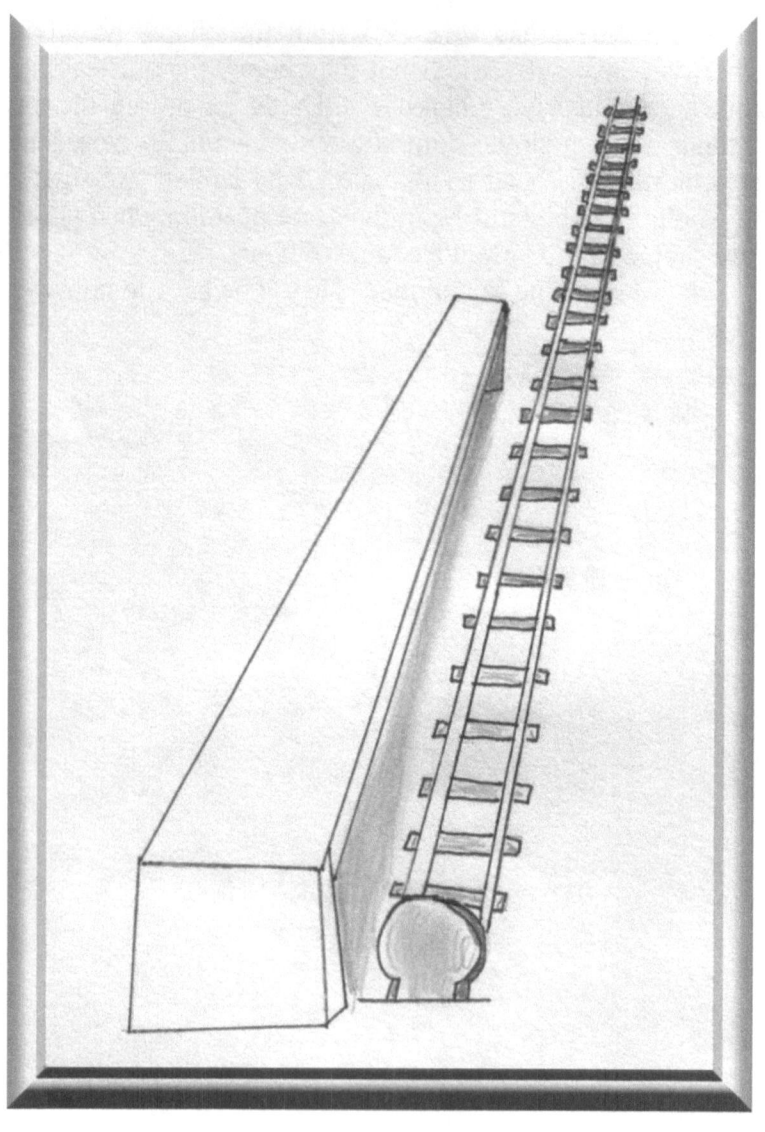

Curse of the Commuter Zombies

Claire allowed an extra hour and five arrivals to pass before she reluctantly concluded that Frank had missed his train. By assuming that he would eventually deliver, in person, an excellent reason he had failed to warn her, Claire was able to determine that everything was fine. Determined but still defeated, she shook her head and started her car. As she exited the quiet train station's parking lot to return to their empty house just up the road but five dozen miles from Frank's office in Manhattan, she rapped the steering wheel and wished that Frank would enter this century and buy himself a damn cell phone. Claire made the two-minute drive home with the radio off, and idled for a moment after she pulled into their driveway. She was having difficulty remaining determined: whenever Frank missed the train, she worried that their ritual peck that morning was the last time she would ever see him; that something terrible had happened. She could never shake the thought, though her experience proved it wrong every time. She was glad that Frank only missed the train once every year or two, and convinced herself reluctantly that everything would be fine. This time she was wrong, and she missed her opportunity to correctly lament the fact that she would never see her husband again.

Earlier that day, just around that utopian quitting time of 5:00, Frank had called Claire from his midtown office, as was his habit:

"Hello?" the voice on the other end of his line said, after just two rings. Frank was always pleased that Claire picked up the phone for him, because he knew she would prefer to wait for the call to run through the machine.

"Hey," he said as he shut down his computer, "S'me. I'll be on the 7:00 train, like usual. I gotta go now, though; can't talk"

"Okay," Claire said, "Walk safe, and make sure you got everything."

"I'll try," Frank said in a singsong.

"Just do it," Claire chanted back.

"Right," Frank said, cracking the only smile of his day, "Bye, my love."

"Bye. See you soon."

Frank's phone was in its cradle for about ten seconds before it rang again. He knew who it was, so he picked it up.

"Yes?" he asked expectantly.

"Frank. I almost forgot."

"No. You did forget. Be honest."

"Whatever. Anyway, don't you forget that you have to pick up that prescription from the doctor on 60th. The one for my asthma."

"Already got it," Frank responded, patting the bulge her package formed in his suit jacket, "Picked it up at lunch. I really gotta go now, so be sure to stay calm until I get home."

"I'll try."

"Just do it!"

The Metro North platform in Grand Central Station was crowded with commuter zombies exercising various levels of mindless patience while they waited for their train, which had not yet arrived on its designated track. It was late

September, but the platform, buried beneath midtown Manhattan, still resonated midsummer heat and humidity. The zombies didn't care, ostensibly; this was de rigueur for their chosen lifestyle. However, they tended to be careful not to speak to each other, for fear of igniting an unexpected fuse in the person to whom they spoke or themselves. Frank, an experienced commuter, avoided even an accidental glance into the blank eyes of his fellow zombies. Instead he cast his gaze into the bowels of the Park Avenue tunnel and attempted to will his train's telltale headlights to appear. His sweaty reverie was disrupted by a mild impact on his right pinky toe. He snapped his attention down to his foot, and saw that the gentleman beside him had dropped his leather satchel on Frank's foot. It didn't hurt much, but Frank was seeing stars anyway -- this fool had broken a carnal rule of personal space. Summoning his civilized demeanor from its handy storage compartment deep within his soul, Frank gently kicked the bag off his foot. His effort, as it had a thousand times before following similar thoughtless transgressions, would allow the perpetrator an opportunity to apologize or at least quietly pull the bag clear of Frank's personal space. In less than a second the bag slid back to its original position, slamming Frank's foot with authority.

Frank turned toward the man for the first time. He was a big man, like Frank, and, like Frank, still wore a tie with his suit. The tie was loosened to allow his thick neck to sweat freely in the stifling heat. Frank couldn't meet the man's gaze because, though he faced Frank, his attention was focused on the empty tunnel.

"Excuse me?" Frank asked loudly. The man ignored him. Frank kicked the bag off his foot, adding a little extra horsepower for emphasis, sending the bag onto the wide yellow warning strip that marked the edge of the platform. The man looked down. Then he looked at Frank. Frank looked back up the tunnel. I can play this fucking game, too, he thought, feeling the blood rushing past his ears. As he expected, the bag landed on his foot after a few seconds. Frank noticed the people crowded near him step back half a pace. He turned to glare at the man. The man, a burly creature of Mediterranean extract and about his indeterminate middle age, glared back.

"What is your problem?" the man asked.

"My problem?" Frank almost squealed in disbelief, "My problem is that you keep on putting your bag on my foot."

"Your foot's in my spot."

"Huh?"

"Your foot. Is in. *My* spot."

"Your spot? This is fucking Grand Central Station! There are no spots here!" Frank shouted over the whistle of the approaching train. The man kicked his bag back toward Frank and followed it, moving his face into Frank's, until their noses almost touched. Someone gasped.

"Listen, asshole," the man shouted, "I been putting my bag down here for ten years! Train's not here, I walk to this spot and wait, then I put down my bag. It's my spot."

"The hell it is! I was standing here. There are no spots," Frank could feel his hands begin to shake. He clenched them into fists to hide the activity, and had no reservation about the signal it sent. Frank was not an aggressive man, but it had been a tough day. A tough decade.

"Yes, there are!" the man shouted against the clatter of the train, which was still a hundred yards distant, "And this one's mine!" With two open palms he shoved Frank away from him, and his bag. Though he barely staggered, Frank felt as though he had been shot. Rusty primal synapses that hadn't connected in years began firing rapidly, supplying signals that Frank could not ignore, and would never understand. Without a thought he stepped back and feinted a swing at the man. When the man dodged the undelivered blow, Frank kicked the bag off the platform and down onto the track. The train, moving slowly, was fifty yards away. The driver must have seen the bag go down, because the train's air horns began blaring repeatedly, perhaps to suggest that the two big guys on the platform avoid doing something amazingly stupid. It didn't work.

"There!" Frank screamed, "Now your bag's got a spot!"

"You asshole!" the man shouted. Frank tensed in anticipation of a punch (he figured a gut shot, because the guy's arms seemed too big to go for his head while confined in the tight suit), but it did not come. Instead, the man stepped off the platform after his bag. Someone screamed. The train had arrived and, though the terrified engineer locked his brakes, 500 tons of moving metal were not going to stop in time, or even in the next twenty feet.

During the instant that the man jumped, Frank felt a rush of an emotion that could only be described as perfect, adrenalin-pumped glee. He was delighted. That feeling lasted until the man landed on the tracks five feet below and fell onto his bag. Then, when the man looked up and saw the train, Frank's hand went out. The man wouldn't take it. Instead, he rolled under the platform to filthy safety. Frank nearly pissed from his sudden relaxation.

The engineer saw as he passed that the man had leapt to safety, and swore something unintelligible as he passed Frank. Frank could also see that he was on his radio already. Fine, Frank thought, now I'm never getting home. The train stopped, but its doors didn't open.

"Fine," Frank heard someone mumble from behind him, "Now these freaks are going to make us all late." Frank spun abruptly toward the voice, but couldn't tell who in the crowd of angry faces had spoken. He didn't push the issue, reading the response he would get by those faces. The zombies had been woken from their stupor by the realization that his behavior will cost them serious delays, inconvenience, and missed drinks. Frank turned back to face the train. He was standing by one of the closed doors. He hoped that they would open and he could get in and become as anonymous as possible once aboard.

That wasn't happening. The man had emerged across the platform on an unoccupied track. Frank could not see him through the crowd, but he did hear his shouts rise above the ambient din of the platform. A wave of zombies began to part from the far side of the platform, the ripple amplified by the noncommittal grumbles of impatient riders already perturbed by the trains delay, and now displaced by a clearly unconscientious suicidal buffoon. Frank watched in stark fascination as the wave approached him slowly. It broke in front of him when a small and deeply confused family of German tourists parted to allow the man passage. Red-faced and furious, the man slammed Frank against the closed train door without warning. Before Frank could respond, the man shoved his bag in his face. The man, and his bag, were filthy.

"Here it is, asshole!" the man shouted, pressing the satchel into Frank's chest, "I got it back! And here is where it goes!" He placed the bag on the platform, and on Frank's foot. This was too much for Frank. His patience had withered years earlier, and his respect for his fellow commuter had become more intellectual than emotional with the last wad of chewed gum he sat on months earlier. Ignoring the herd was all he had, and this madman would not allow him to clutch that thin straw of sanity today. So, with no other option in sight, Frank stared at the man while he gently kicked the bag off the platform again. It got stuck between the train and the edge of the platform, but Frank was able to shove it through with his heel before the man could stop him. The man stared incredulously at Frank (who was smiling) for a moment before he pulled one hand from its position on Frank's chest, balled it into a tight fist, and drew it up to his ear. Without tearing his jacket, Frank noted dully as he waited to be pummeled. He didn't care.

Before the man could release his coiled punch, another hand grabbed the poised fist, with authority. Frank looked away from the man, directly into the tired eyes of a police officer. The cop had one hand on his holstered gun and the other on Frank's elbow; his partner was working on harmlessly releasing the energy of the man's unspent blow. The train doors opened, the commuter zombies filed past Frank and his opponent, offering little more than dirty looks to telegraph their ire at the delay the two had caused. The cops firmly restrained the two men, allowing their grips on large upper arms to loosen only after the train doors closed. Frank finally became conscious of his new situation as the train disappeared into the black tunnel, leaving the four men in relative silence. He attempted nonchalance with a rattling sigh, shook his head, and tried to speak calmly to the cop still attached to his arm. The adrenaline still coursing his veins added a telltale quiver to his voice:

"Officer. I'm not sure what you've been told, but this asshole just jumped off the platform for no reason. I had nothing to do with it."

"Nothing my ass!" the man roared, "He pushed me right off. In front of a speeding train!" Frank felt the cop's grip tighten. He turned toward the cop, raised his hands, and said:

"He's lying, officer. I absolutely did not push him. And the train was going about one mile an hour."

"That makes it better?" the cop holding Frank's opponent asked, in an unexpectedly nasal voice. Frank almost laughed, but judiciously contained himself.

"Well, no," he said, looking at his feet, "But it certainly points out that he might have thought he had time to get his bag, regardless of me."

"*His* bag?"

"Yeah. It's right there, at his feet. He chased after it like it had his life's savings in it, but he still had plenty of time to get it and get out of the way before the train got here."

"Oh? And how did it find its way to the tracks in the first place?" the officer holding the man asked with clear suspicion.

"Yeah," the man added, "How did that happen?"

Frank's fuse burned that last critical millimeter of sanity without warning. He erupted, feeling ten years of commuter hell well up into his throat, pressing his air passages closed, and threatening to crush the rational portion of his haggard brain.

"It happened because this anal retentive piece of shit here could only stand in one damn place, and that damn place is the damn place where I was already damn well standing!" Frank was screaming by the third damn, and even through his anger he could see the cop who held him suppress a giggle.

"So," that cop said, "You're telling us that this gentleman here placed his bag down in your space, and then you tossed the bag onto the tracks."

"Well," Frank said, completely taken in by the easy tone of the cop, "I wouldn't say toss. Maybe more of a gentle nudge."

"I see."

"No wait," the man said, "He pushed me!"

"The hell I did!" Frank cried, feeling his arm instinctively test the might of the hand clamped upon it. He didn't have a chance.

"Tell you what," the officer attached to Frank said, "How about we take you back to our office, and just give you fellas a chance to calm down?"

"Thanks anyway, officer," Frank said, "I'll just catch the next train. Everything's cool, really."

"He pushed me!"

"Huh?" was all Frank could manage. The fight in the man's wide eyes was enough to stifle Frank, miring him in the frightened confusion that accompanies a novel, fate-laced situation such as his. The police officers exchanged a tired and shopworn look of resignation at the hours of work that now lay ahead of them.

"Let's go," one cop said as he began to tug Frank's arm toward Grand Central Station's main waiting room. Frank didn't resist. He followed, feeling the bulge in his breast pocket shift as he moved. He briefly hoped his wife would stay calm until he got home, and then got back to panicking about his predicament. He calmed himself by assuming that someone had called the cops by telling them a man had jumped to the tracks, and was not pushed. Yeah, that was it, he thought; there's always a witness.

Three hours later Frank sat at a steel table in a police station that he hadn't realized existed beneath a terminal through which he had passed five thousand times. He was alone. He hadn't seen his alleged victim, as the cops called him, since they arrived, and he hadn't seen a policeman in at least an hour. Frank had asked the last cop he saw, an old detective sporting a stereotypical rumpled shirt, wide tie, and beer gut, about his phone call. The detective just smiled and said that only works after he's arrested. Not interested in being arrested, Frank didn't protest, and withheld the speech he had been rehearsing about his wife's condition and the medicine he had to get to her. He did not want to take any chances.

Frank wondered, again, what the other man (whose name he had never learned) was still saying about him. It had to be something, because they had not allowed him to leave. But it might also have been nothing, because he wasn't being interrogated or arrested himself. He had simply been left alone, perhaps until his rumbling stomach confessed to all things evil for him. Frank was about ready to stand, again, and maybe pound on the door, when it whipped open. A trim young black man in a very nice suit stepped in. Oh, shit, Frank thought, it's the D.A. The man stepped forward, and held his hand out over the table toward Frank. Mindlessly,

Frank took it, and was startled by the firmness of the young man's handshake.

"I'm Robert Smith," the man said.

"Nice to meet you, Mr. Smith," Frank said, "You the D.A.?"

"Yes, I am," he said, his face contorting slightly, "Didn't detective Willis tell you I was coming by?"

"Detective who?"

"I see. At any rate, yes, I'm the assistant district attorney assigned to this case."

"It's a case?"

"Sir, a man was nearly killed."

"Well, I'm not sure about that. But I am sure he jumped off that platform himself, and that he saw that train coming, and ducked out of the way in plenty of time. Those things I'm sure of." Shit, Frank thought; that isn't at all what I was going to say. He'll never buy that.

"You know what, Frank – can I call you Frank? That's exactly what Mr. Johannsen said. Almost verbatim."

"Who's Mr. Johannsen?"

"The guy who apparently brought us all together tonight. He's still in the next room, and, now that he's calmed down, has become very apologetic. He says he started the whole damn thing."

"He does?"

"He does."

"Then why on God's green earth am I still here?" Frank asked, trying to modulate his voice to avoid new hassles.

"Well, let's just say it took a while for Mr. Johannsen to simmer down, and, since there were no witnesses – "

"You mean aside from the 800 people on the platform?"

"They all, to a person, got on the train. It's a funny thing, too – when this happens, and it does, on a subway platform, there are always a half dozen witnesses who stay behind to keep the perps honest. I guess running away is a suburban thing. No offense."

"Definitely none taken. If me and Mr. Johannsen weren't so obsessed by our escape from work, maybe we'd both been a little more understanding."

"Nicely put, Frank. At any rate, I just wanted to have a quick chat with you before they release you, just to be sure there is nothing you would like to add to this story, or if you feel Mr. Johannsen deserves prosecution."

"Oh, please. No, leave the guy alone. Let him go. That ride can really rip your brain to shreds if you're not careful, and maybe this guy just, um, wasn't."

"I bet he will be now. That'll be it, then. Good-night, Frank," Smith said. He started for the door, and then turned, "Oh, I almost forgot. Earlier we called your wife, just to confirm your ID and to tell her you were fine."

"You called my wife?" Frank asked, feeling that bulge again, "Shit. What did you tell her exactly?"

"Not much, really. See, we called, and when we said we were holding you for a possible murder investigation, she got very quiet and hung up. I talked to the officer who made the call, and she said that she even tried to call back, but got no answer. I think your wife might be a bit angry." Frank felt his face flush.

"I have to go home. Now."

The ride on the empty off-peak train was uneventful and very, very long. Frank sat in his seat, staring at his reflection in the window, and waited for the 20 stops preceding his to be called in glacial progression. He could not shake the sound of his wife's voice on the answering machine, mechanically requesting a message, over and over and over. She never picked up, despite his pleas and apologies. Now his only means of communication was to wait. When his stop was finally announced, Frank was already at the door of the train. He bolted through it when it opened, and ran off the platform. He prayed, really prayed, that he would see Claire waiting for him in her accustomed spot just clear of the platform steps. She wasn't there.

"She probably went to bed early," Frank said aloud as he jogged up the steep hill that led to his house, "That'll be why she didn't answer before, too. Yep, that's it." It was after midnight, he assured himself.

Frank continued this litany until he reached his house, huffing and puffing. The front door was locked, as usual. Frank looked through the filmy curtains that covered the large window in the door, and saw Claire's silhouette reclining in the small gossip bench in the entry hall. Frank felt a wave of relief. She was sitting there, right in front of him. He pounded on the door, but she didn't move. Man, he thought, she must be pissed. But he didn't care. She was right there, and not at the hospital, or sprawled on the kitchen floor, struggling to find a way to relieve the attack that he had assumed accompanied news of his "arrest." Frank dug into his satchel and found his house key. He opened the door quietly, and stepped inside.

"Honey," he said, "Listen. Before you start I just have to say it wasn't – "

Frank stopped. He dropped his satchel, pulled the medicine from his chest with great ceremony, and tossed it to the floor at Claire's feet. Claire was staring at him, at the door. The phone's handset was on the floor, by her feet, silent. Claire just stared.

Final Notice

The flickering electric candelabras spaced infrequently along the dark wood paneled walls failed to enlighten the guests wedged into the dim room. Canned Mozart wafted in near subliminal tones through the general din of numerous animated conversations. An equally subtle scent of roses accented the stuffy air, though there were no flowers. New arrivals and mingling guests ran the gamut of greetings, from tight hugs to loose handshakes with apparent strangers. It was a rare, forced reunion of family and friends.

Henry, always disturbed by the artificial nature of these events, grumbled to himself that he could see only half of his fellow guests clearly. When he had entered the room ten minutes earlier, he spied a remedy in a row of light switches near the door. Now the impulse was complete, and he reached for the switches to flip maybe just one or two of them to the 'on' position. A small hand with sharp black fingernails appeared from nowhere and gently shoved his fingers from social harm.

"Don't do that, Henry," Barbara, his wife of three years, said, "You know you'll ruin everything if you mess with the lights."

"Oh please," Henry sniffed, "As if ruining this puppet show is a bad thing."

"It is," Barbara hissed at him from his shoulder, "So knock it off."

"Okay, okay," Henry sort of apologized, still uneasy in the contrived gloom, "It's knocked. It would've been too late anyway: 'god' is about to intervene."

The glass candle flames brightened sharply in confirmation of his whispered announcement. They shifted from dull amber to soft white, but still prevented Henry from clearly seeing the expressions of his compatriots. Unseen lights in the ceiling came alive as well, but by design added no clarity. Though the ambient change was minimal, it managed to hush the crowd. All eyes in the room turned toward Henry. He blushed, confused by the attention. Before he checked his suit for stains, he realized that their focus crept through him to the main entrance behind him.

Henry dismissed his gaff and rotated to dovetail his attention with the other sixty people in the large room. The double hardwood doors that Henry had closed with accidental yet inspirational volume when he had entered the room had changed. They were paler – less massive. A gap of cartoonish blackness had formed between them, spreading an unnaturally opaque space as the doors whipped silently open.

The change, and the dramatic emptiness of the area beyond the doors, ushered a wave of gasps through the quieted groups. Henry failed to notice consciously that the Mozart had been shut off. The doors stopped short of slamming into the walls, as if unwilling to overshadow the entrance of the little man standing in their frame. Then the blackness faded, or rather was washed in a gentle green hue that offered a superb backdrop to Henry's Great Uncle Eddie, who now commanded the threshold. His arms were folded, and he silently met the gaze of each of his guests. He did not move until he had completed eye contact with each of them. Henry wasn't sure that he would be included in the scan, as he hadn't seen Uncle Eddie in years, and had failed to visit him at the hospital. He hated hospitals.

Eddie did meet Henry's eyes. The old man held his gaze for what Henry felt was a moment longer than the others. Henry did not endure the anticipated agitation. Instead, his great uncle's attention warmed him. He was at ease, forgetting his guilt. Henry wanted to rush forward and hug the crotchety old man, but that was not allowed. He smiled, and his heart stuttered when his smile was returned. Henry thought he heard people whispering softly behind him.

The ambient light dimmed again. Eddie entered the room, striding past Henry without a word or gesture. He began to mingle with his guests, who were now gathered in small clutches, speaking in deferential tones. Eddie did not whisper. His voice was strong, clearly heard by all as he started his obligatory social rounds.

"Fred!" Eddie boomed to a dark fat man standing alone, "Glad to see you could make it. I had some money down on your arrival. Couldn't convince anyone that this is the one occasion that you would attend. Now, don't you mind my remarks, Fred. You know there'll be more later."

"No, Dad," Henry's uncle Fred responded awkwardly as his hands struggled to tear themselves to sweaty shards of anguished flesh. Henry did not recognize the hulking middle-aged man, as Fred had left the family decades earlier, after a terrible row with his father. They hadn't spoken since, but Fred did correspond regularly with his twin sister Frieda, who surreptitiously kept the family updated on his long, slow development into a successful game designer. She lived for their reunion. Fred's beleaguered response speech rolled from his quivering lips like so much loose gravel: "I deserve anything you throw at me. I'm glad I'm here to take your best shot one more time."

"And hear it you will, boy," Eddie snapped. Then he softened, his old gray eyes moistening, "But I can't tell you how good it feels to holler at you in person, Fred."

"Yeah Dad, and for a change I won't mind hearing ... listening ... to it."

"I wish I could hug you, son," Eddie whispered, though his soft tones gently nudged each person's ears with equal clarity.

Eddie's face slackened. He shifted his focus and stepped past Fred without further comment. Fred did not react negatively to the cold dismissal. Indeed, Henry spotted a tear an instant before Fred reached up to apparently brush his hair off his forehead. Guests then gathered around Fred, clasping his hand, congratulating him quietly. Frieda said nothing. She simply beamed at her twin from across the floor, leaving a lump in Henry's throat. Henry's attention returned to his great uncle, who had found another family member – Eddie's brother Jake.

"Jake, you old son of a bitch," he boomed, "I bet you're happy to see me here first, huh?"

Jake thrust out a callused hand to his younger brother, then remembered and retrieved it, conspicuously stowing it in a pocket of his ill-fitting suit. His weathered eyes were glassy as he tried to force a smile.

"It always was a race with us, wasn't it Eddie?" he said. His voice was barely audible, contrasting his usual choleric exposition.

"Yes," Eddie continued, "We both did have a need for superiority. Well, Jake, I think in the end you were the better man. And I love you for it."

Jake opened his mouth to respond, but found no words. Eddie allowed him about three seconds to say something, then turned away. He strode deliberately toward the next group of guests. Jake waited until Eddie was a few feet away before he stiffly crossed to the door, barely enduring the pain of leaving the room and its contents.

Eddie skirted a circle of four people that Henry had assumed were partners in his great uncle's law firm. The three men and a woman, all in easy range of Eddie's ninety-five years, smiled graciously at him. Henry smirked at their visible preparation of the platitudes they would feel were required for their audience with Eddie. Eddie ignored them fully, strolling by without changing his gait. Henry watched in amusement as the partners' loving gazes shifted instantly to vicious glares at Eddie's ignorant back. One of them, senior partner and next in line Ralph Bureaus, took one step after him. He officiously cleared his wrinkled throat.

"Ed," he said in a sharp, yet somehow supple tone, "Ed, we'd like to speak to you a moment. Give you our best." Eddie stopped mid-step. He was motionless for three beats before he turned on his heel to face his partners. He stepped into the center of their withered circle.

"But Ralph. Gene, Linda, Tom. Haven't you already given me your best these last thirty years?"

"Of course we have, Ed," Ralph confirmed, hands remaining clasped tightly in the small of his back, "And you of course have given so much to us."

"Damn straight I have, Ralph," Eddie said, smiling broadly, "Too much. I gave you my name, my sweat, and an enormous amount of my money. And for what?" Ralph,

Gene, Linda, and Tom did not respond. They intently maintained their insipid smiles. Henry thought he spotted a couple of twitching lips in the group. They also continued to keep their eyes on Great Uncle Eddie, though they did occasionally dart away to exchange glances among themselves. Eddie gave them three seconds to respond to his rhetorical question before he continued without prompting:

"For what? For you vultures to sit around plotting my forced retirement the moment I enter a hospital? And, even though my mental strength is as strong as ever, for you to draft a letter to the Board? A letter stating that, as I am incompetent, you will be forced to eliminate my position and continue the firm in my name, but not under my direction?"

"Oh, don't look so damn surprised Ralph. You know I have always been aware of all activity in the firm. Even as a `feeble' old man it was a cinch to keep track of your bungling activities."

"Ed..." Linda tried to protest. Eddie put up a hand to silence her.

"Forget it, Linda," he said, "It's too late now. You're rid of me for good. And I, you. Toss the façade, Ralph. As of Monday, the firm is dissolved. All assets, all liquid funds – including your overrated Christmas bonuses – hell even the building itself have been put in trust for my grand-children. You'll see the paperwork in the morning. Ciao."

With no flourish or emotion Eddie abandoned his disloyal soldiers and resumed his original course through the room. His former partners were frozen in headlights of their own downfall for a few seconds before they collected themselves and shuffled out in a huddle, bumping into each other in their haste. Henry listened with amusement as they exchanged mumbled accusations at each other without pause until they were out of earshot; out of Eddie's room. When the door slammed behind them, subdued cheers circulated the crowd. Someone clapped. Henry laughed to himself, raised his champagne glass to Barbara and his mother, who were seated on the other side of the room. They returned the salute, equally pleased. Eddie, however, appeared to have forgotten his tangential exchange and its aftermath. It was time to speak to his next guest.

He had to bend low to converse. The guest Eddie had approached was Henry's six-year-old nephew Jason, who had talked his mother into letting him attend.

"Well Jason," Eddie said, his voice soft for the first time, "It's wonderful to see that you could make it."

"Hello, Great-Great Grandfather," Jason mumbled. The timid child coyly took one step backward. Jason was small for his age, allowing his frail ancestor to loom above him. Eddie softened at the boy's fear, and took a small step back himself. He also appeared to visibly shrink.

"Don't worry little man," Eddie said, "I'm very proud of you for coming to see me today. You're very, very brave." At this Jason straightened, found his voice.

"I was the only one they said could come," Jason announced, "All the other kids are fishin' or something. They couldn't come. Angela was scared to come."

"Now there's no need to be scared, boy, and you be sure to tell your cousin that. And let that be the last time you tattle on a family member." Eddie's soft voice and pleasant visage softened the force of the censure.

"Great-Great Grandfather, is what Angela said true?"

"What did Angela say?" Eddie asked, raising one eyebrow. Henry scanned the room for his cousin Veronica, Angela's mother. She was pale, hand at her mouth. Jason answered:

"She said I would never ever see you again. That you'd be gone."

"Yes, Jason, that is mostly true. But I have arranged to always be with you, one way or another." Jason fidgeted, struggled to form another question, one that didn't involve tattling, but Eddie held up a gnarled white palm and continued, "That's enough for now, son. You ask your father about things now. He'll be happy to pass all my tired old thoughts to you. Good-bye, Jason." The boy didn't respond. He merely tucked his head into his mother's skirt as Eddie slowly resumed his previous stance and dimension. When fully erect, he smiled at Henry's cousin Marybeth. Barely 35, and she already has two kids, Henry thought, pretty amazing.

"That's a fine boy you have there, child. Don't let him forget me."

"Never, Grandfather," Marybeth whispered, tears streaming, "Never."

Eddie paused again, turned, and took three strong paces toward Henry. He stopped less than an arm's length from Henry's quivering chin. Henry gulped, profoundly apprehensive now that the moment he had anticipated all week was imminent.

Eddie didn't speak immediately. Instead, in the manner he used since Henry was a child, he slowly scanned Henry's six and a half foot frame from head to toe, stretching his neck in an exaggerated motion. As always, he rubbed the back of that spotted pink neck when finished, shaking his head. Then he spoke. Henry caught himself mouthing the litany as it was recited.

"Damned if you're so tall, boy," Eddie said, still rubbing, "You should have been a basketball player. Such a short family, too. Sort of makes you wonder about that mother of yours' checkered past."

"It's good to see you too, Uncle Eddie." Henry stammered, using none of the words he had rehearsed, "It's been a long time."

"Yes it has, son," Eddie said, then added, "Too long. And those eyes. Wrong color; should be blue. Oh well, no matter now, huh?" To Henry's dismay, Eddie turned to leave. This was too short, Henry thought. As if he heard, Eddie stopped, twisted his head and shoulders around to face him.

"One more thing, son," he said, winking awkwardly, "Don't you worry about the hospital. Your father hated `em too. Runs in the family."

Eddie was gone before Henry could form a response. Henry let out a breath. Regret at forgetting his carefully written and rehearsed speech never took root, as his soul was flooded by the wash of Eddie's simple forgiveness.

Eddie moved casually around the room, stopping to chat with each family member and friend present. His mingling was in apparent random order. The time span of each visit was equal, disallowing any notions of favoritism. Even his other two children received the same amount of attention that Henry did, though his conversations with them were certainly more emotional. The only guest Eddie skipped was his wife, Betty, who sat quietly in a corner with Frieda.

Eddie's demeanor impressed Henry. He had been to other events like this. Usually only selected people were spoken to before Final Notice, often with reason: to get in the last word, announce revenge, once even to express lifelong but never admitted love. Eddie's avoidance of such trivial use of the event did justice to his powerful character. Indeed, Eddie seemed to be in a hurry, as if late for an appointment.

At one point Barbara sidled up to Henry. She tugged on his suit jacket to get him to lean over to hear her whisper.

"He sure is in a hurry, isn't he?"

"Yeah," Henry responded quietly, "Betty must want to save a few bucks on the show." They both laughed quietly, then Barbara slipped away again. Blood rushed to Henry's cheeks when he realized that his wife was about to innocently share this parcel of humor. Henry feared that his thought would find its way back to him in the form of Great Aunt Betty's wrath. He hoped not; Aunt Betty's admonishments were rare, but always severe and humiliating. He struck his thigh with his fist, angry that he had said anything. He always managed to misspeak, and preferred to keep to himself. Now a harmless little joke with his own wife might get him in trouble with the family. He couldn't try to stop her. That would only hurt his wife, and amplify the small joke into a family incident. He couldn't win. Henry hated funerals. He wished there was a way to break the nasty tradition, or at least revise it into a more tasteful program.

Fortunately, Barbara didn't have time to endanger her husband. Eddie was already standing at the center of the room, clearing his throat. The guests responded to his gesture by backing away, leaving a large circle of awful green carpet exposed around the rumpled gray man. A group of solemn men in black suits appeared toting bad replicas of Victorian cushioned chairs. They placed the chairs in a circle around Eddie, a discreet distance away. An older, equally serious man in an equally black suit gestured to Eddie's immediate family to take their seats.

Betty, their children, sister Alice, and brother Joe (Henry's grandfather) obliged. Henry took his place in the darkness outside the spotlighted circle of chairs, near the doors. He noticed an empty chair, and that Eddie remained motionless in the center of the circle, staring at an unfamiliar old man clad in a stereotypically black suit that betrayed his station. The man rolled his eyes, then left the room through the double doors. He returned in a moment with Jake, whose eyes were red and puffy. Jake sat in the remaining chair without a word. Eddie bowed slightly in acknowledgment of his arrival, and began to speak:

"Good," he said, beaming, "Now we can get started."

"I'll make this as short as I can. I imagine that many of you are already tired of this nonsense. Besides, knowing Betty, my guess is our time in the room will be up any minute now." A polite laugh circulated. Betty blushed, her smile failing to hide her embarrassment at the truth. Eddie continued, "Just kidding, dear. I'm sure you overdid everything, even if I asked you not to." He refocused on the audience before saying:

"Anyway, I've only a few things to say to you all, and I will be as brief as possible." Henry wished for a chair. He had heard Eddie make that promise in the past. He felt a small hand squeeze his and saw Barbara smiling up at him from the shadows below. She had heard it too. He turned his attention back to Eddie. The energetic little man had paused again. His eyes were closed, as if to gather his thoughts. His head nodded back and forth in silent affirmation of an unheard query.

The lighting adjusted to the hushed anticipation by closing in on Eddie. His immediate family disappeared into gloom, and he became the only perceived person in the room, bathed in pale gray light from the waist up. If Barbara weren't holding his hand a bit too tightly, Henry could easily have assumed that he was having a private audience with his wizened great uncle.

Eddie's eyes snapped open, eliciting a yelp from a few less seasoned guests. Great Uncle Eddie began to orate his Final Notice.

"I, Edward P. McClusky," he boomed his rarely used full name, startling from slumber an unidentified older relative somewhere behind Henry, "Residing at 1325 Palace Street, Fort Lauderdale, County of Broward, and State of Florida, in keeping with tradition of Will and adhering to Probate Law of the State of Florida, do hereby declare this my Final Notice. Any written, recorded, or electronically preserved Final Notice previous to this is declared null and void, by me."

Eddie's voice continued to fill the room after he stopped speaking. His solemn visage slackened, then broke into a broad smile. He turned in a full circle, sharing this smile with all of his guests before he settled heavily into an overstuffed wing chair that had appeared in a new pool of fresh yellow light behind him. He continued: "There. Now that the formalities are done with, we can get underway."

"I want all of you to please listen closely, as I'm only going through this once, and you're better off understanding me on the first pass than retaining a lawyer to interpret the transcript. They're not very good at that. Sorry, Al." He referred to a slim, carefully dressed young man who had stepped into the light to stand by Eddie's chair. He gestured to Al, said, "This is Albert Sherman, one of the three official witnesses to this Notice. Wave hello, Al." Al waved hello. Henry waved back. What the hell, he thought, it's dark.
"Al runs a law firm in Palm Beach. He's available for verification and response to any inquiries. He is not an executor, however, and has no power of attorney, so don't ask him for money. The other two witnesses are, of course, confidential. A Broward County judge can access them, if necessary. Let's all hope we never get to that point.
"There is one more small technical point, then we'll get down to what I'm sure half of you at least are really here for." He stopped speaking to allow the polite chorus of denials from his beloved family and friends, then lifted a palm and continued, "No, no, it's all right. No need to deny anything. Everyone knows his own mind and rest assured so do I. Anyway, back to that last technical detail. I hereby direct my Personal Representative – that's you Betty – to pay all legal debts, funeral expenses, expenses of my last illness, costs of administration, including ancillary, costs of safeguarding and delivering devices, and other proper charges against my estate." Then Eddie paused to smile at his wife, his eyes a bit wet.
"Oh, and Betty," he said, turning to Betty, winking, and speaking softly for the second time, "I'm glad you're here to take care of all this for me. You're doing great, love, and thanks for keeping things simple." Henry could just distinguish Betty's silhouette in the shadows as she slumped

down in her chair, shoulders shaking gently. Eddie extended an open hand toward his wife, paused as if he wished to caress her, and then stiffly retracted it. Jake tentatively patted her shoulder. Eddie returned to his monologue.

"Now for the moment we've all been waiting for. Myself included, of course, and longer than any of the rest of you! Hopefully most of my family won't realize it for many decades, but this is a very powerful moment. A person is rarely afforded the opportunity in life to summarize his successes. It's always the failures that are shared. Too bad.

"It will also be a while for all of you before you are legally permitted to pass final judgment, have the last word, on your own family and friends in the form of material rewards or penalties. That part, I must admit, was sort of fun. So, here we go." Eddie drew a deep breath and folded his tiny arms across his chest.

"First, I am happy to announce that I lived a full and very productive life. I would have preferred a few more decades of declining years to enjoy with my beloved wife and family but hey, there's no room for complaint now.

"I am also pleased to announce that, in conclusion, I am far wealthier than most of you imagine. I have substantial real estate holdings throughout the world, a few prosperous factories and service corporations due to some clever investing back in the nineties...to those of you who told me to sell, I offer a heartfelt `So There!'...and of course the mountain of stocks, bonds, and cash reserves that you all have been drooling over these last few months. No, don't shake your heads in denial. Yes, George, I can see you back there in the dark. I offer each of you a word of advice: if you don't care to visit a rich relative until he lies on his deathbed, restrain yourself; the final visits are revelations. Betty wept at your open greed after visiting hours nightly.

"But enough of these empty thoughts. Let's get to the stuff."

"First, I want it made clear that none of the following comes as a surprise to Betty. We've had many a long hard talk about this moment, and as usual she's convinced me to go along with her thoughtful, caring ways." He stared straight at Betty as he spoke. His fiery eyes glistened. His voice was shaky. Betty was openly sobbing now, resting her head on Jake's shoulder. Eddie gathered himself and resumed the officious tone left behind after his opening paragraphs:

"I hereby bequeath to Elizabeth Hansen McClusky, Betty, my beloved wife and best friend for 65 years, the family homes, lands thereon, and possessions therein in Fort Lauderdale, Florida, Greenwich, Connecticut, and Nice, France, to administer, live in, sell, or give away as she so pleases. Hell, they were always really hers anyway. Damned if I could keep one of those places running for a week.

"I also leave exclusively to Betty my 51% stake in Assemblers Corporation, full ownership of Superconduct Windings, Inc., and my 65% stake in TransPac Communications. Letters officially placing you on the board of each of these companies have been delivered. You can run 'em if you feel like it, babe, it's up to you. I hope you do; those companies comprise our core, and you've put as much into them as I have. Besides, they're a lot of fun.

"Finally, I leave to Betty all benefits and control of the Edward P. McClusky Residuary Trust. Just to remind you Betty, the interest income alone on that trust is over three million a year. It ought to pay the bills for a while.

"And, for the record, all jewelry, furniture, antiques, and other tangible and intangible assets currently in Betty's possession at the above estates are hers and no one else's unless otherwise mentioned by me later on. She can do what she pleases with them, regardless of who gave them to me as gifts or what sentimental, ha ha, value they may have.

"I notice none of you have left yet. Well, nudge your neighbor awake, it's time to dispose of the rest of my holdings.

"Let me remind you all one more time that any recipients forthwith owe your good fortune to Betty. I wanted to leave everything to her, but she insisted that she would not be happy with so much, and that I should share the wealth. Strange girl. Lights please." The candelabras flashed to life, flooding the room with a dim amber glow that caught a few lip smackers by surprise. They resumed their sincere expressions before too many noticed. Henry wasn't surprised that the greedy people barely knew his great uncle.

"First, the remaining property. I own the last big ranch in Montana, 67,000 acres. It's still working, and requires skill, dedication, and a resolute need to protect it from developers. All current debts, mortgages, and obligations have been met by my estate, and I have established a support trust of five million dollars to see that the new owner is given ample chances for success. Now, who should get this parcel? Who deserves it?" Eddie was smiling, pacing the inner circle of chairs like a ringmaster. No one moved. He stopped.

"No, really, I'm not kidding. Who thinks this estate is coming to them? Don't be shy." He resumed his pacing, and the guests began fidgeting. Then, to Henry's shock, almost the entire inner circle stood, and Henry's greasy cousin Sidney from California stepped past the old chairs and into the circle formed by the immediate family, cynically taking his chances. Henry's knees wobbled at the sight of his own grandfather leaping to his feet to claim the prize. Barbara whispered that Joe probably was merely volunteering his business prowess to preserve the ranch. Henry barely heard her, did not acknowledge. His throat was too clogged with emotion to speak anyway.

Jake remained seated. His hand was still clutched by Betty's, though her eyes had dried. His face and neck were red. Henry understood the man's anger, as Jake currently oversaw the ranch, and would be forced to work for or be fired by one of the volunteers. Fred also remained seated. His head was bowed, as if he wished to be overlooked.

Eddie shook his head, tsking the greed of his siblings and children, "You know, I was hoping you would control yourselves. I really was just kidding. The ranch and all its assets, tangible and intangible, is the property of my big brother Jake, who taught me more about hard work and integrity than any man, living or dead. And I love you for it.

"It's yours, Jake, under two conditions."

"Anything, Eddie, you know that," Jake said, rising from his seat as the others resumed theirs in a gamut of humility that ranged from abject to horribly feigned. At a slight nod from Eddie, one of the men in black ushered Sidney from California out of the room. Jake was still red, but stood tall, keeping Eddie's gaze.

"Yes, I do know that," Eddie said, "Just two things, Jake: first, let Betty come visit whenever she wants, and let her take any personal memorabilia she might still have there. It's been years since either of us visited the ranch, but she might have left something. Second, when hell finally freezes and it's time for you to present your will, be very careful about to whom you leave it. I want that place to last forever. Keep it out of the hands of the monsters that money creates."

"You have my word, on both counts."

"I believe I do, Jake. That's all there is for you, brother. I know how profoundly you wish to leave. Feel free to. Al will send you a transcript." Another tear welled in Jake's weathered eyes. Without hesitation he sat next to Betty again, taking her hand.

"Bless your big heart, Jake," Eddie said. Betty beamed. Eddie circled silently for a moment to let the dust of the transaction settle. Then he fell back into his chair, sighed, and resumed his disposition.

"To my other siblings," he pronounced as Alice and Joe stood, gnarled hands clasped, "I leave nothing. Alice, Joe, I mean no disrespect. I should, at the unforgivable way you tried to lay claim to Jake's ranch. However, I'm sure you had completely justifiable reasons," he raised a wrinkled palm, "No, Joe, I don't want to hear them.

"No, my true intent is to highlight your own successes. You need nothing from me, and I have a feeling that when you get home – okay, sometime long after you get home – you'll realize I'm right. Also, I'm sure that if you or yours ever need anything, any help or attentions, Betty will be there for you. I love you both, now sit down." They sat, bewildered.

"And my children. Fred, Frieda, Lizzie. I should do the same for you, but I can't. I love you so much, I am impossibly proud of your full lives and countless little victories. Even you, Fred. I've been to bookstores, you know; I read newspapers. You can't hide from me, boy, remember that." Fred lifted his head for the first time, brushed that lock aside again, and allowed a brief smile to crack his humbled visage. Frieda could not contain herself, and threw her thin arms around Fred's bulk. Henry heard sighs all around him as the last Eddie McClusky Family Story came to a happy ending.

"Frieda, Lizzie, don't feel left out. You're my family, the future, and you let me leave with great hope. But again, you're both successful on your own like your aunt and uncles. Still, you are my kids.

"To my children I leave the sum total of all my Swiss Bank accounts, fifty million dollars, to be divided equally among them. Frieda, since you've proven yourself a wizard in the communication arts, I assign you to see to proper distribution of this and the grandchildren's trust, which I'm coming to now.

"To my grandchildren, and great grandchildren, living now or born after my demise, I leave in trust all assets, funds, and future profits from the sale of such assets and funds, including the building and the vultures' Christmas bonuses, of the now defunct McClusky Holding Company.

Frieda, Al will recommend a reliable executor to see that this fairly huge trust is properly executed. Maybe by the time it gets to my great-great-great grandchildren someone will finally count it.

"Okay family, that's about it. There are a few more odds and ends I'd like to distribute first, for no particular reason, but I don't feel like broadcasting, so Al, here," Al obediently reappeared behind Eddie, "Al here has a list, signed by me. I would again like to point out that all you greedy, distant, uninvited family members get nothing, so you might as well leave." Unlike Jake, about thirty people suddenly sighed, turned, and shuffled out of the room, their hopes dashed. No apologies were offered, no embarrassment was evident. After the door shut behind them, Eddie continued, smiling mischievously.

"Al has instructions to delete from my final list of goodies anyone who just left. Their own greed stole their prizes." Eddie rubbed his hands together, bowing his head as if trying to recall any missed points. He shook his head and straightened. He clapped his hands together loudly and held them clasped before him.

"Well," he said to the remaining guests, "Just one more technical matter and we'll be finished with this tedious message. Before closing let me say once more that I lived a good, full life, and am honored that I was able to share it with all of you. I wish the Fates had allowed me more time to get to know some of you." Fred straightened, tears no longer controlled, and managed a shrug. The simple gesture was ample statement of his loss. Frieda held on tight to her brother.

Eddie continued, "But, most of life is out of our own control, and I bow to that great equalizer." The candelabras again dimmed, leaving all but Great Uncle Eddie lost in shadow. The pale gray envelope of light again surrounded the patriarch as he lifted his chest and cleared his throat in preparation for his final oration.

"I, Edward P. McClusky, being of sound mind, do solemnly swear that all that came before, within the proscribed limits of this holorecord, is my irrevocable will and Final Notice."

Before his last syllable filled the room, the gray light winked out. The room was doused in blackness for a few seconds before the weak light from the candelabras poorly washed the room in an ugly yellow glow. Mozart once again hummed from the walls.

Uncle Eddie was gone.

Betty screamed. She leapt from her chair to the spot where Eddie's image last stood. She spun on her heals, arms outstretched as if trying to grab any residue of his vacated image. She collapsed sobbing to the floor, broken. Her children, barely more coherent, huddled around her, trying to comfort her with their presence. Eddie's siblings sat quietly in their chairs, introspective, unable to separate their grief from the fact that their younger brother had suffered that haunting finale that they, to date, had managed to cheat.

A few minutes passed. Other family members and real friends remained silent and still, either out of respect for Betty or a temporary numbness imbued by the wrenching reality of the moment. Henry felt the latter, the ethereal hammer of Eddie's exit still bludgeoning him, allowing him to think nothing.

In time Jake drew Henry's attention as he rustled uncomfortably to his feet. He crossed stiffly to Betty's family, still huddled on the floor. He fished Betty out, helped her to her feet. His firm grip steadied the shaken widow. She smiled at Jake, whose dead calm was having an effect on all others. Eddie's wish was fulfilled. Jake was in control, his family intact.

The new calm brought with it the ambiance that met Henry on his original entrance. Animated conversations abounded once more among the remaining two dozen people. The anticipation now gone, people were able to speak more easily. They were able, free now, to tell stories about their father, husband, and uncle. Henry was lost with Marybeth in a childhood reminiscence involving Eddie, police, and a stolen candy bar when Barbara came to his side, tugged his sleeve. Henry acknowledged her gesture, finished his story, and then turned to his wife. She was holding a sheaf of paper, looking excited.

"Henry," she said, breathless, "Uncle Eddie remembered you! Look. He left you his hundred-year-old Piaget watch! It's worth a fortune. Plus you get third choice from the `odds and ends' that the others skipped out on. One of them is an old gas car! Isn't that great?"

Henry took the list from her and scanned it. Three pages of single spaced lines listed the variety of baubles that Eddie thought might become treasures to their new owners. Jesus, Henry thought, did the old man miss the whole point? He looked down at Barbara's pitifully exuberant face.

"So?" he asked.

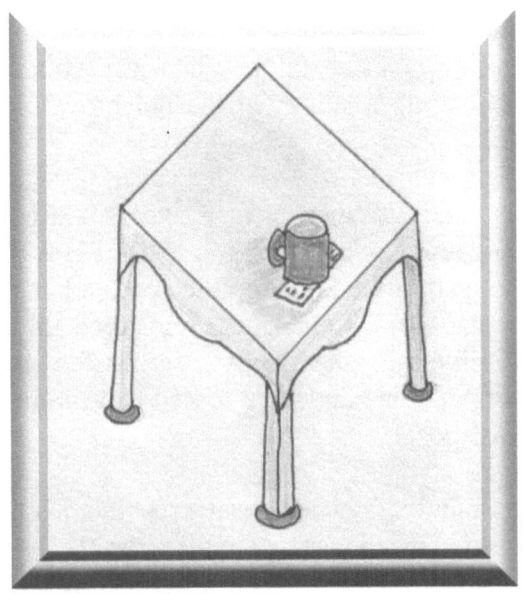

Ring Wearers

Every morning Bob carefully places his coffee mug in the same worn ring on his kitchen table. The same worn ring: a light beige circle that offers the only break in the perfect varnish that protects the rest of the table. The ring is old; almost ten years now, since that bright Sunday morning.

That morning Bob's six precious numbers, silent partners since his youth, finally appeared together in a new place, and not just on the tiny sheet of pale pink paper carefully folded in his wallet: on the morning news. Now they were famous. He knew they were his, of course, but had to compare to the listing in the paper anyway. And when he did, when those numbers matched, his euphoric face fell hard on the table in a heartfelt faint. When it hit, his coffee mug bounced, depositing a splash of the hot brown stuff on the perfect table.

Mary, his wife then of many years and enmeshed in her morning routine, chose that moment of Bob's unbridled bliss to wander into the kitchen. She spotted her dear hubby slumped on the table. Rather, she registered the mess he'd made of it. Fuming, she dabbed the coffee up with the nearest bit of paper at hand, then tossed that saturated bit into the garbage disposal.

The sound of the disposal crushing his fate jerked Bob back to consciousness. Still joyful, he saw the newspaper, the tidy spot where his mug had lain, but not his pink paper, and he knew. Mary would know shortly, but only for a moment. And the ring was born that day.

And so Bob, alone and retired to his pension and some insurance money acquired a while back (almost ten years), took another sip of the brown stuff and replaced his mug carefully into the ring. The same worn ring.

Swimmers

"**W**hat the hell are you doing here?" Bart demanded.

"What time is it?"

"8:45," Bart responded before he caught himself. Bart Homespun, Fester Savings Bank's manager, struggled to maintain his composure. He winced when the bundle of keys he clutched pierced the skin of his palm. He also hoped the socially debilitating blush that plagued him since childhood hadn't already rouged his stretched cheeks. Bart had just completed the time-consuming task of unlocking and dragging open the massive vault door. The chore had been typically uneventful until the reassuring rattle that accompanied the tumblers' release of the vault's inner gate startled the young man sitting cross-legged in the center of the room. The adrenaline coursing through Bart's veins caused him to displace confusion that the interloper was roused by the small lock in the gate, but had not heard the three-inch bolts lining the vault door when they thundered free. The man, surrounded by a loose jumble of thoroughly browsed safety deposit boxes, grinned broadly, honestly, and without fear or malice. He couldn't have been much older than twenty.

"I thought you opened at nine?" the intruder complained, projecting some resolve of his own.

"We do, asshole," Bart couldn't believe he was arguing, "Now shut up and don't move!"

"Or else?"

"Huh?"

"Isn't there supposed to be an 'or else?'"

"Jesus, who the hell do you think you are?" Bart shouted. At last remembering oft-rehearsed robbery protocol, he hit the alarm button installed beside the vault threshold, inches from his hands. There was no deafening claxon, but there was a sudden flurry of activity in the bank lobby.

"Uh, oh" The thief said, standing, "I guess I best be going."

"No, you'd best be staying, right there," the hoarse voice of Gene, the bank's security guard, commanded from behind Bart. Bart stepped out of the line of fire from Gene's cocked .45 automatic. Contrary to popular myth, the safety was off, and the barrel steady as a rock.

"Oh? But I must," the crook whispered. He patted the bulging pockets of his loose-fitting faded jeans, and then raised his arms as if in surrender. Gene took a step closer, but paused in shocked witness as the thief drew a breath, lowered his head, bent his knees, and jumped into the air. He executed a graceful swan dive before arching fingertips-first into the steel and concrete floor; not against it, or onto it in submission to the gun pointed at him, but directly into it, fully immersing himself in an apparent still pool of black and white checkerboard water. Long before Bart had registered what he had done, the thief slipped beneath the surface of the floor, leaving nary a ripple to betray his passage.

Bart and Gene stared, then blinked, then stared again. Time passed in shared silence while the two men pondered the significance of the escape. Eventually -- probably just a few seconds later -- Millie Turner, the head teller, edged timidly into the doorway. Seeing nobody but Bart and Gene staring at a floor littered with fifty broken safety deposit boxes, but nothing else, she stepped in front of them.

"What's going on?" she asked.

"No!" Bart screamed, "You'll fall in!" His instincts raging, Bart spread his arms wide and hurled himself at the unwitting spinster, knocking her to the floor near the pile of pilfered steel boxes. Millie screamed in terror at the perceived attack. She pushed Bart away with surprising force, scrambled to her feet, and ran from the vault before her boss could touch her again. Bart shrugged coyly for Gene, who hadn't noticed the incident. No one else came in, but Bart assumed that the rest of his staff was now looking in from outside the vault. They were probably just a little confused, he thought numbly. He looked at Gene. The old man was still staring at the floor, his unspent, unhelpful gun pointing down, its blue barrel visibly quivering.

"Um, Gene," Bart said, resting a hand on the guard's padded shoulder, "You did see that, right?"

"Saw it," Gene whispered.

"Good. Then we're both insane. Come on out and make sure nobody else comes in here. But if this guy, um, surfaces, try to grab him. Tom -- the police -- should be here in a minute."

"Okay, Mr. Homespun."

"Good. I'm going to deal with Millie now. Wish me luck."

"Luck."

"Oh, and Gene?" Bart said, squeezing the old man's shoulder.

"Sir?"

"You could probably put the gun away now."

"Oh yeah. Right sir." After the pistol was holstered, Bart patted Gene's shoulder and stepped out of the vault. The six employees who had already arrived for work melted into the background (figuratively this time), avoiding contact with their confused, and possibly contagious, boss. Bart ignored their reaction. He found Millie, an employee at the branch longer than Bart was alive, carefully poised behind her desk near the tellers' windows. He plopped into the vacant customer's chair across from her. Millie's eyes were wide, like prey, and did not leave Bart's. Bart shook his head, smiled sheepishly, and reached to touch her gnarled hands, which were primly folded on the desk. Millie yelped and whipped her hands off the desk, to her lap. Oops, Bart thought, that was real bright. He sat back, lowered his eyes, and for once didn't mind the blush -- it might amplify the sincerity of his apology. Millie appreciated sincerity.

"Millie," he said softly, visibly folding his hands into his own lap, "I'm so sorry. I thought you were in danger." She regarded him for a moment and, when she sensed that the threat had passed, Millie cleared her throat.

"Of?" she asked, absently fingering her white lace collar.

"You didn't see? We had a break-in."

"Yes sir, I did see that," Millie said, the characteristic edge back in her deep voice, "But I must say I could have avoided the pile of boxes without any help, or violence, from you."

"No, you don't understand. The thief left through the floor. You were standing on the tunnel entrance, and I didn't want you to fall in."

Millie didn't respond. She just gazed past Bart. She hadn't seen a tunnel, only Mad Mr. Homespun and his groping man-fists.

"Never mind. Anyway, Millie, please forgive me. I meant no harm. And don't call me 'Sir.' You know I hate that."

"That's quite all right. Mr. Homespun," Millie said, curling the edge of one thin gray lip slightly upward. I'll take it, Bart thought, and rose to his feet. He tried to ignore Millie when she shied reflexively from his movement. He was on his way back to the open vault when Tom Hayes, the Fester police department, arrived. Per that same never enacted but oft-anticipated protocol, Tom hadn't used his patrol car's siren; he probably hadn't used his patrol car, given that town hall was right across the street. Tom was tapping gently on the locked glass door with his baton. Bart veered to the door, turned the key that was still in the lock to admit his childhood friend. He left the door open in anticipation of the arrival of the rest of the cops, state troupers no doubt, who were obliged to respond to the alarm.

"Bart," Tom said.

"Tom," Bart responded, mimicking Tom's officious surliness.

"Everything okay here?" Tom asked, stone-faced. He was already looking around.

"Well, yes and no," Bart reported, "We were robbed, but the guy got away. No one was hurt." He heard Mille pointedly clear her throat behind him.

"Oh?" Tom asked, pushing past Bart, "How?"

"He dove through the floor. Just over there," Bart said from behind as he followed Tom into the vault.

"Whoa. Nobody tried to go after them, did they?" Tom said, opening up his notebook.

"Nope. We really couldn't actually."

"Why?" Tom asked, fingering the snap on his holster, "Was he armed?"

"Nope," Bart said as they entered the vault, "No hole."

Officer Hayes stopped, looked askance at Bart, and irreversibly affected his investigating officer routine. He glanced at the pile of steel boxes, then around the vault, then back to the floor, then directly at Bart.

"No hole, huh?" he asked.

"Um, nope," Bart said. He waved in Gene, who had been hovering around the doorway, waiting nervously to be called into the game. Gene nearly slid to the marble floor in his haste to reenter the crime scene. Bart grabbed the old guard's elbow, steadied his arm. He nodded toward the undistinguished spot on the vault floor, and said, "Gene. Tell Tom what you saw."

"I'm not totally sure," Gene said pensively, rubbing his chiseled chin.

"Awe, shit, Gene, don't do this!" Bart snarled, "You were here. You saw."

"Oh yeah, I'll give you that. I was here, for sure. Definitely was a perp here when we arrived -- male caucasion, early twenties, slim, short black hair, gray eyes, wearing jeans and a brown t-shirt, apparently unarmed. He eluded capture, however."

"How'd he manage that?" Tom asked, titling his head toward the cannon on Gene's hip.

"Oh," Gene said, glancing nervously at Bart. Bart nodded confidently and may have winked to help ensure that it was okay to continue. Gene stared at Bart for an instant, effectively projecting his profound doubt about that into Bart's soul. He continued to play, however, and said, "How? Don't know exactly. But he had great form."

"Were you asleep?"

"No sir," Gene exclaimed, indignant, "No way would that happen!"

"Then what did happen?" Tom snapped. Bart knew Tom well enough to sense that the officer was growing visibly suspicious of his two witnesses. He suddenly wished that he had never broken up with Tom's sister back in the '90's.

"That's hard to say," Gene said, his husky voice slightly atremble, "I guess you had to be here."

"Well I wasn't, so give it a shot."

"Okay, here goes. Seems the perp just up and disappeared. We couldn't find him anywhere. Might as well have just dove through the floor, like Bugs Bunny on his way to Pismo Beach."

"He *did* dive through the floor," Bart chimed, "You saw it Gene."

"I'm not sure what I saw, sir. But I sure don't see a hole now, so I guess now I couldn't tell you where he went, really." Oh, shit, Bart thought.

"Thanks Gene," Tom said. He scuffed his shoe against the area of floor Gene and Bart had indicated, and stood in the spot for a few seconds before he turned to Bart, "You got anything to add, Bart?"

"Nope, except that he really was here, and he really did dive through the floor."

"Sure he did, Bart. Okay if I get a few statements from your people?"

"Of course. Unfortunately, Only Gene and I saw the thief."

"I see," Tom said, scribbling some notes in his pad, "I just have a couple more questions for you, for now. Who locked the safe last night?"

"You know the answer to that, Tom," Bart said, "I did. I always do."

"Just gotta confirm it," Tom said, still scribbling. He looked up from his pad directly into Bart's eyes, and asked:

"You didn't see a guy in there last night, did you?"

"Jesus, Tom!" Bart said, "Of course not. What the hell?"

"Easy Bart," Tom said, hand raised, voice officious, "You know I gotta ask."

"Yeah, yeah."

"Okay, then, I'll be visiting with your staff for a bit now. Please follow me out and be sure not to touch anything. The State Police detectives, should they ever find their way to our fair city, will probably have some more questions for you later." He nodded and exited the vault, leaving Gene to stare dumbly at Bart. Bart smacked Gene upside the head. Gene did not recoil; he understood.

"What the hell, Gene? Are you trying to leave me out to dry?"

"Sorry Bart," Gene said, "I don't know what I saw anymore."

"So, you didn't see some kid do a Greg Louganis into solid steel? There's a shocker," Bart said. He sighed, draped an arm over Gene's damp shoulder, and led him from the vault, speaking softly, "I can't blame you Gene; they're all going to think we're nuts if we stick to a story like this. Nuts. But we gotta say something, don't we? If we don't, the police will assume that we had something to do with this."

"But we didn't," Gene said loudly, suddenly pale.

"I know that. But the cops are going to believe what they can, no matter how many papers I delivered for Tom when we were kids. I sincerely think that the image of a man passing through two feet of concrete and steel will never conform to their belief system."

"Yeah, you got a point there, boss. And maybe you shouldn't have dumped his sister back in the '90's."

"Tell me about it."

"So what do we do?"

"We stick to the truth, just like we said it, and hope for the best."

Two weeks, and four grueling hours at the county seat's unemployment office later, Bart sat at the counter of

Fester's Tasty Bitz, admiring the soapy sheen on his third cup of coffee.

"There was a hole," he whispered into the cup. A crumb from his doughnut dropped from his chapped lips and into the coffee. He stared at the resultant ripples, which were really there, for a moment, and said, "There was a hole."

"Bart," Gretchen said from across the counter, wiping her hands with a dirty dishrag before jamming a few errant brown locks back under her bun, "You gotta get off it. People can hear you, you know."

"Hear me?" Bart laughed, "That's a real trip. If they could hear me, I wouldn't be explaining my need to collect $288 dollars a week to that sleepy woman at the welfare office in Busby who came as close to anyone actually giving a shit as I'll ever get."

"Unemployment Office; and I give a shit," Gretchen corrected, polishing the clean red counter with the same rag.

"Whatever. Neither of 'em would've given me a moment if I'd mentioned that damn hole either," Bart said, dropping another crumb into his coffee to relive the effect. Gretchen threw her rag at Bart, who allowed it to bounce off his face without reaction. Then she sighed deeply, and looked around the diner to confirm that she had another minute. She did, of course; this was Fester.

"Bart," Gretchen said softly, leaning over the counter until her angular face, unmarred by the diner grease and cheap makeup that challenged its natural beauty, was inches from his, "You know what I mean. It's bad enough that you got fired, and that the town's concluded you're a fruitcake, but don't start actin' the part for them." Bart heard her, but her words were muffled by the rush of blood in his ears caused by the intriguing way her breasts were squashed by the edge of the counter. Man, I am losing it, Bart thought.

"Gretchen," he said, "You're right. I do have to start dealing with this. Tell you what. Go out with me tomorrow night, and I'll start putting it behind me the moment I pick you up." Gretchen smiled brightly.

"That's a deal, sir."

"Good."

"Now," she asked casually, without backing away, "Will we be doing our usual dinner and a movie, or do you have a special night planned to celebrate your upcoming sanity?"

"Way to blow the romance right out of that moment, Gretchen," Harry Bromfeld rasped from his near permanent position three seats down the counter. Gretchen frowned at Harry, and then pretended to ignore him. She waited for Bart to take her hint.

"Of course we will," Bart said, happy to have his mind scrambling something other than images of vanishing thieves and amnesiac bank guards. He put his hands over Gretchen's, leaned forward, pecked her thick lips, and stood.

"I have to go now," he said with conviction.

"Where?" Gretchen asked.

"Seriously," Harry muttered.

"Shut up Harry!" Gretchen, Bart, and the young couple at the booth by the door all shouted in symphony. He did, but couldn't conceal his cynical smirk.

"I don't know yet," Bart said, "I'm going to walk around a bit, sort things out, and maybe start figuring out how to put all this behind me without running away."

"It's about time, Bart," Gretchen said. She spoke sternly, but he felt her relief. He knew she knew he meant it. He never doubted she would. But he did manage a frown of his own.

"Gretch, it's only been two weeks. Give me a break, huh?"

"Two weeks is a long time in this town, Bart. You gotta show people your stuff quick, or else they remember only the bad, forever. And then you gotta --"

"Run away," Bart finished, "I know. Well, I'm not. I'll see you later."

"At Murray's?"

"At Murray's. Bye, Harry."

"Bart."

Bart left the diner. Outside, he walked past his car and turned up Main Street, sporting an honest smile for the first time in two weeks. An insane thing happened, he thought, and I got fired because I was the one who witnessed the insanity. Or thought I did. Now it's done. Tom didn't throw me in jail, even though he really wanted to.

"That's it, then," Bart said aloud.

"What's it?" a voice asked from Fester's only alley. Its unexpected presence and clarity brought Bart to a muscle-wrenching stop. Bart peered into the narrow passage. It was empty. Bart shook his head, and was about to turn away when he noticed an odd shimmer in the brick wall of Klein's department store (Klein's went bankrupt in the '70's but everybody still allowed the empty shell its original given name).

"No," he said, "Not now."

"Oh, come on, dude," the wall said, "After all you've done for me?" A head emerged from the bricks, followed by the rest of the body of the young man who had robbed Bart's bank -- the casual magical crook who had simultaneously stolen Bart's future and deleted his dignity.

"Excuse me?" Bart said. Though a wave of real anger surged through his chest and passed dangerously near his closing fists, all he could manage outwardly was a pathetic, almost snobbish sniff. And, of course, the requisite blush coated his clenched cheeks. Though his initial presentation said otherwise, fear rapidly had no place in the moment; indeed before a few silent seconds passed he was no longer blushing. He stepped close to the man and continued with an unintended hiss, "You robbed my bank, you screwed with my head, and you made my whole town think I'm insane. Which part of that was for me?"

"Bart," the man said with a shrug, "You stuck to your story. That kind of integrity will follow you to your grave."

"And that'll be when? In six months when I starve to death after the unemployment runs out?"

"I thought it goes for a year now?"

Bart suddenly grabbed his hair with both hands and shouted, "What the hell am I even talking to you for! Help! Police! Tom!" Bart expected he would need to make a grab for the thief, but the man just stood in front of him, arms folded, smiling. Bart stopped.

"What?" He asked impatiently, though he already knew the answer.

"And what do you suppose the cop will find when he gets here?" The man asked, correctly.

Bart's urgency had already been trumped by the embarrassment that still lingered from the last time he tried to tell the truth. He calmed himself, and asked, "Then what do you want?"

"Want? I don't know. I hadn't given it much thought."

"Why are you even talking to me?"

"I like you, Bart."

"I'm honored. You got a name?"

"Steve."

"Last name?"

"Nope."

"That so I can only tell the cops that a demon named Steve stole the most prized possessions of half the people in town?"

"Nope. It's just Steve. Guys like me don't need a last name."

"Guys like you?"

"Yeah. Swimmers."

"There are more of you?"

"Oh, yeah. Tons."

"Where?"

"All around. I'm the only one in this town, and I just moved here myself. Mostly we hang in the big cities, where half the people are ghosts anyway. We fit in better there."

"Why are you telling me this?" Bart asked. He noticed that they had been walking, and were nearly through the half block of unkempt weeds that folks liked to call Fester Memorial Park. Bart thought it odd that no one noticed him with this stranger (or, worse, wandering alone if he were truly insane); they had been staring at him for weeks. Steve had an uncanny sense of timing, Bart decided.

"Don't know. Lonely maybe. Or maybe I thought it was time to teach someone else how to swim," Steve sort of sighed. Bart stopped. Okay, he thought, I am nuts, because this conversation is going exactly the way I would expect it to go. He bit anyway:

"Teach me?" he asked.

"Yeah, sure. There's nothing to it, really. Mostly you need to want to."

"So then I can rob banks too?"

"Sure. But more important, you can do whatever you want to do. Good or bad. Or neither."

Bart asked the question that was asked of him three hundred times: "Why did you take all those people's stuff? There was fifty grand in small bills just lying there."

"I told you I just moved in. I'm shy. I find browsing their treasures is a great way to get to know people. And I did plan on putting it all back. Really. It would have been fine except you surprised me -- or I, um, lost track of time."

"Steve, you're a sick fuck. Or I am. Either way I lose, though, so I think it's time to end this."

Steve ran a hand through his thick black hair. He frowned almost prettily for a moment, stared into the space behind Bart's left ear, and finally shrugged and said, "Okay, then. I really thought you'd be interested."

"I'm not," Bart lied.

"Fine," Steve said. He absently fastened a loose button on his faded denim jacket, and continued, "Guess I'm out of here, then. At least I tried."

"Yeah, sure," Bart snorted. He had to act indignantly; it was the only emotion left that he could still control. He started to stalk away, indignantly.

"Oh Bart," Steve called after him, "Just one more thing." Bart stopped. Why am I stopping? He thought, c'mon feet, pick it up! They didn't.

"What?" Bart asked without turning.

"Has anyone looked in those safety deposit boxes in the last couple of days?"

Bart turned, felt that surge again, but kept calm, "What the hell's that supposed to mean?"

"Nothing, I guess," Steve's smile was perfect, "Except that now I feel I know the folks around here a little better."

"Tell me you didn't put every thing back?"

"Best as I could. Swimmers don't have much use for treasure, you know. Slows us down, physically and spiritually. You should remember that."

"You put it back?"

"Uh huh. And if the bank still had a *real* manager, they would have noticed by now," Steve laughed, "But the idiots tossed him."

"You put it back. So my job, my career, is over, and nothing was even stolen?"

"Mm-hmm. Go figure, huh?" Steve said. He paused for a moment, then held his steel gray eyes to Bart's and asked, "You really call that a career? Dude, I did save you. Ciao." Without warning he disappeared down into the sidewalk. Steve's laughing eyes never left Bart's as he descended, as if aboard a tiny elevator, into solid concrete. The last thing Bart saw was Steve's hand. It was closed in a fist with pinky and thumb extended toward the sky.

The sharp stab of pain rendered by his failed knees' contact with the sidewalk helped shake Bart of his urge to swim after Steve. He rolled to the grass, grabbing his legs and swearing loudly. His curses flowed more from anguish than pain. Before they subsided, a crowd had gathered to gawk at their town's new crazy man. Bart noticed them, and returned their stares.

"Oh fine," he shouted through unwanted tears, "Now you see me! I don't suppose any of you saw the guy with me?" Someone snickered. They hadn't. The small crowd shifted as Gretchen shoved her way in. She shook her head and knelt beside Bart.

"You people!" She shouted over her shoulder as she examined her fiancé, "Don't you have lives?"

"Sure," Joey Miller, who should have been in school, shouted from the back, "But Mr. Homespun's is way more fun."

"Bart," Gretchen whispered as she helped a wobbly Bart to his feet, "Didn't you just decide not to be crazy, like five minutes ago?"

"I guess I got better," Bart said. He straightened up, dusted the crease of his rumpled suit, and spoke to the crowd, "Okay folks, that's it. Nothing more to see here. Millie? That you lurking back there? Behind Ed Jones?" It was. Millie stepped from behind the huge farmer, pulled her cardigan closed, and nodded.

"Shouldn't you be at work?"

"I had an errand, sir," Millie said.

"No need to explain, Millie. Not any more. And yes, I know it wasn't your fault I got fired."

"I helped," Millie said, her voice cracking. She noticed that she stood alone in the street now; the rest of the crowd had already dispersed. Suddenly nervous, she turned toward her bank.

"Millie wait," Bart called. She didn't stop. "Don't worry, I won't jump you."

"I'll guarantee that," Gretchen called. I know I didn't need that, Bart thought. Millie stopped.

"Millie," Bart asked, careful not to step closer to her, "Could you do one last thing for me? One small favor?"

"I'd have to hear it first, sir."

"Millie, please stop calling me sir!"

"Is that the thing?" Millie asked, looking relieved.

"No Millie. I just want you to have someone recheck the safety deposit boxes."

"Why?"

"No reason. Just have someone do it. Hell, grab some customers and do it yourself."

Millie stood still for a moment, regarding Bart with a gaze he would have sworn carried hope, if he knew what hope looked like. Then she turned and left, striding quickly to the bank.

"Why did you ask her to do that?" Gretchen asked, leading him back to the Tasty Bitz for another cup of coffee and some careful supervision.

"I guess just to help the ungrateful wretches around here realize that their stuff was back. Maybe it never left."

"Huh?"

"Nothing. Don't mind me. Listen, now that I think about it, don't mind me at all. I'm okay. I have to go do something now. Something else." He extracted Gretchen's hand from the crook in his elbow. The way in which he gently kissed her cheek sent a ripple of panic through Gretchen. She let go of him. She let him walk away, down Main Street and toward the edge of town. He did not turn as he walked, and she noticed that his back was straighter than it had been in years. When he reached the edge of town, about a hundred yards along on the empty street, Gretchen groaned and shouted:

"Bart! Where the hell are you going?"

"Thought I'd get some swimming lessons," he said softly, though his words reached her easily. He waved once, and turned away. Gretchen looked at her feet, puzzled. She raised her head and shouted:

"But you're an excellent swimmer!"

Bart was gone.

The Six Souls' Secaucus Summit

Did you ever awaken confused, disoriented, and convinced that you just experienced someone else's dream? Perhaps you did. No, not in the Edgar Cayce-ethereal-person-to person contact manner, but perhaps for the instant of that dream you understood your role as a single fiber enmeshed within a vast network of thought whose confluence forms a single soul. Occasionally, that soul gets its wires crossed, and you bump into strangers during your dreams. The concept is not as far from natural as you might think. For instance, ants have existed as colonies of separate but clearly united organisms for millions of years. Is there a rule mandating all advanced life to be comprised of separate individuals walled off from each other by all but often clumsy physical communication?

Consider therefore this cosmic option: Humanity is not a vast chaotic herd of six billion individuals littering Earth's surface, but rather a group of six "major" souls who divide their experience among the thoughts, dreams, and daily lives of billions of human beings. These souls have existed since the dawn of intelligent life, and have enjoyed being greater than the sum of their sentient parts for uncounted millennia. The souls physically exist in an ethereal realm, removed from the mundane world of humanity in general, though always interested in the condition of their parts.

Occasionally they will visit their human condition, or allow one mind to experience their true nature. These visits and allowances could clarify many mysteries, including ESP, real magic, clairvoyance, miracles, Carl Jung, the French, and why people actually liked "Dumb And Dumber." They also could explain nationalism, religion, and other global phenomena that target specific groups of people.

It is the activity of these groups that caused the souls' rare descent from their lofty perches. By replacing the souls' authority and innate mythology with modern technology, humanity threatens to rend the fabric of its own collective being. The six souls are aware of this. However, as each soul defines and experiences reality differently, communication is difficult on the astral plane of their everyday existence. Therefore, in order to deal with the crisis properly, the souls have agreed to take human form for a short time. For this major summit of the forces behind the wisdom and consciousness of all humanity, they choose to brunch at Howard Jonson's, in New Jersey...

A chubby Asian sat reflectively on the red vinyl cushioned bench that lined slightly dirty windows offering a sunny panoramic view of NJ Rte 3. From his carefully chosen central position at the large three-sided booth's long Formica table, he called the meeting to order: "I wish to express my sincerest gratitude to each of you for manifesting corporeal form today. The grand event of the resolution of the fate of our souls can only occur while we occupy a condition that generates appropriate human emotion and physical reaction to our otherwise uniquely impenetrable thoughts." He cleared his bouncing throat regally. With small black eyes gleaming from an empty cherubic face, he somberly reviewed the five faces of his variably attentive compatriots gathered around the table. He patiently finished his sweep, waited in silence for a few heavy seconds, and then finally asked: "Now, could someone please pass the syrup?"

"Here you go," Europa responded cheerfully as she started a cruet of maple syrup moving across hands toward the ancient. She brushed back a lock of blonde hair to clear her huge blue eyes, and continued, "But Sino, dude, why did we meet at a Ho-Jo's in Secaucus? I was hopin' for Le Cirque myself."

"The reasons are many, young one," Sino stated, "But the greatest are threefold. First, our locale for gathering must enjoy neutrality. None of us, not even Shaman, enjoys a firm presence in this land called New Jersey. Second, our discussions must be had inconspicuously, and the diners at Le Cirque may be more able to acknowledge the significance of our presence and conversation than the patrons at this lesser establishment. Third, and perhaps most important – I am most interested in fueling my occasional flesh with pancakes, and Le Cirque just can't touch Howard Jonson's."

"Cool," Europa said, grinning around a plastic straw, "But you could've just said 'because I said so.' We'd have played along."

"Your thoughts might not be shared, child," rumbled Brahma as he brushed a bit of doughnut powder from his Armani suit, "Sino, your logic is sound, but does the rationale for our summit truly exist? My time and energy are likely better spent elsewhere. There's been a great flood, you know."

"Yeah," chimed Bantu between chomps on a sausage, "What he said. This whole body thing is fine; I do it all the time to properly understand my minds. Unfortunately, I have a whole continent coming apart under me, and it's all I can do just keeping track of the casualties. My time is precious these days. Whose fate is so deeply dragging that we need to meet like this? We haven't done this since, since..."

"The Christ," Shaman mumbled, "And look what that did to me."

"Oh, quit feelin' sorry for yourself, Sham Man," Europa said, resting a hand on the tall brooding man's twitching leather-clad thigh, "After all, your loss was my gain. Right?"

"Your gain is indeed what we have come to consider, dear Europa," Sino interjected from across the Formica table. His volume silenced the others, and sent a child in the next booth into a sympathetic rain of colic tears. Sino did not respond to the parents' dirty looks. He lowered his tomato juice, the tiny glass almost concealed behind his puffed fingers, and studied Europa. His eyes, little black suns forever setting behind Pop-n-Fresh cheeks, examined her long blonde hair, fresh skin, bright smile, and perfect teenaged body. Europa could not discern whether he was pleased or annoyed by the physical presence that she chose – Sino always seemed to be smiling. In a moment he drew a long breath, and then spoke again. His words pierced the silence with unchallenged authority that rang subliminally in the ears of other diners and rattled the silverware throughout the restaurant:

"Where hides the constituency of your soul, Europa? We offered you a grand opportunity when we allowed your emergence at the last summit: a chance to become the minds of the next age of man, to guide the spirit of mature humanity. Yet your minds are disparate, independent, and interested only in themselves. They are more primitive in behavior and desire than the stock with which we originally provided. Moreover, this germ of individuality and greed has infected the world. Our world. We must consider carefully how to cure your inaction."

Europa did not allow Sino's words to echo through her colleagues as intended. Instead, she responded instantly.

She innately understood the purpose of their meeting, and was prepared. She placed a thin finger on her Mary Kay cheek and said, softly, "What are you talking about, old man? You think that because I don't keep shop the same way you do I've failed? Be serious."

"Don't toy with us, girl," Bantu hissed, "We made you; we can expect something from you in—"

"Oh puh-lease," Europa said, extending her hand, palm out, and looking away, "Spare me the theatrics. You didn't make shit. You shed me. I am the construct of the discards of your beings. All of you, except maybe poor Shaman here."

"We fortified you with our best minds," Bantu argued.

"Yeah. Minds that kept interfering with your ability to keep a tidy house. You loaded me up with three million dissenters, questioners, and thinkers, then dared me to build a world with them." Europa pinched a greasy sausage between two fingers, regarded it silently as it dangled limply before her. Then she shook it collectively at her elders while continuing sardonically, "Well get the Kodak boys, 'cause I got your world right here. I'm real sorry if it interferes with the 'wisdom of the ages,' but hey, I did what I could with the tools at hand." She shoved the sausage in her mouth, smiling as she chewed.

"Silence, child!" Sino shouted, slamming a ham-sized fist on the table. The impact sent crockery flying and raised the eyebrows of increasingly less tolerant patrons. That reignited the baby, setting his father to mumble angrily to himself about the disturbance.

"Sino, please," Shaman whispered without much conviction, "She's done. And you must remember the profile we desire."

"Nonsense. This is New Jersey. Who would listen? And why is that? Because this child dares to leave her minds free to develop on their own! They learn; they draw their science from the Ether. They elevate their material world above that of the reality of spirit. She has let them spread their disease to the souls of the entire planet! You are a failure and a disgrace, Europa."

"Why? Because I'm not into shepherding followers? I'll call your disgrace and raise you a dozen failed religions, fat man. Not to mention all the useless civilizations my thinkers also swept under your musty rugs. Right, Shaman?"

"Fuck you, bitch," Shaman whispered. His brown eyes glistened.

Opinions and accusations clouded the cluttered table as the group struggled to strain their ancient opinions, biases, and judgments through the simple human machinery that they had chosen to convey them. The chaotic conversation must have appeared bizarre to a bystander, as each person spoke in a different language (Sino, Mandarin; Bantu, Swahili; Shaman, Navajo; Europa, bad English), but all understood each other perfectly. Well, at least they all heard each other. The din rose steadily until the silent, hooded woman seated directly across the table from Europa raised a closed fist to her trim dry mouth, and coughed once. Then it stopped. Five heads turned in unison toward Sumer. She let them wait a few minutes, and then lifted her eyes to each of them, apparently in unison.

"As one of the primary progenitors of this issue, and of young Europa's world, I would like a word," Sumer said gently, in a language unheard on earth for twenty centuries. She looked down at her untouched bagel with cream cheese and waited. Her sudden, softly spoken and totally unexpected words surprised the other five souls; they rarely heard from the elder, in any form. That she chose to attend was honor enough, but to add to the discussion piqued their interest. Bantu enjoyed the novel sensation of a chill racing down his spine.

"Of course, mother," Sino said, bowing his great round head, "We would be honored by..." Sumer looked up, and pulled back the blue silk hood that had concealed her sharply chiseled features. Her deep-set green eyes narrowed behind rose tinted wire-rimmed librarian spectacles.

"Spare me the speech, boy," she snapped, her ancient tongue raising the eyebrows of a tweed-clad gentleman at the snack bar, "And never address me so; I am no creature's mother." She peeled her glasses off with long, dark fingers and leaned back from the table. Her robes rustled against the booth's plastic cushion. She looked at no one, but all felt the fiery pierce of her gaze, including their waitress, who had arrived to refresh the coffee. The bewildered girl set the pot on the table, smiled nervously. The young woman then retreated to the kitchen, where she shook her head, loosened her ponytail, and headed out the back door for a smoke. Sumer blinked, slowly, while meticulously cleaning her glasses with the edge of one of her veils. She spoke softly, but there were people in Philadelphia who were sure they heard the echo of her words:

"I am not convinced that this child has chosen the wrong path."

The gasps from Sumer's eternal kin were audible, and Brahma stopped chewing his toast. He raised a painted finger as if to interrupt, but Sumer shook her head: "Hold your counsel Brahma, until I have completed this thought. Then you may strike."

"We did indeed release our unwanted aspects into the tepid cauldron from which Europa emerged. In the short time that has since elapsed, we have chosen to refrain from observation, much less caring to note what harm we wrought. This was done in clear defiance of our very nature, which exists to incessantly communicate our feelings. We have remained aloof, content in our little unchanging universes. Our arrogant silence has allowed her minds to dominate this world's structure. The domination by these rogue husks has affected each of us. Shaman ignored, and lost, his minds. Bantu chose to hide in the frightening biology of the Earth. Sino and Brahma have forced their minds into a dizzying spiral of procreation. I, perhaps most unwisely, have reacted to the new order by propagating a lethal religion whose noble foundations have been forgotten. All this was done in our effort to fight the power of Europa's ignorance."

"Hey!"

"Do not interrupt, child. I understand that, when we resume our standard forms shortly you may hold the best cards, but I will still control the terrorists. You can be proud, but be wary always."

"Now. As I was saying. In our halfhearted effort to confront our error, we did many painful things: crusades, jihads, world wars, plagues, overpopulation, dictatorships, terrorism, cable television, and so much more. We have all reacted in one way or another to Europa's pathetic handling of her charges. Yes, those charges, those nonconforming minds, did thrust her into existence because of our pathetic laziness; but they were hers. She chose to allow them to grow beyond their mortal capacity, to reach for the stars and to build weapons, political systems, and societies that threaten their own reality. Remember, though, they do not challenge ours. Not even you, Shaman, who chose to vacate yourself from your charges the very century Europa's husks found them. What were you thinking?"

"I was tired," Shaman mumbled. He rested his chin atop a closed fist, and seemed to be carefully studying something over Sumer's shoulder. Sumer disregarded his posture and continued:

"You still are, I know, and also quite weak. I am sure that we all feel your exhaustion, and understand its root. Your minds had grown far too attached to you, and you in turn allowed them to know you too well. Close contact means cohesion, cohesion means vast energy spent. What were you thinking?"

"I liked the attention."

"Shaman" Sumer sighed, tapping a long black pinky nail on the edge of her teacup, "When we resume our true forms you and I will address at length your desired entropy. The subject has been neglected long enough, and must be resolved. You are the purest of us all, Shaman, the closest to the Truth, yet you have no eye for practicality. Imagine letting Europa eliminate so many aspects of your precious soul, with lowly germs alone! Again, what were you thinking?"

Shaman shifted his unfocused gaze down, to his untouched omelet. He said nothing. After a long and utterly silent pause, Sumer continued:

"It is amazing, the animosity that human form can engender. Forgive me, Shaman, as I forgive the attitude the current chemicals that are your body must foment in you."

"What about me?" Europa snapped, "I could use a little of that, too."

"Silence, child," Brahma growled, "Your interruptions grow tedious. Let Mo—Sumer – speak."

"Thank you, Brahma," Sumer said, almost smiling, "Now calm yourself; you are frightening the human children over there. Look at them; the untainted young. They know us. Children always do and, though the legends may do this tired land of refineries and wretched retail some good, we do not want to instill decades of nightmares with but one outburst." Brahma looked around sheepishly, nodded, and resumed munching his steak in silence. Sumer cleared her throat again and addressed Europa directly:

"Now, back to you, child. Your antics attempt to tear asunder the fabric of our being, to end existences that have endured since this world took its first breath. We do not appreciate the gesture."

"Well, bitch," Europa said, eyes ablaze. She held Sumer's glacial gaze, and fought a traitorous flutter that invaded her blustery speech when she continued, "Live with it. It's happened before. You guys were out of circulation for almost a tenth of this world's existence after you offed the dinosaurs."

"We did not 'off' the Great Races, child," Sino corrected, "Their civilization became too advanced, and they threatened the survival of nature Herself with their ceaseless tampering with the environment. In addition, they forgot the source of their wisdom. Action had to be taken, to preserve the souls, and to keep nature intact."

"Gee," Europa said, index finger firmly against her cheek, eyes skyward, "Now why does that sound familiar? Huh? What is up with you losers? You fall asleep at the wheel, and then try to pin the wreck on the kid in the car seat. Please."

"That is enough, Europa," Sumer said quietly, "Do not assume that I have forgotten the dinosaurs. We were once twelve souls. The nine that were absorbed by the cataclysm were my elders, and my creators. You cannot know sorrow until you hear the death song of a soul, especially one as old and once plentiful as Gr'Alth' Na. The void of their absence still clouds my dreams."

"And your judgment," Shaman whispered. Bantu hurled his full coffee mug at Shaman, but Sumer caught it before it reached the dark man's furrowed brow. Not a drop was spilled. She gently set the mug before her and, without glancing at Bantu, spoke to Shaman.

"Perhaps your wisdom eclipses ours. Nature always favored your counsel. You are correct, of course; the actions of Europa have invited another cleansing. Unlike the Great Races, whose civilization was millions of years strong, this cleansing would require little effort from us. Indeed, we would need only walk away and watch the nuclear, or – what is the latest threat? – Nanotechnic display as the world bleeds out her latest chaotic infection. Perhaps, Shaman, I am being selfish, even humanly selfish, by maintaining a grip on my minds. You did not endure the pain of the last bath, the death of billions of minds, of nine souls, of civilizations whose achievement mightily reflected eons of labor. I do not intend to endure that agony, and subsequent loneliness, again."

"Nor I," Brahma mumbled, "The loss made time real for me."

"And choked the life from too much of this world," Sino finished, "I was not present at the last sweep, but I shudder (yes, shudder) at the prospect of abandoning my charges, at the erasure of so much of my, of our, selves."

"So what I hear you guys saying," Europa said between rounds of blowing bubbles in her chocolate milk, "Is that I managed to open the door to another planet-wide disaster."

"Yes, child," Sino said, "And a purification of such nature should still be eons away. Your tenacious ignorance has forced the civilizations of humanity to develop millions of years prematurely."

"So? Can't that be a good thing?"

"Absolutely, young one," Bantu said, waving off the waitress while he spoke, "Unfortunately, you spurred only the growth of knowledge and the vast power that accompanies it. You eschewed wisdom, which can only come through ages of careful attention. Even the dinosaurs had wisdom (perhaps too much, true). Knowledge without wisdom is power without focus or control. Only pain can result. Sadly, the pain will not be yours."

"Cool!" Europa chirped, and then gasped, covering her mouth. She stammered, "No, not cool. That's not what I meant. I was just relieved. Dammit, I hate this whole body thing; it totally screws me up!"

"That's why we do it, child," Sino said calmly, "So we all can qualify the damage our decisions can cause."

"Seriously, though," Europa said to Sumer, "Why won't this bother me?"

"Because the conflagration your minds are destined to create will delete them so quickly that you will cease to exist before you can feel the pain."

"Oh." Europa said softly. She regarded her milk in silence for a few minutes, then asked, without looking up, "Will I take any of you with me?"

"Most likely," Sino sighed, "Though who will succumb, we cannot know. The rest of us will suffer on to nurture what DNA survives the doom. We have done it before, but –"

"We are not ready to now," Sumer finished, "It is too soon." She slapped her palms on the table, then turned them over and raised a corner of her thin mouth in bemusement. She looked carefully at each of her charges before continuing:

"That is all I have to say. I leave it to you who control the fate of billions to sort out the details of rescuing our current species before it goes too far. Europa, if you enjoy life, I suggest you pay attention. Brahma: slide out that I may leave." With no further word, Sumer slid across the vinyl patch Brahma cleared for her by heaving his seven foot frame from the booth. Sumer threw a $10 bill on the table, gently rubbed a lapel of Brahma's suit for an instant, and walked out of the restaurant. Brahma sat and returned to his breakfast. No one spoke until the vintage black Rolls Royce pulled out of the parking lot.

"What a woman," Europa said, picking up the money, "She even overpaid. I mean, she just had a bagel. Hell, she barely nibbled it."

"Please, girl," Sino said, "Spare us. Unlike you, Sumer chooses, always, to complete a transaction."

"She's a god," Europa hissed.

"Well, yes," Bantu responded, sipping coffee, "But that has nothing to do with our plans to deal with the shit you got us into."

"What?" Europa whined, "Why are you guys pinning this on me? You made me! Your other attempts to curb my soul failed (yeah, don't think I'm not aware that the Black Plague was your baby, Sino. That hurt!). Why do you think anything you try now will work? Maybe Miss Fussypants left because she knows what you've really got to decide."

"Oh?" Sino asked, "And what might that be?"

Europa smiled widely, but thought to keep her perfect teeth concealed. She slid from the booth. On the way out, she carefully rubbed body parts with Brahma and Bantu. She crawled into a neighboring booth, kneeled against its high seat-back behind Sino, and began gently rubbing his shoulders. Caught up in a moment of human tactile appreciation that he hadn't experienced in a thousand years, Sino allowed her the gesture. So, oddly, did the young couple at the booth Europa had invaded. After a moment of gentle massage, Europa spoke to her elders:

"You guys have to decide how much force will be necessary to eliminate this little virus you let me create; this virus called modern man. You don't give a crap about me. I know that. I'm as much an outcast as the minds that created me." She paused, waiting, in a distinctly human fashion, for the denials. The four souls remained silent. Only Shaman seemed disinterested.

"Go on," Sino said softly.

"With what? The speech I been rehearsing for 300 years, or the massage?"

"Both. Please."

"You old softie. At any rate, though I am not part of your aged club, I have managed to become, in an incredibly short time I must add, a soul whose minds are virtually unstoppable. I mean, what'll you do? One of Sumer's jihads will fail, as they always do. Bantu could attempt another disease, but my little soldiers keep on outsmarting the bugs, and besides, why risk it? Look what AIDS did to his own unwitting kiddies. Brahma, I'm sure you could keep up the breeding, expanding your influence, but time is not on your side. Sure Sino, you've got the nukes, but then you're all back to nursing DNA for a thousand centuries, and nobody wants that. So you see, guys, you'll just have to adapt to my brave new world, at least until I can catch up to you all."

"You forgot me," Shaman said softly, though the depth of his intensity drew an involuntary gasp from a Latino man at the counter. Europa glanced down at Shaman, her eyes half closed.

"No, Shaman. I did not forget you," she said, her tone somewhere between sympathetic and dismissive, "The world forgot you." She lifted one hand from its work to gently caress Shaman's cheek, where the tear should have fallen.

"Perhaps," Shaman said. Then he surprised Europa by raising his gaze until it met hers, and smiling broadly. He held the expression for a full minute before Europa ceased her kneading and absently slapped Sino's shoulders in frustration. Sino chuckled.

"What!" she exclaimed. She suddenly became agitated, and her temples began to throb when she noticed that the other three appeared to recognize and approve of Shaman's smug behavior.

"Why Europa," Shaman said pleasantly, "I thought you would know. Don't you ever listen to your minds? Even to your fellow souls, when we are able to communicate properly?"

"Well, sure I do, but I've never heard a peep outa yours, at least not since the Casinos started up."

"You should listen. Sumer's displeasure in me is not in my abandonment of my minds. Their cohesion is stronger now than it has ever been. No. Her anger stems rather from my inaction. She wants me to wake up."

"You're asleep?"

"Uh huh."

"So?"

The four souls laughed heartily. There was no joy in their raucous display, only recognition.

"This isn't good, is it?" Europa asked, biting her thumbnail.

"Potentially not, child," Brahma said, wiping an easy tear from his eye, "But only potentially." He calmed, and then returned his attention to the latest doughnut he was devouring. He seemed particularly pleased with the dunking part.

Silence fell upon the group. They seemed to have either lost interest in speaking, or gained interest in the rare pleasure of corporeal ingestion. Eating, Sino reminded himself. Europa rubbed her temples, adjusted her hair, and snatched a full coffeepot from a passing, acquiescent, waitress. The puzzled woman removed the pot that Brahma had recently finished, and disappeared. Europa returned to the booth, but jammed herself in beside Brahma, across from Shaman. She was careful to keep her knee pressed firmly against Shaman's. She filled Sumer's clean cup with black coffee, took a sip, and tried to hold Shaman's now constant stare. His brown eyes were dazzling, yet haunted with an image that forced her to look away. She waited for a few more minutes before she broke the silence gently:

"So, is anyone going to share Shaman's little secret with me? Or do I need to guess?" Oops, she thought, after she spoke. She touched a finger to her pouting lower lip, and waited. Bantu licked the butter off his fingers, still savoring the English muffin he had finished, and spoke:

"There is nothing like butter. Nothing. Anyway, since we're all here for a good time, we'd be happy to play a game. Go ahead and guess. You're a smart girl; I would imagine you would get it right very quickly."

"Well," Europa smiled, "I guess there's no point in calling any of you patronizing. Are you serious?"

"Please," Sino said, "Humor us. Your communication skills surpass ours in this tender forum. We articulate far more effectively as a group, so your singular response may be to our benefit. Besides, you may think of things we have not – "he paused, waited for Bantu to stop chuckling, then continued, "You may stumble upon an acceptable cure for your disease of biological independence that we ignored."

"Yeah, sure," Europa sighed, "I'll play. What's to lose?" Bantu stifled another chuckle by ramming a freshly buttered English muffin into his mouth. Europa looked around the restaurant, tapping her nails on the table pensively. She hummed an old Cream tune, "Strange Brew," while she scanned those patrons who were stout enough to finish their meals in spite of the barrage of disturbances her table had been delivering. There were several, thankfully of various ethnic backgrounds. She spent about three seconds observing each group. First was a Rockwellian family saying Grace over their half-eaten entrees; next was an Asian man at the counter, who had either fallen asleep or was lost in thought. A pair of Arabs at a back booth were arguing fiercely and pointing toward Manhattan and their watches. A Jewish woman nearby looked troubled as she fondled the oddly shaped charm that hung by a gold chain from her neck. Europa closed her eyes, allowing the scattered messages the minds in the restaurant projected to congeal into a single image of their parent souls' intent. They did, and the music of their mingled thoughts, their improbably shared mortal dreams, coalesced into a unit of understanding that flung open her wide young eyes. She shook her head; cast those eyes directly at each of her colleagues. She linked vision with Shaman last and longest. Finally Europa looked down at her hands, which had folded gracefully in her lap. She laughed a little too loudly, releasing more of a frightened cackle than a knowing guffaw.

"Oh, you assholes," She said, "You shopworn sons of bitches. It's that old time religion, isn't it? You're planning another messiah? Maybe a kazillianth ineffective jihad?"

"No, child," Sino said, "We've learned our lessons about the limits of our current race. We plan on something much more subtle this time."

"Let's see," she said, raising her hands to count off pretty fingers, "Subtle, Sham-Man, and a desperate play for the survival of your ethereal selves. No messiah's (thank you!)." She paused, cast a final net across the innate hope embedded in the minds of the humans around her, and snapped her fingers loudly.

"I got it," she exclaimed, "You're going for magic." Shaman smiled.

"It is what I have left. My minds are few, but the seed of faith, the desire to believe in the impossible, is still buried deep within them, and within all the minds of mankind. I have already begun to nurture that dream."

"Yeah, I've seen that Wicca crap on the Internet."

"That Wicca crap was no accident," Brahma said, "And it is the antithesis for your science. We hope to share the thoughts of Shaman across the world, though a few souls..."

"Like Sumer, maybe?"

"A few souls may disagree with the tactic. Sumer, and I, seems to share the deepest dissent. We have spent several millennia nurturing our souls toward order and consistency. Magic confounds that order, and invites individual acts."

"Yes," Sino interjected, "But the acts would be in the name of harmless faith, rather than technical invention or blind experience. I have already felt the infiltration of Falun Gong in myself. We sense a complete cleansing in less than thirty generations."

"That sounds effective," Europa said, "You guys should follow his lead. How long is a generation again?"

"Sure," Shaman said, "Thirty generations ought to allow you with enough time to obliterate some of us from the world completely. Sino chooses, in his wisdom, to underestimate the power of wishful thinking. I do not. I expect that the esoteric revolution I am fomenting in your own back yard will accelerate Brahma and Sino's efforts."

"What about Bantu?"

"Fear not, child," Bantu laughed, "Like my dear sister Sumer, I never let go. Our souls will draw strength and cohesion from Shaman's magic, even if we do lose a few minds to the inevitable holy wars. I have already begun stirring the pot by allowing this disease AIDS to spread unchecked, thus forming a fine foundation for faith in magic. That's right, child, the destruction, the sacrifice, was no accident."

Silence invaded again as Europa tried to absorb the concepts thrust upon her. She felt ill-prepared to deal with the thoughts while still confined to the machinations of biomass, but then assumed that was the intent of the meeting. She would have ignored the others, as usual, if they had attempted to contact her in the normal state. She refilled her coffee cup once more and patiently considered its mist. In time Europa, the youngest and currently most powerful of the six remaining souls of earth, raised her head, but glanced up at no one in particular.

"That's it, then," she said, "I guess I'll deal with it. Bantu, you gonna eat that last doughnut?"

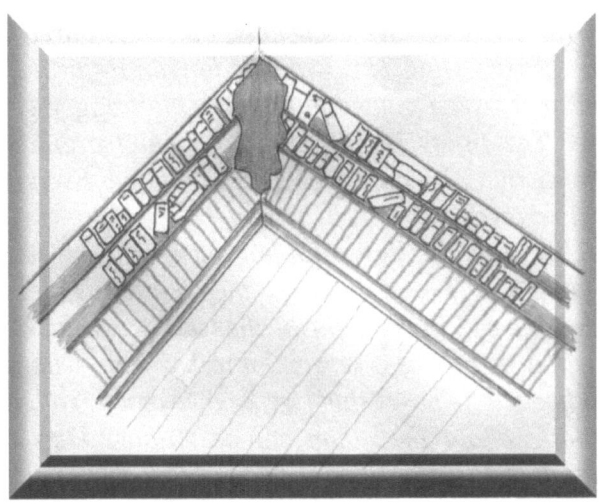

Hiram, Lydia and the Void

*E*lm Street lay quiet, peacefully dim in the amber wash of incandescent lamps. It was an unobtrusive neighborhood in Pillard, an insignificant farm town. Not a very worldly place; indeed, if asked, few of the residents would know what a pentagram was, or care. But then, every town must have its educated few.

The lights of 301 Elm burned well into the night, though the little shop had been closed for hours. Every night the front display windows would glow until the morning sun retired them. This was not a standard activity in Pillard, where the bars even shut their doors before twelve.

The neighbors were curious, but none dared inquire after the owner's vigil. This was not done in Pillard. Besides, everyone that asked got nothing more than angry grunts in response. The lights simply stayed on, and eventually the nocturnal activity became accepted as routine. Even the ugly rumors died away.

This night the lights did not burn until dawn. Shortly after midnight they went out. First they flared, as if to expend the night's energy in one flash, then all was black. At the same instant there was a scream of terror from within, but it went unheeded. Those that were awakened rolled over, complaining about the damn cat next door. They did not understand why the hairs on their necks stood. Some did not even notice.

Hiram Grouper smiled broadly. After ten years of saving, his dream was finally real. There it was, spread out before him in so many piles of paper, leather, and dust. His own bookstore. He had acquired it at the recent auction of the sizable estate of the widow that hung herself a few months earlier. She was a crazy old bat, Hiram knew from rumor. Ever since her husband disappeared in the thirties, she had kept to herself and her wealth. The gossip never reached a definite conclusion as to where Mrs. Banister found her funds, since no one had the courage to ask her. Her only visible means of support was the bookstore, and this was the first day its doors were opened since the night Mr. Banister vanished.

Hiram did not care for trivia of that nature. He had what he wanted, and could even afford to lose some money while he enjoyed his new occupation. Lydia cared. She stood behind her husband, waiting for him to finish basking in his moment of supreme glory. Hiram was a simple man, filled with simple thoughts and dreams, and she loved him for it. However, that did not prevent her from wishing occasionally that he would set higher goals for himself. The aspirations were there, when they met in college, but Hiram had to get a degree in literature, contrary to all her pleas for law school. Lydia curbed her dreams, for his sake, and in the end was glad she did. They weren't much anyway.

But why had he blown all their savings on this ancient bookshop? There wasn't one new book here. She wouldn't complain; she had promised herself once never to complain.

"Well Hiram," Lydia said, walking in, being sure to kick up ample dust, "Here it is. Your very own out of print book shop. And with no money left for new titles."

"That doesn't matter, Lydia. There will never be a Romance book sold here anyway. Besides, there's a market for vintage books."

"How about vintage dust? Vintage, he calls them," Lydia sighed, pulling a cobweb from her bleached hair. She put her purse on a chair and sat on it, to wait for Hiram's triumph to subside. He was at the counter, playing with the antique register. He hit No Sale to watch the rusty tag pop up behind the glass.

"Hey," he said, holding up a wad of cash, "There's money in here. The old lady really did leave in a hurry." The discovery sparked Lydia's interest. She snatched it from Hiram and counted it.

"75 dollars. Well, it's better than nothing."

"I wonder why she left it behind?"

"Who cares?" Lydia snapped, pocketing the crumbling cash, "Let's just be thankful it's here; it may be all we ever make."

Hiram ignored her and began his venture into the store.

Time and several bottles of pledge proved that the major difficulty in the store was dust. The shelves were properly stocked and everything was in order, but it was all abandoned to a blizzard of dust. For three days Hiram and sometimes Lydia worked steadily, clearing shelves, dusting books, coughing often. They had started at the door, and now the warped back wall was in sight. Hiram gave the back left corner a collective glance, as he did before starting each section. Lydia stood beside him, facing the other way. She was admiring their handiwork. This store isn't half bad, she thought, once you get through the grime. She was feeling much better about the store. That morning she visited the local library and nosed through price books. There was a fortune in collectible books littering the store. The thought was enough to make her softly whistle a tune of delight the rest of the day. Hiram wasn't completely hopeless after all.

"Well," he said, "This is it, the last section. Occult."

"What's a `colt'?" Lydia asked, her arm resting on a cleaned firearms shelf, head cocked toward Animals.

"Witchcraft, mostly. Parapsychology. The science of forces science knows nothing about, you might say."

"Yeah, I suppose I might," Lydia said, dropping the subject. When Hiram was getting his degree, her major was waitressing. She said, "I think I'll go practice on the register some more," and returned to the side of the store she understood.

"Fine," Hiram said, content to work alone. He pulled aside a blanket crumpled in the corner. It revealed some open books, a smashed candle, and a drawing on the floor.

"Hey," he shouted over his shoulder, "The old lady left a mess for us. And the rest of the store was so neat. Only dust. She must have been Jewish, too. And proud of it."

"Why's that?" Lydia asked, insincerely.

"There's this star on the floor. My God, it looks like... yes, it's paint. Now how are we going to get that off?"

"We could always move Religion over there."

Hiram laughed. He appreciated his wife's sense of humor. He then addressed himself to the dusty shelves at hand.

"That old lady sure liked her magic books. I've never seen so many in one place before," he said, blowing dust off a hefty copy. It was ancient, leather-bound, and must have weighed thirty pounds. Once clean, Hiram recognized the raised lettering on the cover as Latin. He whistled. "Wow, this one must be worth a fortune." Lydia had a hand on it before he finished his sentence.

"What is it?" she gasped.

"I don't know, I failed Latin twice. We'll check it later. Maybe it has a history." He set it down, in the star. Lydia's eyes followed the treasure to the floor. She started to turn to the language section to find a Latin-English dictionary, but her eyes lingered on the book. The hairs on the back of her neck stood. She felt a shaft of fear pierce her spine, with the book as its source. There was no reason for this, so she shook her head to clear it and left the book, forgetting the matter. Hiram hadn't noticed, so why should she?

Hiram returned to his cleaning, spotted a rag tucked in the corner. He pulled at it, but it stayed put. He pulled harder until it gave, sending him to the floor. The cloth in his hand was nearly the size of the one that had covered floor.

"But it was so small," Hiram said.

"What?" Lydia asked, sensing another rare find. She had translated the cover, but it meant nothing to her. "Hiram, what's `Necromancing'? It sounds kinky."

Hiram did not hear her. He was lost in the mystery of the growing cloth. He laughed at that, being reminded of the Hardy Boys. "Well," he said, "They always did unravel the riddle."

"What? Don't talk to yourself Hiram, it isn't healthy."

Hiram said no more. Curious, he began feeling around the corner, searching for a crack or crevasse that the rag could have been tucked in to. There was none. There was nothing. Not even paint.

Hiram pulled his hand back in terror. Lydia jumped.

"Hiram! What is it?"

"Nothing," Hiram's voice shook.

"Why'd you get so upset about nothing?" Lydia asked indignantly. She did not like jokes.

"No," Hiram said quietly, "I mean nothing. There's nothing there..."

"You okay?"

"Nothing at all," Hiram continued in a soft monotone, wide eyes never leaving the corner, "No wall. No floor. Just air."

"I don't see a hole," Lydia said, backing a subtle inch from her husband.

"No hole," Hiram said, in the same voice, "Just nothing." Lydia believed him, intuitively. She also felt compelled by the same instinct to move the book. She gave it a little kick, but it was too heavy. Hiram was leaning toward the corner again.

"Hiram no!" Lydia cried. He did not acknowledge.

Pressed by curiosity, Hiram leaned once more toward the hole. He grimly thrust a hand in the corner, and it disappeared. Hiram felt a slight tug, but ignored it. He wanted to feel around back there. He reached his arm in fully, his body pressed against the floor. He was slipping, but failed to notice.

Her husband's disappearance did not escape Lydia. After the initial shock of his vanished arm wore off, she became very aware that the rest of Hiram might follow the lead. Her eyes were drawn again to the book, inches behind Hiram's shoulder. She bent to pick it up, but was distracted by Hiram's scream. He was being sucked into the corner. Lydia grabbed his free hand and held tight while the rest of Hiram slipped through what should have been solid wood. Their screams of terror were lost in the wind that thundered past them, down into the hole. It was absorbing everything in the store-- books, shelves, the vacuum cleaner, Hiram. Everything but Lydia. She did not understand enough to question this. She did know that the book had something to do with this, and it would have to be moved.

Hiram was gone now, save for his left arm. Lydia took the risk of losing more of him to bend down and grab the book. She picked it up.

Like a switch had been thrown, the room was silent. She could not hear Hiram either. She didn't have to hold him anymore either. She sat back in relief, and set about finding a way to get the rest of Hiram back. She wondered why his hand was becoming so dark.

An icy vise of fear gripped her throat. She leapt to the corner and pounded on the wall. It was quite solid. Without thinking she snatched the book and threw it back into the pentagram. Hiram's hand blushed again, and immediately began to sink deeper into the corner. She clutched what fingers still remained in sight. His hand kept sinking, and hers followed. Lydia would not let go, though every inch of her body pleaded for freedom.

One of her hands fell in the hole, and she pulled it out. Wait, she thought, I can pull my hand out. Before she gave the matter any due consideration, she slid down the hole with Hiram.

Lydia expected to be tumbling in an abyss, dropping to hellfires a million miles below, but she fell into nothing. An almost tangible nothing. She was utterly alone, though she knew that somewhere her body still held her husband's hand. She could not think of her body, only of its absence. The word took on an entirely new meaning for Lydia. Everything seemed to be absent, except her thoughts. She had no idea what was going on, and it never occurred to her to try to figure it all out. She was just a housewife from Pillard, and the closest she had ever come to something like this was The Twilight Zone.

Having nothing to do, her thoughts turned to Hiram. She wondered where he could be, if he was smart enough to get them out of this hole. She wished she could be with him. She wanted to be home like she never had before. Her mind wandered. The moment she first realized her love for Hiram entered her thoughts. It was in the park one summer. They were together under a great oak tree, basking in the sun as much as the warmth of the moment. Hiram was telling her his dreams, and she was accepting them with every bit of her soul. She loved Hiram. From then on he was hers. A squirrel played a few feet away.

She gasped after landing from a fall that amounted to inches. Thick red grass cushioned her. She stood on a lone knoll under a cool oval sun, alone. Her only company for the miles she could see around her was the tree that stood a few yards away. It took her a moment to realize that it was a tree; she had at first taken it for a cliff. Its trunk was wide enough to conceal two bookstores. Lydia was not sure it had a top. She wondered at it, recognized it, tried to explain it, then shut it from her mind. This was all too much for her. It was as if her thoughts were coming alive for her, or at least trying to, in their own misshapen way. She figured that she was hallucinating. Isn't that what people do when there's nothing else? she thought.

She wanted Hiram. He had to be somewhere, she knew. She had had an iron grip on three of his fingers moments earlier, and was sure they hadn't parted. She shook her head at the illogical feeling that she still clutched Hiram's hand. Still she felt herself flexing her fingers to be sure that they too were alone. They assured her they were. Lydia decided that something must be done, so she set out to explore this new world, figuring that getting lost would be impossible with the tree as base.

After about eleven feet Lydia dropped to the ground in frustration. This was not going to work. The red grass went on for endless miles in every direction. There did not seem to be any horizon. She hadn't thought about a horizon.

"That's it!" she exclaimed, leaping up at the revelation. Why hadn't she noticed what she was doing? Like a dream she had turned a memory into reality, and like a dream it was imperfect. She was always in control, but did not know it. She still knew nothing of her predicament, but now she did not have to think about it or fear it. She began to walk, in no particular direction. What she sought lay wherever she walked, so in a sense there was no direction. Lydia giggled at the high-brow logic she was concocting. She was gaining confidence now that there would not be absence. She felt no fear, or even much apprehension. Lydia never was very good at being afraid. She set her mind back to Hiram. The tree. The park. The first moment of union.

Something blurred past her, buzzing like a disturbed hornets' nest. What looked like a furball on fire stopped inches in front of her. Knowing it could not harm her, Lydia reached for it. The animal timidly started, regarded Lydia with large, imperfect eyes, and buzzed away. A path began to form before her. She found that she chose not to take it. Moments later a new one formed, and she followed it.

Lydia no longer questioned her actions. She had made her path unconsciously, but following it would be all her own. She envisioned a horizon in the distance. Rippled slightly by a low mountain range. This time she would be more careful; no more flat red grasslands or high-powered squirrels. The horizon had been easy, since it was the most distant object that could be imagined, but Lydia was finding it difficult to create the simplest of closer objects. Her oaks were too large and she gave up on animals after two purple rabbits and a wretch of a creature that resembled a bird but flopped around on the ground in a boneless frenzy. Her attempt at a local Seven-Eleven resulted in a giant coffee cup boiling tons of Fritos onto a large red shoebox. The path was beginning to fade as well. She turned back to align herself with the tree, but it was gone. She had been walking for ten minutes.

She sighed, and sat on a failed lounge chair to assess the moment.

Lydia was lost. She had no definitions for the things she was doing. And, with her education, if someone had told her she would have given them a blank stare. But there she was, trapped in a world not her own. Yet it was a dreamland of her own making. Her own making. That was the most frustrating aspect. All this was hers, but she did not have the capability of making it home. Lydia fought back a melodramatic tear that persisted on rolling down her cheek. Hiram would have answers. "If he did, then where is he?" she answered aloud, not realizing for a moment that it was she that spoke. Another tear welled. There certainly can't be any of this, she thought, slapping her leg rather hard and standing up.

Still with the same answers, she sat again. Lydia tried to think all this through, but as usual no thoughts came to mind. Then she dramatically snapped her fingers and smiled. Wait, she thought, that's what got me on this chair in the first place. Thoughts. I've got to avoid them. That shouldn't be too hard.

Lydia got up and walked again, in a lighter mood. She hummed an old tune, and completely resigned herself to a pleasant, mindless walk in this new country, living but for the moment, one step at a time. It wasn't hard. Most of her life had been a mindless walk.

There were no more strange animals, no more big trees. For a time there was nothing more than a pink sky and an emerald desert. Then the scenery grew more familiar. Lydia was not surprised, nor did she expect it. That was simply the way her world turned, and she lived with it that way. She did find herself feeling somewhat smug when Elm Street found her.

She walked into the bookstore, the silly cowbells ringing. It took a moment for her eyes to adjust to the dim interior. Everything was as she had left it, if not cleaner.

Lydia's knees wobbled with relief when she saw a man at the register, checking the drawer. she leapt to the counter, ready to cry in relief.

Lydia gasped loudly. It wasn't Hiram. She tried to leave, but the door had become a solid wall of books. The gray man in shirtsleeves and suspenders spoke, his voice strong for his apparent years.

"Hello young lady," he said, "Are you the one that took my 72 dollars?"

"Your what?" Lydia squealed, "Who are you? Why won't you let me leave? What have you done to my husband?" She stopped, deciding to save some clichés for later. Besides, she knew this man. It could be no one else.

"You're Mr. Banister, aren't you?"

"In the flesh. And who might you be? I hadn't thought a woman would be able to use my book."

"Times change. I came with my husband," Lydia said, looking around the windowless room, "But I think he's lost."

"He'll turn up. He has to."

"He does?"

"Of course. All Void travelers must come here. You might call my humble dwelling a gateway to other worlds. The Statue of Liberty of dimensions. One must be processed through my Ellis Island before one can move on."

"You're a talkative old man."

"There is little else to do around here."

"Except process space travelers?"

"Correction: Void travelers. There is no space and time in the Void."

"How can that be?"

"No proper Void would have them."

Lydia was silent for a moment. Then, "Wait. Aren't we the first to come through? Your bookstore was empty for all those years."

"Ah, but the bookstore was only the point of my exit. Many others have had their own. But they all must use my machine, my book. They always have."

"Always? Its only been about thirty years since you left it. I don't see how your book ever got out of the store."

"Thirty years, is it," Banister smiled, "Dorothy must have only passed away in your time. She never did understood, poor fool." Banister was silent for a moment, lost in thought, then he continued:

"The last traveler was shocked to discover that my book would not be formed for yet another century beyond his time. The Void knows no time. In truth, I've nearly forgotten it myself. In my world there can only be Now. There never was a Was, nor will there ever be an Ever. Eternity works that way. I understand your confusion but do not fear; it is all much simpler than you think. Simpler even than your terribly linear home world. There my book has existed for millennia. More advanced worlds have been using it for eons. But you say I can only have existed for a short stretch of recent history. Frankly, I cannot see how I ever lived in such a difficult dimension. So flat, so terribly primitive.

"I am sorry, young lady. I suppose I can ramble if I am allowed. But none of that is important since, for the moment-- if you will pardon the phrase --we are out of time. I can only sustain this linear activity, live in time, if I may, for but a few carefully compounded moments. We must begin the processing. Tell me. What sort of world do you wish to be prepared for?"

"My own," Lydia snarled, "With Hiram." She was tiring of this vacation from reality.

"That would be most difficult," Banister frowned, "Most travelers do not return to their world until they have truly mastered Adjusting. Perhaps we should start with a land more easy to picture. What's a `Hiram'?"

"Hiram is my husband!" Lydia's voice squeaked, "I don't want an easy world, I want my own. I want my husband back. You don't understand. I'm not a traveler. I'm lost and I want to go home." Once more she fought tears that insisted on surfacing. She had never thought she would need Hiram like this. She knew he would have no way of taking her back to Pillard, but it would be a supreme comfort to have him with her.

"How sad it is," Banister sighed, "I never know what to say to those that stumble into the Void. It is so very hard to return to a point of origin. Or any point for that matter. Points have a terrible time of remaining constant in the Void. Those that do fall in resign themselves to becoming travelers."

"Well I'm not most, and I want Hiram and I want to go home. Now, can you tell me where either of those are?"

"Where? Young lady, I tell you again, there is no Space in the Void, no Where. You must properly bring desired space to you. That is why I am here, to assist you in your creation."

Lydia was ignoring him. "Can you find Hiram?"

"I can try. Accidental travelers never read the instructions in the book. I imagine that some never find me. How did you?"

"I pictured the town," Lydia snapped, "Now where is Hiram?"

Banister's jaw dropped. "You...created me?" he gasped, then rubbed his chin, "I had thought that impossible. Silly pride. There may yet be hope for you, young lady."

"Where's Hiram?" Lydia slammed her fist on the counter.

"Easy girl. I apologize for my rude behavior. But you are truly unique. No one can envision before I show them how, not successfully... it must have something to do with your starting point--"

"Look mister, my fist is going to have something to do with your face if you don't find Hiram," Lydia said softly, leaning toward Banister.

"Sorry. Did he come through with you?"

"Yes," Lydia sighed, "He was first. I was holding his hand. In fact, it feels like I still am." Lydia was relieved to see Banister smile at this. Surely, she thought, in the eternity he's been at this job, he's taken care of a few cases like this.

"That is good. The two of you are indeed still joined. But, you are a special case, girl. Perhaps you can indeed return home with Hiram. But you must do what no inexperienced traveler has done before you. I think you can. There is a special quality in you, a true evolutionary step up. I had not thought it possible for a Human to move with such ease through the Void. And still retain your Hiram. What a pleasure this Now has been."

"Please stop talking and tell me how to get home," Lydia begged.

"Oh, it is quite simple. You need only to forget me."

"What?"

"Forget me, but retain all else. I had not realized that you were halfway home already, and that I was in your way. I merely interrupted what was probably the beginning of a successful journey."

"So I was already on my way home. Probably?"

"Oh yes. You see, your attempt should not have worked at all, under normal circumstances, but then you are far from normal."

"Thanks. Now what do I do?"

"Nothing but what you were doing so well already. Simply forget me and continue assimilating. Make the store your store. Try not to convince yourself that you are home, just Be home. Know; understand your presence in your own personal reality. If all goes well you will have home again and I will have been no more than a dream."

Banister continued, but Lydia had stopped listening the moment she had her instructions. She was furious for not realizing this in the first place. Needlessly furious, since she had no way of coming to the right conclusion. She forced her anger to subside; there could be none of that. There was traveling to be done.

She needed only to continue as she was, turning the abstract into concrete. She stared steadily at Banister, fighting to erase him from her mind. She needed to see the panel of wall directly behind him. She found herself thinking about a dust rag that she had left on the counter beside the register. Its presence grew until it was all she could think about. Banister wavered in front of her, like a mass of hot air was rising between them.

There was a brilliant flash of light and a clap of thunder that knocked her over. Then there was nothing.

She was in the Void again, but took no notice. Her mind was completely fixed on the dust rag. It was now grasped in Hiram's free hand. She could see only his hand. She struggled up his arm, found his chin. His mouth. When she looked into his eyes there was another flash of light, more thunder. Lydia's body was wrenched and twisted, but she did not let go of Hiram's hand, or his eyes.

Once more the register was before her, but this time Hiram stood in Banister's place, cleaning the counter with the blessed rag. Lydia spun around. The door and bay widows were in place, living afternoon sunlight filtering through. Everything was back, once again in complete detail. Hiram was back too. She was around the counter and in his arms in an instant, but they did not let go or say a word for minutes. Finally Hiram spoke.

"Thanks for holding my hand, little girl," he sounded and looked like he had just woken up.

"Was it real?"

"The Void? Can I call nothing real? I'm not sure. But, dream or not, we went through something. I heard that gatekeeper toward the end. It felt like he found me, like my soul was being reeled in. But I never went all the way. I could only feel your conversation and hope that he was right about you. I guess he was."

"I guess so," Lydia said, not believing how calm they were. Perhaps they did both think it a dream. She finally let go of Hiram and backed a way a step, said, "What do we do now? Make believe it never happened?"

"That would be the sane thing to do, wouldn't it? But Lydia, what have we found here? It's a genuine miracle! Think of where we could go, what we could see as travelers. Think! And the keeper said it was done all the time..."

"Except that there is no time where he lives. Besides, I think it was all just a dream; I want it to have been. Hiram, why don't we set the book aside, paint over the star, and think about being travelers in thirty or forty years."

"But Lydia, Think of what we could do. We could create our own worlds, like gods..."

Lydia laughed, "Hiram, you couldn't even create yourself. And we'd probably never return home." She was silent for a moment, then continued, "What am I saying? None of this is real. It can't be."

"But Lydia..."

"No Hiram!" Lydia shouted, then hugged him again. In a moment she put a finger on his lips and said softly, "Hiram, a week ago all your dreams came true. You wanted nothing more. Please don't make my nightmares come true. I won't go into the Void again, not at least for many long, wonderfully dull years. And you can't go either. I don't want to be another crazy Old Lady Banister." With that she parted from Hiram and walked to the corner. She noticed that Hiram shied, keeping his distance until she had lifted the great book and placed it carefully on the bottom shelf of the travel section.

Three weeks after they had moved in, the couple at 301 Elm Street disappeared. They took nothing, even left their store open. The Ugly rumors still persist.

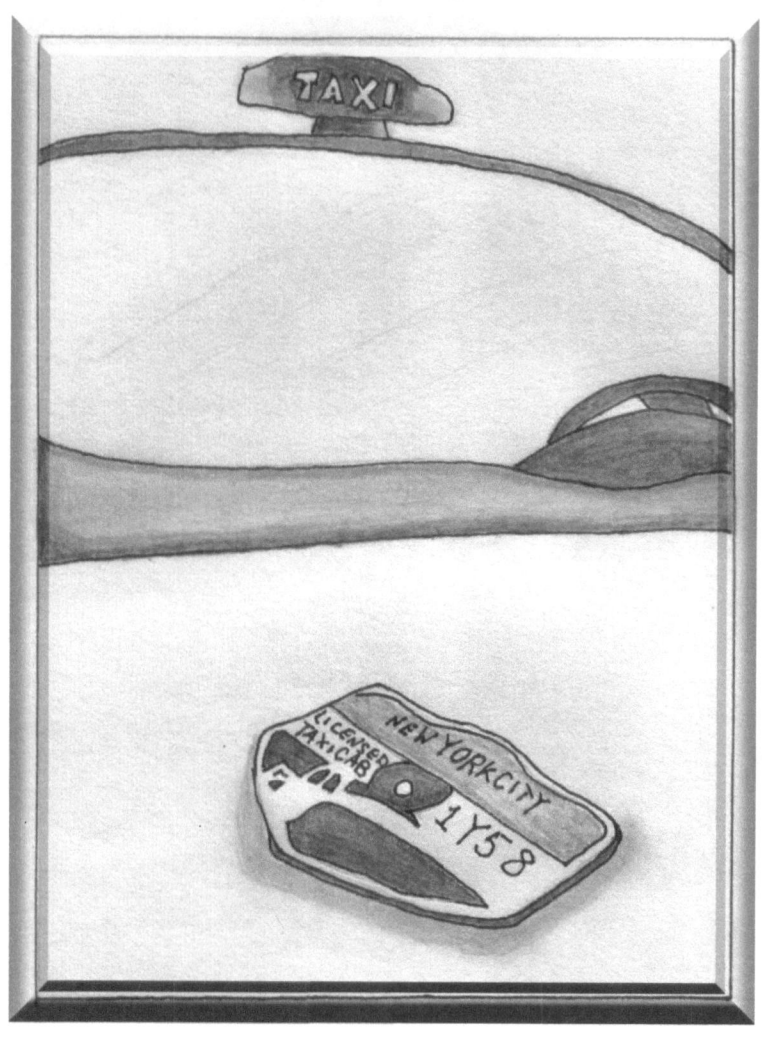

Medallions

Claude and Muffy's practiced strut onto the gray 5th Avenue sidewalk was foiled by the slap of the late afternoon October chill. It twisted their lofty postures, forcing them to yank their useless silk collars tight against their skinny white necks. The sans-coat-devil-may-care image they preferred to project was vanquished by nature. They hated nature.

Howard and Muffy Gentry wanted to be seen as the perfect monied couple. Their obese egos would not allow them to agree that any passerby would have seen them as a couple of shivering waifs, pale and fragile enough to actually be threatened by the merely brisk October air. If they were not thoroughly engulfed by silk and jewels, that passerby might surrender a dollar.

"Afternoon Mr. and Mrs. Gentry," Howard, the doorman, boomed cheerfully as he eased the polished brass door shut behind them. His flabby jowls were tightly tucked into the exaggerated gilded collar of an immaculate red wool topcoat. He rubbed his own arms more as a weather report than in effort to get warm, and continued, "Bit nippy out here. You folks might want to send up for wraps before you head out."

"Thank you no, Howard," Claude sniffed to the doorman, "It's a short ride. I am sure the car that you have yet to produce for us will be heated."

"Where is Flora with our luggage?" Muffy snapped to no one in particular. Her answer came in the form of a thud against the foyer door. Howard lurched for the gold handle, drawing a grimace from Claude.

"Really Howard," his snarl dampened by a shiver, "The car." His faulty command elicited a rude giggle from Muffy.

"Sorry sir," Howard said over an empty epaulet, "Duty, you know." He pulled the door open and was able to grab three of the six Louis Vuitton cases before they clattered to the floor, free of Flora's tiny white knuckles.

"But I was here first," Claude whined, "Never mind. I'll get a taxi myself. Your failure to have one waiting will most certainly not ring well with Mr. Snipes." He stepped into the street.

"Sorry sir," Howard repeated mindlessly, setting the cases to the pavement. He joined Claude, continued: "But I thought that when you ordered a car, it would be the usual service. I left a message with Serge at Skytop, but he only called moments ago to, um, confirm your current status. I was going to ask you."

"Shut up Howard!" Claude snapped, freezing the portly doorman's damning excuses. He scanned the street for neighbors, saw none, and said, "And blast your incompetence. Now step aside, here's one now." He stuck one bony finger in the air, his pose as majestic as possible. A battered yellow Caprice far up the avenue slowed appreciably at his gesture. Claude crooked his finger, wagged it a bit. As if its driver came to a decision, the cab suddenly sprinted to the curb beside them, forcing Claude and Howard to leap for safety. Claude recovered nicely, silenced Flora's titters with a glance, but could do nothing about Muffy's. He bent toward the cab's opening window. Howard tried to step between him and the cab.

"Sir please," he insisted, "Let me call you a proper taxi. It'll take but a moment."

"This one's fine," Claude said, his creased eyes inches from Howard's puffy lips.

"But sir, it has no--"

"Out of my way, little man," Claude yelled, shoving Howard who, of course, allowed the frail tenant to push him aside.

"Fine sir," Howard said.

"Kennedy Airport?" Claude asked/demanded of the dark skinned driver. He assumed that, like all NY hacks, English would not be in his repertoire.

The driver nodded inanely, said in a heavy Middle Eastern accent, "Kennedy, sir, yes, quick quick."

"There Howard," Muffy said softly, unable to hide the thick sarcasm irreparably embedded in her collagen-lipped slur, "Everything is just fine. Now load our bags, please." She stepped back.

"Yes, of course," Howard said, his jovial tone and visage quite natural. The trunk popped open as he hefted the three bags he had rescued earlier. He placed them in the decaying metal cavity, careful to conceal the window to the street that ancient rust had opened. Flora handed him the other three cases, which he deposited with equal care. He surreptitiously patted Flora's callused hands, which were prematurely aged from over a decade of loyal, unappreciated service. She smiled, sharing an obvious secret. The Gentry's had already taken their seats in the back of the cab. The door remained open, waiting to be closed by lesser hands than Claude's. Howard counted to five before stepping over to it. He leaned into the dark car.

"Sorry for the confusion folks," He said drawing out the pathetic ruse, "I will endeavor to remedy my oversight with exemplary behavior."

"I'm sure we'll be discussing your 'future behavior' with Mr. Snipes at our earliest convenience," Claude hissed softly through his thin blue lips.

"Of course, sir," Howard said, gently closing the door.

The tattered taxi's tires squealed as it launched from the curb. Flora and Howard watched until it was gone. She touched his elbow, whispered in his ear:

"You should have told him."

"I suppose," Howard sighed, "I suppose." He wrapped his neatly tailored arm around Flora's thin shoulders, turned her around. As he opened the door for her he paused, looked in her eyes, continued, "But would he have listened? He announces constantly that he is a born and bred New Yorker; he must know. Ah, hell, I guess I finally got sick of speaking unheard words." He hoisted his blue lips into a tired smile, shut the heavy door behind her, and returned to his post.

"Perhaps you should have shown more compassion, Claude," Muffy noted after they turned east on 59th, "What with our situation and all."

"Our situation is an annoyance. It is temporary, and certainly not news to be shared with a hapless doorman," Claude said, looking out the window as the grizzled driver yanked his cab into rush hour traffic. Well, not out the window. He was unable to see past his own reflection. He noticed and removed a bit of pimple material from one of his tiny nose pores.

"It won't be our charity, Claude. You saw the looks Flora was tossing the old fart. You'd think they had a thing. The tramp."

"Maybe she's his daughter." Claude ventured.

"Oh Claude," Muffy guffawed, careful to catch any coarse laughter spit in her hand, "You know that can't be true. I mean, Howard is so Irish, and Flora is Puerto Rican, or some such. There's just no way. I can tell."

"Whatever. I just right now want a retreat from this town, the co-op board, the IRS, Clemmons at the firm. All of it."

"Well now, dear," Muffy said, linking her arm in his but still not touching him, "That's why we're taking this wonderful trip to Cannes." She took pride in feeling her teeth remain firmly clenched while she gently forced the word 'Cannes' between them.

"You're so right. And damn the cost. And damn the cold in this cab," Claude declared. He reached to tap the divider glass with his Princeton ring, but stopped mid-swing when he noticed the partition was missing. He augmented his heavy sigh with a wimpy slap on the greasy seatback.

"Driver," he shouted, "Some heat back here. Now."

"Sir. Heat," the cabby said, nodding vigorously, "Right away. Heat, sir."

"Good man," Claude said, sitting back. He wiped his hands together, said to Muffy: "That's taken care of." Muffy didn't hear him. She was looking out her own window. The glass on her side offered no reflection, so she noticed that they were taking Rt. 278 south, not north, off the Queensboro Bridge.

"That's odd," She said, her clear polish manicured index finger touching her latest chin, "I always thought we take this road in the other direction."

"I wouldn't know, Sweetums, you know usually I watch the markets on TV, not dull scenery, during these drives."

"Well, it's not right. I think the driver made a wrong turn."

"Nonsense," Claude said, "All cabbies know exactly how to get to all NY airports. Even, I would imagine, Newark. It's in their DNA – along with a few quarts of oil, apparently." He leaned forward again, referenced the hack license taped to the dash.

"Excuse me Mr., um, Williams," he said, "You do know the way to Kennedy?"

"Kennedy, yes. Yes Kennedy," the driver repeated, smiling brightly.

"The airport, right?"

"Yes yes. Airport." Smiling brightly and humming, the driver took his hands off the wheel and mimicked an airplane with his arms outstretched.

"Okay okay! I get it!" Claude shouted. Mr. Williams resumed steering. Claude sat back, nestling unusually close to Muffy. She recoiled a bit. He whispered, "See? No problem. We'll be fine."

"Great. Will that be before or after we freeze to death?"

"Very funny dear. I'm sure there will be heat. If not, well, it can't be more than an hour to the terminal."

"You have the tickets, right?"

"Aren't they waiting by the plane?" Claude asked, visibly confused, "They always are."

"No. No," Muffy rolled her almond eyes, "We couldn't get that this time, remember? The club thing?"

"Oh my," Claude said, slightly touching his fingertips together as he rapidly recounted distant moments, "That means that yesterday, when Cora said my tickets were on my desk, she wasn't speaking figuratively?"

"Good God Claude," Muffy declared. "How stupid are you?"

"Come come," Claude said, his error already forgiven. He checked his Piaget, said, "We still have an hour and a half to the flight. We'll simply tell the driver to scootch back to midtown. I'll stick my head in my office, grab them and we're on our way."

"What about that rube Clemmons?"

"Oh, him," Claude grimaced, then smiled (after ten years of marriage, Muffy could differentiate), "He can be bypassed." He leaned forward again, tapped Mr. William's blue-sweatered shoulder. The driver started, jumping the curb in his excitement, then smiled.

"So sorry," he said sheepishly.

"That's quite all right," Claude said, "Listen my man. We have a change of plans. I must go back to 57th and 5th for an item. Please turn around immediately."

"Yes. Kennedy," The driver nodded vigorously, "Right around immediately."

"Oh shit," Muffy whispered.

"No, no," Claude tried again, slowly, "Back, turn, Manhattan"

"Manhattan. Yes. Kennedy."

"No, you idiot! You foreign imbecile. Midtown. Midtown Manhattan. Back over bridge."

"Oh!" the cabby exclaimed, "Bridge. No Kennedy. I get!" He swerved to the right lane, sped off the next exit into Brooklyn.

"Thank God," Muffy said.

"See? No problem."

"No. No problem," the driver repeated. "Almost there."

"Well, I wouldn't say that." Claude said, blissfully ignorant of his condescending tone. The cab suddenly skidded to a halt. Claude and Muffy were hurled to the floor. As they struggled comically to regain their seats without contacting the sticky floor, the driver leaned over them, regarding them with an all too comprehending and livid countenance.

"I would," He said softly, with no accent or head-nodding. He showed them the chrome pistol nestled in his hand.

"Well, so much for the tickets," Claude said as the cab disappeared down the deserted street, leaving the troubled couple without money, jewelry, or outer clothing.

They stood in the middle of the street, surrounded by debris, gutted buildings, garbage, and absolutely no people. Muffy was already shivering violently. Her thin white arms were wrapped around her pink designer bra more out of vanity than for warmth. Her eyes, wide with terror, did not, would not, release their focus on Claude's pale face. She had no interest in her surroundings, or in seeing what new horror encroached. She took no comfort in the tears gushing from Claude's eye slits, in spite of his attempted bravura. All she felt was cold, and a sharp, adrenaline-pumping intuition that she was about to die. In Brooklyn.

"In Brooklyn!" she screamed, slapping Claude's bare chest violently, "How could you? You Bastard!" She shivered uncontrollably, either from the cold or her anger. She didn't care which.

"What?" Claude stammered, his feminine hands raised in defense, "What did I do?" Muffy regarded his pathetic stance. His 'artistic' frame and demeanor once intrigued her. Now all she wanted was a man with a little meat on him, who wasn't intimidated by a ninety-pound waif.

"What did you do?" she continued her tirade, swinging violently with each sentence. It kept her warm. It kept Brooklyn away. "You blithering, motherfucking idiot! Where the hell do I start? You lost a seven-figure salary out of sheer stupidity; you lied to me about it; you refused my father's job offer; you planned this stupid waste of the last of our cash trip; you pissed off Howard; you got us in a cab without a fucking medallion; then, and I'm sure finally, you let some ape rob us and leave us here naked in fucking Beirut to die! Do you want me to go on?"

"That's fine, Muff. Just fine," Claude shouted, his attempt at authority sounding more like a desperate squeal, "What the hell did you want me to do? Fight?"

Muffy's rage snapped for the instant that she allowed herself to picture Claude taking useless swings at their assailant, then returned, "You could have at least grown one ball and convinced the asshole to let us keep our clothes. No. Couldn't do that, could you? No, you had to ask him if he wanted them, too!"

"That was sarcasm, Muff," Claude whimpered, ducking her latest, and hardest, swing.

"That was shitty timing, Claude! And stop calling me Muffy. My name is Sylvia, for Christ's sake!"

"It is?" Claude honestly asked. Sylvia caught his blue ear with a blow that drew blood, pounding his next line out, "Of course it is, Mu-Sylvia! I was just kidding. Now stop hitting me. Please!" Sylvia stopped, gasping for air. I was done anyway, she thought.

They stood, silently facing each other, for a few minutes. Each was still afraid to look around. Both noticed that they were still alone, still cold. In a few frigid moments other thoughts began a ragged dance through Sylvia's racing mind. She wondered if Claude noticed her nipples almost ripping through the thin silk of her bra (probably not, she conceded). She hoped there was no glass under her bare feet. She wished Claude would wear the boxers she bought, instead of those awful red briefs. She tried to remember her phone card pin number. Eventually she came back to the cold, and their position in the middle of a frozen street, bathed in harsh fall air rife with the smell of old sweat socks and forgotten garbage. She reached out, touched one of Claude's bony wrists.

"Claude," she said softly, "We have to do something."

Claude didn't answer. Good God, she thought, could he be dead already? Standing up? His skin was certainly cold and clammy, cadaverous enough. Of course, it always was. His sudden demise wouldn't have shocked her. Indeed, it would have been Claude to a tee. He blinked.

"What?" he asked.

"You know, Claude. Do. Something. Other than just stand here and freeze to death?"

"We can't freeze," he said, his tone dismissive, "It's still too warm."

"Damn, Claude, still looking for an argument, are you? Fine. Here's one: What time is it?"

"I don't know. Afternoon, I guess. The man took my watch."

"Yeah, yeah," Sylvia said softly, "Your pretty watch is gone. Try looking up. It's probably late afternoon. What else do you suppose will be gone in a couple of hours?"

Claude scanned her with renewed fear, "You're not going to leave me, are you?"

She smiled, "I won't say the thought hadn't crossed my mind once or twice but no, I'm here. What else?"

Claude stared at her blankly. She sighed. Since his world had just completed its destruction around him, she supposed that there was no more time for games. She took his hand, rubbed it a little.

"The sun, Claude. The sun will be down, real soon," she fought to control her condescending tone, "Do you remember the weather report?"

"Oh, shit," He said, suddenly scanning their surroundings. It was the first time she heard him use that word, ever. Claude was waking up. He continued, "Muffy. Sylvia. We have to do something fast. You think it's cold now? There's a front coming... the weather forecast called for temperatures close to zero tonight. We can't survive that."

"Now we're on the same page," Sylvia said through her chattering teeth, "So what do we do?"

"I don't know," he said thoughtfully. She could tell he was thinking. And that was one thing Claude was good for -- his mind could race like the wind when pressed. He continued, his voice clear, "We could walk. This desolation can't go on forever. We can walk to the river, find a bridge back to Manhattan. Maybe run into a cop on the way."

"Not to be negative, but which way is the river?" Sylvia asked gently. She omitted her opine that there probably hadn't been a cop in these neighborhoods since the seventies. Claude spun on his bare heel, a full 360 degrees. He searched the overcast sky.

"I, I don't know, exactly. Definitely in Brooklyn, I think," He said, squinting, "Maybe Queens. Couldn't be the Bronx; I'm pretty sure we didn't cross over any more bridges."

"Do you know which way is west?"

"Um, no."

"Me neither. I guess I should feel just as guilty for not paying attention. So, do we go back to panicking now?" That drew a smile from her beleaguered little husband.

"Not many other choices, huh? Do we dare ask for directions?"

Sylvia was about to nod, then realized that they hadn't seen a soul throughout the whole robbery. The crook hadn't even told them not to scream. The guy had found the moon, she thought, right in the center of the universe, to do his business.

"From whom?" she asked sincerely.

"There must be someone in these buildings. You remember how those tenements we owned in Yonkers were always littered with squatters and drug users."

"Not the most helpful of people. Maybe we ought to steer clear of the buildings."

"I guess looking for a phone is out of the question," Claude sighed, "And eating or finding our clothes should be relegated to fantasy."

"You're right about that. But there must be something we can put on. Maybe in that abandoned car over there…"

"Let's hold off on that as long as we can, okay Sweetums? The thought is still too repulsive."

"Yeah. We might be naked, but we are still human. Should we start a fire?" Sylvia suggested. The rush of the moment was wearing thin, and the early evening's frigid air had resumed its inexorable grind under her pale skin.

"With what? You have any matches? A lighter?" Claude wasn't being sarcastic.

"You're right. Plus, a fire would be a thug and junkie magnet. Forget it." They resumed their staring contest. They were content to remain frozen in the middle of the street, passively waiting for a useful idea to drift into their emptying minds. This went on for a few more minutes until Sylvia stepped forward, fell into Claude's arms. He was as cold as the air.

"Oh Claude," she whispered, "This is bad."

Night fell. Vague shadows nipped at their fleshy heels. These harbingers of impending cold and dark chased them slowly, unconsciously, to the east side of the street. Unconsciously enough that neither noticed that the elements were offering them a compass, a hint at salvation. By the time gray twilight surrendered to the blackness, they were huddled at the edge of the sidewalk. Neither of them sat, as they were unwilling to touch their naked thighs against the grimy concrete. Sylvia stared at the stars that had begun to spread above them.

"Look, Claude. The sky is finally clearing. I've never seen so many stars."

"Well, there had to be a bright spot somewhere along the way. At least the lack of streetlights are giving us a nice evening."

"My God, we really are on the moon."

"It could well be," Claude said, drawing her into his sunken chest, "I think the moon might be warmer, though."

Sylvia tried to stretch her chapped, oddly frozen lips into a smile, and failed. She longed for the extra body fat the diet books said she was supposed to be carrying. She straightened up, drawing Claude with her.

"Claude," she said, "We have to do something. Find shelter. Fast."

"You are so right. I've been watching this building for a long time now, and I think it's empty." She could just see his gesture toward a nearby brownstone.

"I really don't care at this point, as long as there's something that burns inside."

"You should care. The monsters will be out soon, I'm sure of it. It'll be bad enough to be found on the street, but to trip over them in their den would be disastrous."

"Don't talk like that, Claude. They are people," Sylvia said, running out of strength for lectures. Suddenly she jumped, instinctively startled by a thing she sensed more than saw; a heaviness in a nearby shadow. She clamped her hands around Claude's elbow, and whispered, "In fact, don't talk at all. There's someone on the corner. Over there."

"I don't see anyone," Claude said, way too loudly, "Of course, I don't see anything. There's no light at all."

"I don't see him either, Claude. But I know he's there. So whisper, for God's sake. We have to get off the street now." She braced herself for his sarcasm, for the fight. Instead, he turned toward his building.

"Let's try in there then," he whispered. Sylvia nodded. She had also studied the building that was just up the street before the sun vacated. She was sure it was the same as his choice; as it was the only one standing, alone and intact, on the ravaged block. She remembered noting that some glass was still in the windows on the upper floors when she swept its surface earlier, searching for attackers. Monsters. She clutched Claude's hand, terrified of losing contact with him in the cold blackness. She followed him, realizing that in a past lifetime she would have asked him at least three times if he knew where the hell he was going. Not now, she thought, not now. She smiled at her unnatural flash of faith.

They helped each other through the tiny, invasive breeze their movement fostered, and were almost carrying each other by the time they stubbed their bare toes on the building's high stoop. Sylvia scaled the first two concrete steps before she realized that her body was not interested in climbing the next ten. She stopped. Claude clutched her upper arm, tugged gently.

"No, love," he whispered, "we can't stop. Not here."

"But Claude. The steps."

"Ignore them. You have no choice. Imagine they're the steps to that brownstone in the west 90's that we always wanted." -- But could never have because the upper west side wasn't a neighborhood for us, Sylvia finished silently. Claude hadn't mentioned that place in five years. She thought he had forgotten. She took a step, felt the skin on her leg protest the move. She ignored it, endured the climb by imagining what her husband (her husband!) suggested, and reveling in the sweet fact that he remembered. In time she realized that the entrance was near. She could smell the rich odor of decay, as if the building itself were flatulent.

The rotten entry hall wasn't locked, or even obstructed by a door. They felt their way in, knocking off paint chips and bits of paper from the walls, until they found a doorway. Claude passed through it, felt nearby walls for a light switch. He found one, and flipped it. Miraculously, a lone bare bulb dangling ten feet above their heads glowed dimly, almost brown. To Sylvia, it might as well have been the sun.

"Find some matches. There must be something in this mess," Claude said, "I'll try the kitchen." Sylvia watched him fade into a black doorway, awestruck. Her weasel of a husband had actually surveyed the place while she was basking in the light. Helluva time to find out you married a man, she chided herself. She began her search for something with which to start a fire. As she scanned the battered living room, she noticed that her movements had become twitchy. Her ceaseless violent shivering probably had something to do with that, though the cold wasn't as sharp as it had been outside.

The room was devoid of anything useful like clothing, or even curtains. She found some oily rags in a corner, and examined them. They were too small to provide any kind of cover, so she dropped them. Maybe we can burn them later, she thought; if we find something that can start a fire. She inspected the worn hardwood floors, the only wood in the room. Good wood, she thought, but we'll need a jackhammer to get it up, and probably some gas to get it burning. She hadn't noticed any power tools lying about.

A crash sounded in the other room, followed by a flurry of muttered curses. A side effect of Claude's investigation, Sylvia guessed. He must be okay, she thought, so I'm sure he won't mind if I don't investigate, or call after him. She hadn't been able to move her lips for several minutes, and was reluctant to attempt parting them. Colagen, she thought, freezes well.

Claude stumbled out of the kitchen with what appeared to be a coil of rope in his hand. He held it to the light.

"No matches?" Sylvia asked, wincing. Her lip fear was well-founded.

"Nope," Claude said, "But this might work just as well. What's up with your voice? You okay?"

"Fine. Never better," she said. Now that's my Claude, she thought. "What are you going to do? Do you need anything?"

"I'm going to start a fire. I need an electric outlet and some rags."

"I got the rags. How are you going to do it?"

"I ripped some wire from the wall in the other room. I figure I could put two pieces into a socket, touch the other ends over something that'll burn and, ta da!, warmth."

"Aren't you a little concerned about burning down the building?"

"Only a little. Besides, we could light it in the oven, be safe."

Sylvia was amazed, but not convinced. She said, "What about the monsters outside? Won't they want to come in and warm up too?"

"Good point. I wish we could cover the windows somehow. Hell, that dim bulb is probably a handy beacon on its own. But then, we might get lucky; maybe there really is no one out there."

As if on cue they heard the throb of a poorly muffled V8 engine nearby.

"Oh shit," Claude whispered. He ran across the room and shut off the light. They were blanketed in blackness again. Sylvia fought back panic, groped for Claude. She found him, clung tight. They gingerly shuffled to the slightly less black area on the wall that signified a window. As a unit, they gingerly stuck their heads out into the night to see what terror was coming.

A large car from the seventies was crawling toward them. Its high beams flooded the barren street with white light and black shadows. Four of its occupants hung from open windows. They were scanning the buildings as the car rumbled along. Sylvia could hear Claude's breathing speed up as the Cadillac stopped in front of their building.

"Holy shit," he whispered, "You don't think they live here, do you?"

"They couldn't," Sylvia sighed, "They're alive." Claude squeezed her hand gently. She felt that he knew she wasn't kidding.

The four men -- boys really, Sylvia could tell in the wash of the headlights -- stepped out of the car. One of them reached into the passenger side front window, removed a dark object from the seat. Sylvia gasped, sure it was a gun, and that the boys knew about them and were coming in. Instead the boy clicked on a powerful spotlight, and began a meticulous scan of the building. Claude grabbed Sylvia, started to drag her to the floor. It did not take much effort; she was already convincing her knees to bend for her again, one last time. They did, and she dropped noisily to the wooden floor. The splinters that were driven into her ass by the impact felt like machetes. She struggled against crying out, but the tiniest of yelps managed to squeeze through her frozen lips. The light stopped at their open window. Its invasive incandescence offered them a good look at their sanctuary. However, neither of them cared to inspect the battered apartment as the light showed them every corner.

"Shit," they heard from below, "Ain't nothin' up there at all, Shaquir. Especially no white folk. Hell, they be flashing their white asses at us by now, looking for a ride."

"Ain't what Lupey say," another voice said.

"Lupey a crack head, bro," the first voice said, "Forget what he say, man. There ain't nothin' here for us."

"Damn straight," the second voice said, "Let's get back. It's cold out here, man."

The light blinked off, returning the terrified former aristocrats to their blessed darkness. Doors slammed, an engine roared, then faded away. Claude and Sylvia didn't move for a minute or two, until the demand for basic survival stirred their whipped souls. Sylvia heard Claude's joints crack when he rose. She swallowed panic when he shuffled away, sure he was just looking for the light switch. She was proven right when the bulb glowed softly again, illuminating Claude's gaunt and shivering body with dim yellow light. He attempted a brave smile, crossed back over to her. He was bent over almost double by his ceaseless and fruitless attempt to ward off the cold.

"So Claude," Sylvia said as he helped her to her feet, "What about that fire?"

"Comin' up, homey," Claude tried to joke. Sylvia didn't try to laugh. She followed him around the frozen apartment, more to keep her blood flowing than to help. She longed for a coat, a blanket, a plastic garbage bag. Fond memories of the six floor- length fur coats hanging in her closet spurred a rueful smile.

Claude was back in the kitchen, working in near darkness. He had two lengths of wire stretched out across the counter. One end of each was jammed in either slot of an electric outlet, the other ends were carefully separated on the blackened surface. He was standing still, rubbing his chin, and not shaking. After a puzzled instant, Sylvia realized her husband was thinking.

"So what's the plan?" she asked, surprised at the effort it took to breath out the question. Claude paused before he answered, with what Sylvia took for a look of concern. She suddenly felt a few degrees warmer.

"Simple," he said, "All I need to do is touch these wires together to get a spark. I'm guessing that the current is low enough that I'll be able to do it a few times before a fuse blows."

"Okay," Sylvia said quickly in an effort to speed his moment along, "Sparks. Then what?"

"These greasy rags you found smell like oil or something. I'm betting they'll light right up. Once they're burning, we just have to start up the scraps of wood I found, and we're warm."

"How long will the wood last?" Sylvia asked. The pile was quite small.

"Not very," Claude responded, looking around, "But hopefully long enough for us to find more wood."

"From where? We're not going outside, are we?"

"Now's not a good time for this, Muff," Claude said, emphasizing the nickname, "Let's get a flame first, then we'll find something. Hell, I don't know, maybe a door or something. Of course, I'm sure I won't be able to get it off its hinges."

"Fuck that," Sylvia said, "We'll bring the fire to the door. What about the smoke?"

"We hope. The ceilings are pretty high in here, and the windows go right to the top, so hopefully there should be enough ventilation."

"'Nuff said," Sylvia said, "Let's do it."

"Okay," Claude said. He selected one of the rags, bunched it up, and then laid it on the counter. He picked up the wires and, with no warning, tapped their exposed ends together. Per his plan, a tiny shower of sparks erupted. They were out before making it to the rags.

"Shit," he whispered.

"Do it again," Sylvia prompted, "Put it closer."

"No kidding." Claude rested one wire against the rag, then touched the other end to it again.

The rag burst into flame, eliciting a yelp from both of them as they jumped back. Claude grabbed another rag, set it near, but not quite on top of the first. Still slightly blinded by the flash, Sylvia edged closer to the warmth. Once the second rag was blazing, Claude dropped a couple of slivers of wood in. They didn't ignite fast enough for him so he dropped a couple more pieces on. Smoke filled the room, but the fire refused to be snuffed by Claude's overzealousness. The kindling burst into warm yellow flame.

Sylvia wanted to cheer, but lacked the strength. Instead she took Claude's cold hand and kissed him lightly on the cheek. Claude appeared not to notice. He was staring at the kitchen's dilapidated cabinets, grinning broadly.

"There's our wood," he said.

"Where?" Sylvia snarled, slightly annoyed that he had ignored her special gesture, "You going to rip those off the wall?"

"Nope. Just take out a piece or two." He punched a shelf, swore as his fist bounced uselessly off. He tried another, with the same results. Sylvia saw the condition of the shelves in the firelight, and understood what he was doing. She also would have helped, but was having trouble moving her arms. She wondered where Claude found the strength.

Find it he did, though: his third try was met with a resounding crack as the shelf came apart in his hand. He tore off his booty, laid it on the fire.

"That won't do too much," he said, disappointed at the foot-long shard of painted wood that slowly began to glow in the tiny blaze. He didn't punch any more cabinets. Clearly it was taking too much out of him. Sylvia began opening drawers, looking for a tool that might help him. By the time the third empty drawer squealed open, she realized what she was doing.

"Wait a minute," she said. She gave a yank, pulled the drawer out of the counter, laid it carefully on the fire. "Ta da!" she said. Claude was beaming.

"Duh," he exclaimed, though he did not seem hurt but her one-upmanship. They stopped speaking, huddled by the growing fire, trying to ignore the smoke.

Three drawers and an hour later, their heating system had warmed Sylvia's senses enough to allow other priorities to enter her shaken thoughts. As long as the fire burned, they would not freeze, but they were still very hungry, very tired, and very alone. Sylvia wondered what time it was. She assumed that it must be nearly dawn, but feared that time had slowed, ensuring that the nightmare would continue.

"We have to start thinking about getting home, Claude," she said.

"I know, dear," Claude said gently, "Little else has crossed my mind since the taxi stopped. But it would probably be best to wait for morning. That way we can see where the sun comes up and get our bearings."

"Good thinking," she said, strangely pleased that her mouth was moving properly again, "When do you suppose that will be?"

"Couple hours, I guess. It better be; we're on our last drawer." His tone had changed, Sylvia noticed. His voice had deepened somehow. Claude wasn't shrill anymore, and he hadn't called her Muffy for hours. Suddenly a word surfaced in her thawing mind: sincere. The trauma they were suffering had sown sincerity in her empty husband. She wrapped her arms around him, and tugged gently downward on his waist. He was compliant to her tender gesture, and followed her down to the floor.

They held each other in silence. Sylvia listened to his nasal breath. It was still repulsive, but somehow bothered her less. She was, she realized, willing to let the shrill whine hover close for the first time, ever. She also realized that her nipples stood erect again, but not from the cold: she was excited; turned on, for the first time in years.

"And here we are, too weak to move, much less do something about it," Claude said.

"Yup," she said, not caring to acknowledge that he had read her mind, or at least noticed her breasts. She nestled closer, "I have an idea, since we're parked here until the sun and God return."

"What's that?"

"Let's just sit here, and enjoy each other's company. Forget the circumstances, forget our history, drop our relentlessly fabricated personas, and just relax."

"I could definitely go along with that," Claude whispered. She could see his smile in the dim orange glow of the fire. He looked content.

"My God, Claude," she said, rubbing his arm, "I can't believe the alarm clock we needed just to wake up."

"Seriously. Spain would have been nice, though."

"Nice, yes, but it would have been so much emptier than this room. No matter how much we paid."

"I think you're right Sylvia," Claude said.

"I love to hear you say my name," Sylvia said, nuzzling his neck. She bumped her nose on his Adam's apple, but really didn't care.

"I guess I reached the heights of artificial snobbery by forgetting it, didn't I?"

"Hey, I let you forget it, didn't I?"

"What a pair," Claude said. He raised his right hand, presented it to Sylvia, and said, "Nice to meet you. My name's Claude. I'm your husband."

Sylvia, eyes blurred, took his hand, shook it, said, "It's a pleasure Claude. I'm Sylvia. Your wife." Claude pulled her closer, kissed her deeply. It hurt a bit, but she did not care. They held the kiss until they were out of breath. Then they separated, just slightly, and sat silently in each other's arms. Sylvia thought without words, swimming instead in the emotion that this frigid, terrifying day had born from the ashes of their spent lives. In time she opened her eyes. She noticed that her forehead still touched his. His eyes were already open, and focused only on her.

"Well," she said, "Looks like we might only need one bedroom after all."

"Good," Claude quipped, "Because that's all we'll be able to afford from now on."

"Forget that, Claude," Sylvia whispered, "We'll have plenty of time to make repairs."

They hugged again. They were silent for a few more minutes, until Sylvia noticed that Claude's tiny chest was heaving in a most alien manner. It took another minute of close concentration for her to realize her husband was crying. She found strength somewhere and gave him a mighty hug.

When she let go, Claude asked, "What was that for?"

"Because I love you."

"I love you, too."

"Claude," Sylvia whispered, "Do you realize that's the first time we ever said it?"

"No. C'mon, we've said it a million times."

"Not in less than ten words. And certainly not without qualifiers."

"Damn," Claude said, "I don't think we left the cabby a big enough tip."

"I guess we owe Howard for letting us take the ride."

"We sure do. I hope he can ever forgive us."

"Don't count on it," Sylvia said, "We bought our ticket."

They were quiet for a few more minutes, holding each other tight while they watched their fire, the one on the counter, die. Claude reclined a bit more, brought her with him.

"Maybe we should get a little sleep," he said, "This nightmare is far from over, so we should be as rested as possible for tomorrow's adventure."

"You got that," Sylvia said, "I can't wait to explore Brooklyn in my underwear."

"Don't worry," Claude said, "I think we'll have a little better luck finding clothes in the morning. We got a little more adept at survival last night than we were coming in."

"I think you're right, babe," Sylvia smiled, "I think you're right." Without another word, she nestled close to him and drifted off to sleep. Her fears of the night, the cold, and the coming adventure were soothed by Claude's gently heaving chest. Just before she finally drifted off, she heard a distant church bell toll twice. She was sure she imagined it, but was happy to drift into a welcome sleep with that hopeful note in her ear.

The glare of the winter sun forced Howard to shade his eyes in order to identify the woman approaching. It was Flora, and her face was ashen. Howard was immediately concerned.

"Flora," he said, "You just left. What is it?"

"Oh Howard," Flora said, almost stumbling into his arms. She clutched his lapels, buried her cheek in his ruffled shirt.

"Flora?" Howard asked, sensing the answer.

"They found them, Howard."

"The Gentry's?"

"Yeah. They found a couple, half eaten by rats, in a tenement in Brooklyn. They were in each other's arms. The coroner figured they must have frozen to death about a month ago. He identified them from dental records"

"Right after they left," Howard said. He slapped his forehead, "Ohmygod! The taxi! The one without the medallion!"

"We should tell the cops," Flora said.

"You're right," Howard said, "I'll get Fred to take my place, we'll go right now. Jeez, I should've kept them out of that cab."

"A flight of angels couldn't have kept them out. You did what you could, Howard."

"No, I did what I did. I meant no harm to the poor bastards, though."

"I know."

"What a way to go, though, huh?" Howard mused, not willing to spend guilt on such awful people, "They probably blamed us, and each other, and the rest of the world, right up to their last breath."

"No doubt. I'm surprised they were in each other's arms."

"Hey, even serpents snuggle to keep warm."

The Stoop

She is fifteen, high school pretty, and alone. Her day begins in a twin bed in Mom's dim four room flat, and ends in that same somehow smaller rack after being filled by little more than two packs of smokes:

Adorned in carefully planned attire as yet seen only by her hamster, Frieda, she haunts her building's decrepit front stoop. She feigns a need for a stroll to the street oh, every ten minutes or so, because someone, maybe that guy with the tuner Honda, will drive by and notice her.

A commotion down the street summons her from the top stoop step...she leaps to the sidewalk gaining nonchalance just in time to spot a giggle of girls, middle-schoolers she once played with before she came of age. She recoils into the shadow of her front door, careful to avoid eye contact with her passing past comrades. She knows why she mustn't chat, but wishes desperately she could.

Suddenly a noxious buzz fills the street; as if a bicycle approached with very large baseball cards rattling in its spokes. It's the Honda, ripe with what's-his-name from the football team! She jumps again to the street, then arches her back and puffs her cigarette just so. And the Honda stops. The passenger door comes ajar. She opens it, hoping that this time he'll turn the thunderous music down enough that she can hear his voice.

Ten breathless minutes later he screams away, and she is resigned to her stoop. She perches on the top step, rests her chin in her hand, her elbow on her knee, and just watches some hapless debris being nudged gently out of sight by a weak spring wind.

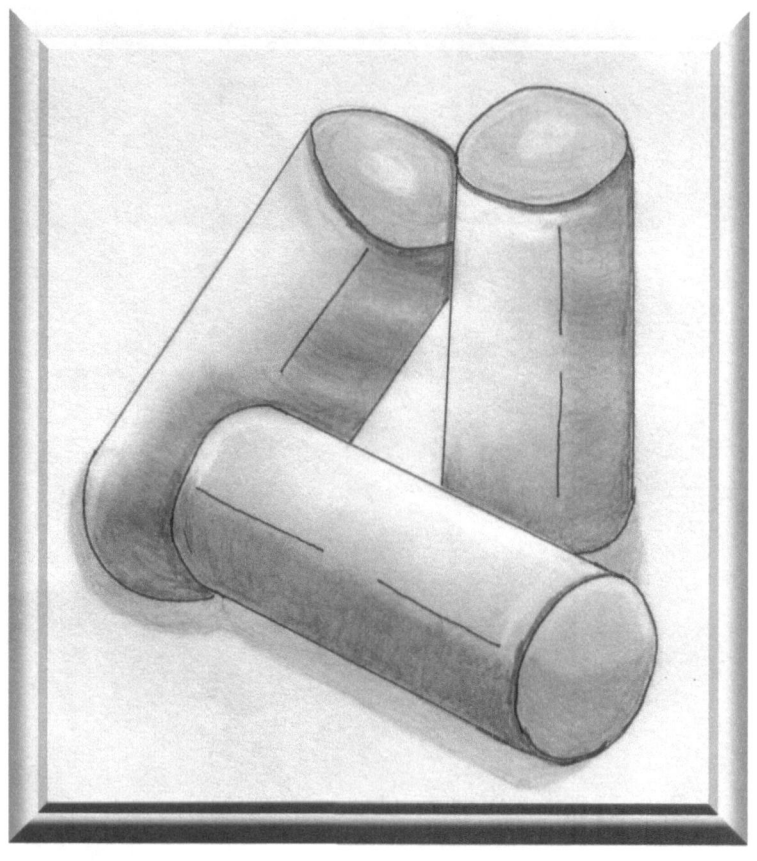

The Need for Reseeding

Noah rubbed his bald head, as was his wont, and surveyed his happy world. His wives were silent, his children plentiful, and his barge the largest and busiest the river had ever borne. Noah was rich, comfortable, fat, and over forty. He was a god.

"No, Noah," a voice boomed from behind him, "You are not."

Noah started violently in a hoppity sort of way, knocking loose his sandals. Recovering quickly, he spun awkwardly on the hot sand of his front walk to see who had the audacity to address him so, after even more rudely reading his thoughts. Only the bank of the river filled his view. It was as he had left it moments earlier: clean, flat, and devoid of any living soul beyond the slaves working the great barge that so admirably marred the scene.

"Huh," Noah said aloud. He sighed and returned his filthy toes to their sandals, shaking his head at his imagination, and at his behavior, which made him appear the doddering old fool he so feared.

"Over here, old fool," the voice boomed again, just to his left. Noah's neck snapped in that direction; this time he was not alone, or foolish. Noah turned to fully face the young stranger lounging on a boulder beside him. Noah straightened to his full three cubit height to best intimidate the man.

The stranger smiled, showering Noah with the glow of perfect white teeth, as though he had eaten nothing all his life.

"Very scary, old man," the stranger said. His voice had moderated to that of a smallish man, striking Noah, to his relief, as perhaps a bit womanish.

"I am indeed, stranger," Noah snarled, now confident enough to heft his walking stick in both hands like a club, "And you should hold that thought while you consider the consequences of sneaking up on me." The man failed to cower. Instead he rose to his feet. The action never seemed to end, but eventually the man was fully erect, and his head hovered a full cubit above Noah's. Sure, but he's as thin as a dying sapling, Noah thought; I can take him.

"No, you can't Noah, so don't try."

"Now cut that out!" Noah shouted, "And tell me why you so disturb me."

"I need a favor."

"What's a favor?"

"Ah, my work at its zenith," the stranger said softly, shaking his head, "I'm so impressed." His long black hair shimmered in the sunlight when he shook his head. It was clean; Noah did not know quite what to make of that.

"Huh?" Noah asked, wondering where he would find either zenith or favor to trade with this tall beautiful fellow, so that he might go away. The man rubbed his smooth chin slowly, almost sadly, Noah observed, and gazed at the river as he spoke.

"Noah," the man said with a tone Noah himself reserved for blank-eyed children, "A favor is a task that you perform for a friend, asking nothing in return for your service, save perhaps that friend's good graces."

"That's insane," Noah announced, "Do a thing for nothing? Why bother?"

"Which takes us to the crux of things, Noah, and the real reason I need you."

"You need me?"

"Yes, I do."

"What's a crux?"

"Never mind that; we'll see that those concepts wander into your cortexes when they are just a bit lumpier. I need you because you are a great and powerful man in this fledgling world, and I must task such a man to take the lead in a very special and terribly demanding adventure that will change all things."

"I'm great and powerful?" Noah asked, rubbing his hands in delight. The rest of the man's speech was gone.

"Sure, Noah," the man sighed, "The powerfullest."

"Well!" Noah exclaimed, delighted at the recognition.

"That," the man said, "And you have a big boat."

"You mean my barge?" Noah asked, still confused by all these odd words.

"Yup. That very one. It is a facet of (oh, bother), a participant in, the favor."

Noah folded his arms. Certain territorial instincts were ignited by the man's arrogant reference to Noah's, *his*, barge, and Noah made little effort to ease the fires his fears kindled. He crooked his neck, squinted, and said softly:

"What do you mean, my barge will be part of the favor?" he asked softly, sure that he sounded quite threatening. The man was nonplussed; he only smiled.

"Yes, yes, Noah. I understand. The boat – excuse me, the barge – is your treasure, your livelihood, and the secret of your success. I don't include it in the favor lightly."

"Well that's a good thing, because it isn't light, you know."

"And yet it still floats. Doesn't that bug you?"

"Sure does. Some people think I'm a sorcerer or something. I'm not, of course, but it's good for business," Noah said conversationally. Then he stymied his sudden relaxation and resumed his air of general suspicion, saying, "Hey, you're not some sort of sorcerer, are you?"

"Of course not," the man said, rolling his eyes, "Nothing I do is magic."

"That's a relief," Noah said, "Got enough crazies around here as it is – seems like a new sorcerer, prophet, or even god is popping up every day. I'm getting a little tired of it. I'd be more so if a little superstition and fear weren't so good for business. Hey, you never said your name. You got one?

"Nope."

"That's new," Noah said, though he wasn't surprised. Plenty of people in his grandfather's day passed their entire lifetime without a name. The fast pace of Noah's modern era demanded identification, though, so Noah was intrigued by a man who still managed to get by without a moniker.

"So, will you be telling me what this favor is?"

"Getting down to business are we?"

"It seemed time."

"Alrighty then," the man said as he rubbed his own hands briskly. He seemed about to speak, but then he paused and looked out over the river. In time he did speak, without a glance to Noah. His voice had regained its initial massive boom when he said, "Noah, I require that you convert your barge into very special container; an ark we'll call it. That ark will be a repository for an amazing cargo."

"Amazing? Last time I got a description like that, I found myself fending off angry lions from the far south."

"Oh, this'll be better than lions."

"How so? Will I need to finance a guard as well?"

"Good lord no," the man said, smiling oddly at the reference, "This cargo is quite docile. To you it will appear to be 314 casks of wine."

"That's a lot of wine," Noah said, rubbing his chin, "Large casks?"

"Very."

"Well, this barge has easily moved over 200 of the largest made in the past, so we should be able to accommodate you with a bit of effort. Why are you so secretive about wine?"

"I said it will appear as wine. I never said it was wine. I hate the stuff myself; indeed I can't wait until stainless steel gets invented."

"Huh?"

"Never mind. At any rate, yes, your boat can handle the load, even during the heaviest moments of the cleansing. It will take some effort on your part to prepare it, though."

Noah held up his hand.

"Hold on," he said, "What cleansing?"

"Never mind that, either. For now just be mindful that you're fully up to the task I have chosen to lay upon your shoulders, and that the rewards will be great when you succeed."

"Rewards, huh?" Noah smiled, running his tongue across all eight of his remaining teeth, "Now there's a part of this favor thing I can sink my teeth into. What kind of a reward did you have in mind?"

"Well, Noah," the man said, suddenly staring sharply at a spot about one cubit behind Noah's eyes, "You won't die." Something in the man's tone, or in the blaze of his odd blue eyes, froze Noah's blood. Something serious is going on, Noah decided. He drew a deep breath, and asked the first question that wandered without apparent provocation into his numb mind:

"Who will?"

"Everyone."

"Everyone?" Noah asked, glancing toward the busy village just downstream from his anchorage, "Who's everyone?"

"All the people, hell, all the living things for that matter, who are not aboard your ark in two months' time."

"You're insane, right?"

"Nope. I am just very, very powerful, and more than a little pissed at the quality of my work to date."

"What's your work?" Noah asked, growing amused, and a bit relieved that the young stranger was simply insane. That did not matter, as long as he was rich.

"Long story. Real long. Suffice it to say that I'm a creator with an ambition for perfection, but still a few practice sessions shy of my goal."

"Huh?"

"I agree," the man said, sitting on the boulder again. He reclined, cradled the back of his head in his impossibly clean hands, and went on, "Tell you what, Noah. I obviously like you, and intend to trust you with, well, everything, so I'll give it to you straight. I'm the stooge who created this happy little desert world you live in. I built the mountains, let loose the rivers, and, above all, seeded the life that infests an otherwise perfect world. I thought I had managed things well enough and that life was progressing well. I had some trouble with the raptor tribes a few million years ago, and had to chase them off the planet (they simply advanced before I was ready) – "

"What's a planet?" Noah interrupted.

"That's what I say," the man said, hands on hips, "Would that you had asked me what a raptor might be! Anyway. after the raptors debacle I thought everything was developing well. I had the code set for a steady evolution of creatures that would eventually manifest a biosphere unlike any other in the universe. But I screwed up."

"How so?" Noah asked. Though he had never heard it before either, screwing up was the first phrase from the crazy man's tale he dared understand.

"Well I'll tell you. The code was perfectly efficient; more so than in the age of raptors. I found that I could leave it be, go nurture a few gas giants, perhaps even whip up a galaxy or two while things took care of themselves here. But then a strange thing happened: One of the skinniest, lamest, most destined-to-fail iterations of the code developed a feature I hadn't anticipated. Do you know what that feature is?"

"I don't even know what an iteration is, or a raptor; how could I guess at a feature on a skinny lame animal that I've likely never encountered?"

"Ah, Noah, you're a very deep man. That might be one reason I chose you."

"That, and my barge?"

"And the barge, yes. So you're not going to guess?"

"I'm not going to guess."

"That's fine. If I would never have guessed it, how on earth would you?"

"What's earth?"

"Never mind. At any rate, that paltry creature is mankind: you, Noah, and your bald bipedal ilk. And do you know what that feature is? Not your thumbs; I planned that one. No, it was your brain. Don't ask; suffice it to say it's a thing inside your head that does important stuff. Anyway, all of a sudden, right out of the blue, your ancestors started thinking. The code had inadvertently established a trait for very large brains in your development, without accounting for the fact that that kind of mental capacity would bring about self-awareness millions of years before another creature should have possessed it (as I said, those raptors were quite a problem, and I actually wondered if intelligence were really a thing worth revisiting at all)."

Noah stared at his thumbs for a moment, and then said gently, "You know I don't understand anything you are raving about."

"Of course I do. But you'll indulge me? I'm on a roll."

"Of course I will," Noah smiled. He liked this crazy man.

"At any rate, I was away while this intelligence was developing these last few million years, and things have gotten way out of hand. Indeed, this big brain coding has begun to spread across countless other species. You know how you can joke with your donkey, and argue into the night with your dogs?"

"Of course," Noah said, smiling at the debate about public morality that had kept him and his pack up half the night just the previous week.

"Well, that wasn't supposed to happen. I meant to allow one intelligent species per domain. The whales have the oceans, the ant colonies have the dirt, and you have the lands' surface. That's it. But my negligence allowed that rule to be broken, in spades. Now thousands of species, in every domain save the dirt (gotta love the ants' ability to stymie competition!), are at a level of intelligence that I had reserved for just you three. And, when thousands of species are aware, thinking, fearing death, starting religions, fighting wars, and inventing shortcuts, mayhem ensues. And it did."

"It did?" Noah asked, not remembering a visit from the Mayhem clan.

"Trust me; it's all swirling in the toilet now, and it's only going to get worse. I have to fix that."

"How?" Noah asked. He was intrigued by the swirling, and he wondered with unexplained visceral pleasure about what a toilet might be, though he opted not to ask about that either, lest the man judge him ignorant.

"Good question; and yes, well chosen. Basically I'm going to let loose a single infinitely self-replicating bacteria that will eat every living thing on the surface of the land, converting it all to a five kilometer – sorry, a 10,870 cubit tall wall of gray goo that will erase all evidence of this intelligence plague. Then I'll start all over again, with mankind again the sole possessor of awareness on the surface. Like it was supposed to be – in about six million years." Then the man fell silent, appearing to have had his attention fully taken by the muddy waters that meandered along the bank.

Noah could reckon very little of what the man had said. He wasn't even sure what a cubit was. Something about an arm, he remembered being told once. But that goo thing sounded impressive; though he had trouble imagining things called "thousandeighthundredandseventys" piled ten high to form it. This man could imagine formidable beasts indeed!

"More formidable than you'll ever know, my friend," the man said wistfully.

"Stop doing that!" Noah shouted. He then paused, paced a bit, and when no questions, decisions, or thoughts entered his head he spoke softly to the man:

"I think I've had enough entertainment for this day. I'm a very busy man, and have no more time to waste on such prattle." He turned and began to stride purposely toward his hut.

"Of course you don't, Noah," the man said. His words, or rather something in them, caused Noah to stop. When Noah turned, the man was right behind him. He gently wrapped long fingers around Noah's elbow and tugged him back toward the river. "Let's walk," he said.

And they did. They strolled in silence for a time, away from the village and Noah's property, out toward a patch of land currently being farmed by an unruly tribe of apes. Noah should have felt nervous getting this close to the hairy village without a guard, but he did not. Instead, he felt at peace, and quite interested in the man's proposal, were it ever to come. When the road became a wavy thin line of sand fording tall grass, Noah cleared his throat:

"Will we be walking all the way to the Elephant city?"

"We could, you know. But no. This is far enough. Will you do me my favor, Noah?"

"What is it, exactly? In words a sane man can understand."

"Simply hold those casks in your barge for about a month – sorry: a moon cycle. Endure the cleansing; it should be like a flood of porridge to your senses, so you'll understand how to stay afloat. When it eventually subsides, and I am sure it will, simply smash the casks and go about your business. You don't even need to remove them from the ark first."

"Why would you want me to smash them, after caring so for them?"

"You'll see. Okay, you won't actually see. But you'll get it. I think. Your kids will, anyway; or their ancestors. Some bozo will no doubt start a religion over it eventually."

"That certainly clears things up for me. A 'month' is a very long time; I can make two, even three trips with the barge in that time, to several trading places. That is much work lost. Will you be able to pay me enough to financially justify the time spent floating about with your wine?"

"Noah," the man said, resting a hand on Noah's shoulder, "When this is over you will be the richest man in the world."

Now that is something I can understand, Noah thought. He felt himself believing the man's bizarre tale, and wondered if it was his inner greed that clouded his judgment.

"Probably," the man said, "But I have a feeling that your inner goodness will prevail in the end."

"I thought you weren't going to do that anymore."

"Sorry. So, will you carry my casks?"

"One moon cycle?"

"Give or take."

"And 314 casks of wine."

"314 casks."

"When would we leave?"

"In six months."

"Six moon cycles?"

"You got it."

"And where am I taking those casks?"

"Nowhere in particular. All you really have to do is keep them afloat."

"What's in them? I know it isn't wine."

"Smart man. Call it seeds, Noah."

"Seeds? You mean for planting?"

"Yup. For replanting that code, and getting everything right."

"Let's not go there again, huh?"

"Sure. But you'll do me this favor? You'll make your barge an ark for my casks?"

"I will," Noah said, half disbelieving the words as they exited his mouth.

"Great. I'm glad to hear that. With that, I must be going – things get weird when I hang around too long."

"Weird, huh?" Noah asked.

"Yup."

"What a shock."

"You'd be amazed," the man smiled. He started to turn, then he stopped and touched a finger to his lower lip, "Oh, I almost forgot, Noah. A couple more things."

"I knew it," Noah said, folding his arms, "There's always a complication thrown in after my word's been given. Well, be aware that I don't – "

"Spare me the speech, Noah," the man said easily, "These are small things. First, tell no one of this coming adventure. They won't believe you anyway, and might kill you out of fear."

"I can do that," Noah said, having already figured that, "What's the other thing?"

"You're taking your family with you."

"No I'm not," Noah said defiantly, folding his arms. Half the reason for the barge was to have a place his family will not be, save a few healthy sons. He continued, "My family does not travel with me. There would be no room even if they wanted to."

"This time they are, and you will make room."

"Fine. I guess it is your show, after all," Noah conceded, much more quickly than he had expected to. Then he felt a wave of panic, "You mean my whole family? All seven of my daughters, and their good-for-nothing husbands?"

"That would be best; as many as you can cram in, anyway. Keep in mind that you'll never again see anyone left behind."

Noah heard what the man said, and didn't disbelieve.

"I guess I'll need a bigger barge."

"That you will. An Ark, it will be," the man said. He then took Noah's hands in his, looked him in the eye again, and said, "Thank you Noah. You will not see me again."

Without another word, the man turned and walked toward the river. Noah felt emotionally swollen by the man's exit, with parts of him twisting in ways he had never experienced before. He stared at his toes for a few seconds in a vain effort to shake off the odd feelings inspired by his insane business partner. Finally he gathered himself, summoned his sensibility, raised his head and shouted after the man:

"But if I don't see you again, how will I find your cargo? How will I be paid?"

The man was gone. Noah spun around, but there was not trace of the man, or anyone, in any direction up or down the river. He was alone. Noah sighed, shook his head, and started home. He had barely taken a step when he noticed that the path was again a wide stretch of good flat dirt, and that his hut was just up the hill to his right amid well-trampled grass. He stood quietly for a moment while his wife Shirah stared at him from the hut's small entryway.

"A big barge," he mumbled as he climbed the hill.

A full growing season passed, and Noah never did see his odd new business partner again. Not in waking life, anyway: during sleep his dreams were plagued by visions of the man and the sticky gray flood he had described to Noah that day. When awake he found himself preternaturally driven toward preparing his barge to take on 314 casks of wine, many passengers, and stores enough for a moon cycle. He told nobody about the dreams, and failed to explain to his sons why they were adding a third deck to the barge. They did not question him, either, as they tied countless reeds and stared at him dumbly. They knew better than to raise questions of the old man, especially when they were so bent by the gravity of his instruction. He spoke of nothing to his wives when they demanded to know why they had to make so many new clothes while simultaneously drying fruits and brewing far more beer than even Noah required in a season. Still, taken as they were by his resolve, they did their work with minimal mumbling.

Noah was equally amazed by his resolve. He had assumed that, after the rush from the visit dissipated, he would dismiss the man's request as insane and go on with his life as if the stranger had never occupied that afternoon. But something within him drove him. It forced him to blurt orders and plans that he hadn't realized needed delivery. It led him to break a dozen contracts with his regular customers while he modified his barge, earning both their ire and the label, 'Madman of the River.'

And so, in less than six moon cycles Noah's barge was ready for its cargo, and had been fitted with accommodations for his entire extended family. Though he hadn't yet told them they were going with him on an unusual journey, they began to get the hint when his slaves started packing their belongings into the new third deck of the barge. Noah smiled when some of the slaves balked at carrying goods to such a great height: that third deck was over 30 cubits high, far higher than they had ever before risen above the earth. But, perhaps because his son Japeth was particularly adept at persuading them, they went. One slave had asked another of his sons, Ham, why no slaves' belongings were being loaded. Japeth got curious about this himself, and relayed the query to Noah.

"Because," Noah barked, adequately.

Noah stood on the riverbank for many hours on the day the ark was finished, both to admire his handiwork and to quest inwardly for the still elusive sane explanation for his efforts. To carry all those casks, which had yet to arrive, Noah was obliged to raft two barges together, and even this was barely enough room for 314 casks and supplies for his entire family. In addition, he had to attach a second reed hull to the sides, in order to keep the great tub from rolling over at the first ripple of this gray wave. All held together with tar, pitch, and a whole lot of luck.

"300 cubits long," he said to himself, rubbing his smooth dome, "Thirty high. Almost as wide as the river. And still no cargo. I truly am insane."

"I'll offer no protest to that, Dad," his eldest son, Shem, said from just behind him. Noah was too tired to be startled, but not too angry to smile. Shem didn't see the smile, as his eyes were steadily gazing upriver to the Northwest. Without removing his palm from its position of shielding his eyes, Shem continued, "But that's not important now, I think."

"What is?"

"That gray cloud that seems to be crawling on the ground toward us from upriver."

Noah prepared his response to Shem's jest, but it froze in his throat when he turned his gaze up river.

"Saddle up!" he bellowed.

The gray goo required the rest of the afternoon to reach Noah's docks, affording him just enough time to corral his sons, a couple of daughters (sans husbands, who were off on a hunt in spite of his direction; he didn't care much), his wives, and two slaves from the south named Osi and Isi. Noah stood at the large doorway high up on the new hull, specially constructed to accommodate the casks that had never arrived. He shook his head at his gullibility, but was relieved at least that he had been convinced to build such a sturdy craft in which to weather the coming storm.

Apparently the inhabitants of possibly every nearby village wanted to share in his good fortune, as they had begun to gather on the shore below him. The gangway was narrow, steep, and easy to release from the hull, so they were hesitant to climb it. Instead they milled about below, alternately shouting pleas for help and arguing amongst themselves for position at the ramp (an argument the elephants and lions handily won, save with each other). Noah mostly ignored the fray below him while he leaned against the heavy door frame, watching the coming flood. He guessed that most of the people gathered would fit aboard, though there was not enough food for all of them to eat for a full moon cycle. And the lions, though, generally a sensible crowd, always made him nervous. All might not be lost yet, he thought, there is always a hearty profit in rescue. Realizing he must make a decision quickly, he glanced at the hold behind him for one last gage of available space.

Noah gasped. There would be no passengers today, it turned out, because there was indeed no space. The cavernous hold that he had prepared, and which was empty save for a curious echo just a moment earlier, had become crowded with huge, shining casks, the like of which he had never before seen. They stood as tall as he, but half again as wide, and were polished so smooth that he could see his reflection in every one of them. And they filled the hold, perfectly, from corner to corner, deck to deck. If he hadn't built that third deck, there would be no room for his family, much less the rabble outside. He returned to the open hatch, and bent down to the thin reeds holding the gangway fast. He untied them, and let the wooded ramp fall into the water.

"Sorry folks," he shouted over the panicked screams of the crowd below, "There is, alas, no room aboard. You'll need to find shelter elsewhere." With his words the crowd fell silent for a few heartbeats. Then they looked at each other. Then they looked at the approaching goo. Then they looked back at each other. Then they repeated. Then they panicked.

Noah pulled the great doors closed, curious about his lack of compassion for his neighbors. If the crazy man was correct, he surmised, then all those people were doomed to a terrible end. Some of them were his friends. Indeed, a few of them were his family. And between the goo and the sudden cargo, the crazy man was making great strides in overall credibility with Noah. But he really didn't care much about those people, and he wondered why for about eleven heartbeats. Then he was climbing the ladder to the top deck, shouting at his sons to cast off, and be ready to deflect the adventurous few who dared and succeeded to climb the sheer, slippery side of the ark to perceived safety.

"So," his wife, Judy, asked for the three-thousandth time from her position beside Noah at the rail, "Do you think a moon cycle has passed yet?"

"Oh Judy, Judy, Judy," Noah sighed, rubbing his head, "How many times must I say I have no idea?"

"Just a few more, I suppose," Judy snapped back without breaking her useless, ceaseless search into the black nothingness that surrounded them, "Until you have an idea. Because I know you will, somehow." She smiled when she spoke, but Noah assumed that was sarcasm dripping from her full young lips (Judy was just twenty – Shirah, the mother of his sons and several daughters, was below decks scrounging for food among the dwindling stores). He smiled, wrapped an arm around her thin waist, and said:

"But Judy, I may never know. This stuff we've been floating on for so much time is as much a mystery to me as you."

"So I've heard. But you knew it was coming, right?"

"Yes."

"And you knew we'd need something this big just to survive, right?"

"Well, yes, I suppose."

"And you knew almost to the day when to finish this – what did you call it? – this ark so we could be safe, right?"

"Well. That, was mostly luck, I think."

"Sure sure. So do you think a moon cycle has passed yet?"

"Judy!"

"Noah! It would be nice to know. We're running out of food, you know."

"I know," Noah whispered, "I know." Now he searched the ink himself, though he could not tell whether he could see only a few cubits, or if the air was truly clear and simply carried no light or matter for an unknowable distance.

The goo had indeed arrived, as the man had said. Noah's sons had to fend off only a few desperate creatures before the entire river valley, and everything else, was buried in the stuff. They watched in awe as the mountain of goo passed silently beneath the floating ark. Everything was obliterated; the land, the river, the distant mountains; even other barges that had initially risen alongside the ark. It was all gone, and quickly, as the formerly crazy man had promised. Then the sun was erased as well, by clouds so perfectly dense it was impossible to discern day or night. Nothing remained but Noah, his family, some stores, and those casks.

Of course Noah had tried to open a cask or two. The man had not forbidden such action, and his initial curiosity and later fear of starvation led him several times into the hold with his heaviest tools. Though he and his sons swung hard and broke several mallets and stones, their efforts failed even to smudge the shiny surfaces of the casks. The mighty containers had no lids, seals, or latches to worry loose, either: that smoothness was uniform, perfect, and really, really annoying.

Beyond that, it had been a fairly uneventful journey. His sons were disciplined, his wives strong and remarkably patient, and his daughters kept to themselves. There was little conversation, absolutely no speculation, and, oddly, no sorrow. Noah many times admired the strength of his loved ones, and wondered if that was as much a factor in the man choosing him as was his barge.

There hadn't been much to do aboard the ark, either. Shirah and the slaves (okay, the slaves, with Shirah's guidance) handled the cooking, there was no navigation to be done, nor did the ark seem to need any maintenance. Some games were played and stories told after the initial shock of the event wore off, but both grew tiresome after a time. Now each person found a spot at which to sit and wait quietly for the next meal, journey's end, or death, whichever came first.

Noah had managed to track the first few days by reckoning time through his sleep cycles, but that measure, plus any urge to sleep at all, began to fail after a few days. Now all he could do was guess at time by counting the intervals between the rumblings of his empty stomach. He knew with reasonable accuracy that a moon cycle plus about ten days had passed, but he was certainly not going to share that with Judy. She didn't like to be late for anything. His gloomy search was broken by a shrill shout from Japheth that seemed to pierce the emptiness with its volume and urgency.

"I think I see light!" he shouted from his position on the roof of the deckhouse, "No. I am sure I see light!"

"Where?" Noah and Judy asked at once without breaking their scan of the blackness.

"In the sky. Straight up!"

Japheth's volume was enough to draw the ark's full compliment from their holes to the deck. They shouted with glee and pointed shaking fingers at the shaft of light that had broken through the clouds directly above them.

"It seems that the sun has not abandoned us after all," Noah said, hugging his wives and winking at his sons. Everyone was jubilant. The daughters danced amid excited chatter as blue sky cut a growing hole in the blanket that had minimized their world for so long. Then, when the sky had fully cleared, someone took a moment to look over the side. And that someone, a daughter's (lucky) husband who hated hunting, fell silent. His wife noticed his pause, and stopped to look out as well. Her smile twitched for a second, then was gone. In a few moments everyone on deck had fallen into a silent gaze over the ark's high rail. Japheth wept. Noah rubbed his head once more, and wondered.

The sky showed them the world that had been obscured from them for most of the trip, and that world had become very, very simple. It was a gray sea, smooth as a pond on a quiet summer morning, and as shiny as those casks in the hold. That sea stretched in all directions in a perfectly flat horizon that broke on absolutely nothing. Noah's world was gone. Nothing was left except him, his family, those casks, and precious little food.

"Oh my," were the only words able to free themselves from his choked throat.

"I think we'd best be more careful with the food," Shirah mumbled as she gently parted Noah's frozen embrace and started back to her kitchen.

"Dad," Shem asked quietly, though his question pierced every ear, "Who was this guy, really?"

That the days could again be accurately measured was more curse than boon, especially after Noah had scored the hundredth scratch on the wall of his cabin. He wished not to make a new mark every morning he saw the dawn's orange fingers creep though his thin cabin window, but still he did; he thought it might be important someday that he remembered his adventure accurately.

"One hundred days," Noah whispered, "Three moon cycles, plus ten."

"And we're still alive," Shirah said from the bed, where she sat, rubbing the sleep from her eyes.

"Thanks to you, my resourceful wife." Noah said, patting her ample buttocks as she passed close to him to make her way from the cramped sleeping space. She just smiled, rolled her eyes, and gave Judy a soft kick as she stepped over her sleeping bulk. Shirah, the heroine of the journey, and had long since given up insisting that that cask had fallen open on its own as she passed it. That cask, which was filled with a creamy pink jell that tasted of sweet fruit and proved unlimited in supply. Shirah left the cabin to hoist her back end over the side for her morning pee. Noah normally wouldn't see her again until breakfast, but today she raced back into the cabin, tripping over Judy and flying into Noah's arms. They fell on their straw sleeping pallet, with Shirah on top. Her eyes were wide, her hand's clutched Noah's shoulders.

"Noah," she gasped, "Come quick!"

Noah did not need to be asked twice. He let Shirah drag him to his feet with an alarming show of strength. They leapt together over Judy's still sleeping form, and ran through the dank narrow passage to the deck outside. Shirah didn't need to say a word, or even point. Noah knew what she had to show him.

The world had risen back up to them.

Not all of it. Only a few craggy brown peaks of rock, cold tentative nipples of once mighty mountains, poked through the taught fabric of the dismal sea. But it was enough to fill Noah's soul as it hadn't been filled in many cycles. There was still a world under there. Noah had hope. He squeezed Shirah's hand.

"The trip is ending, my love," he said softly.

"Should I wake the family?"

"Just Judy. The rest can form their own joy as they rise. It's much nicer that way."

"Already here, Noah," Judy breathed from his other side. He felt her body against him, and felt Shirah reach behind him to hold her tight, "So, you think that moon cycle has finally passed?" Shirah giggled like a little girl.

"I think so, young love," Noah sighed, "I think so."

The cycle had passed, but the ark still floated in a sea without beaches (and no way to navigate to them if any appeared) for many, many more days. But now they knew that the land was there, and slowly more so with every dawn, and that converted their long ride from purgatory to advent. The days were consumed by happy activity (actually they did the same nothing they were doing before, only now they did it together, in a communal bath of bright hope), followed by nights of easy sleep. They had no idea what had happened, why it had happened, or what would happen in their future. But they now knew that their future was to happen; and that made all the difference.

Within about four more moon cycles enough of the world had reappeared to convince them that landfall was imminent. With a renewed sense of urgency, Noah set about preparing himself and his family for having a world unto themselves. Such an assumption did not impress him, since it had been so long since he had seen a pair of eyes that belong to someone outside his family. It wouldn't be much of a reign, anyway, if one judged it by the barren muddy rock that the goo was leaving behind. But still, it was his kingdom, his world, and his opportunity to make things right so that the guy with the casks didn't come along and sweep up again. So, with the future in mind, he brought his family together for a meeting. He called them down from their sundry perches and quiet spots, and bade them squat about on the floor before him. One of his sons-in-law (Raleph, Noah guessed) was not interested in squatting, so Noah nodded to Shem to knock the lad over. Shem obliged, and Raleph fell to the floor sheepishly amid the giggles of his wife and her sisters. Noah cleared his throat.

"Now that we're all settled," he said, rubbing his hands, "We have something very important to talk about."

"Would this have anything to do with the water receding?"

"Or the fact that there's nothing left alive but us, not even fish?"

"Or maybe we're going to discuss how we have to take responsibility for this new world we've been given?"

Noah rolled his eyes.

"Have I been talking in my sleep again?" he asked.

"No dad," Ham said with a wink, "It's just that you've been chatting pretty much nonstop about all this for the last three moons. I think we've all got it pretty much memorized."

There was a round of laughter in the cabin, which Noah eventually joined. I am getting old, he thought, feels like 600 years sometimes. When the moment passed Noah raised his hands and said, "Fine then. It appears that I've said enough. Save one thing: I meant it all. We're on our own now, and we can't trust that magic cask to feed us forever. As soon as our ark runs aground – which it will in the next few days, I'm sure – we must set about taking care of ourselves and starting our new lives. We've been parked on this stinky tub for almost a year now, and we might have gotten too fat and lazy to work."

"But Dad," Japheth said, "What will we do? We're merchants with no buyers. We could have figured out how to farm, I suppose, but we ate all the seeds before the cask started working, and have you seen any fish?"

"All good points, Japheth, to which I have no answer."

"So then we take it easy and just hope the cask never empties?" Ham asked. Shem smacked his little brother on the back of his head.

"No. That would be wrong. I think we were saved from the destruction for reasons other than just my barge. I think there might have been a higher purpose this crazy man had for choosing me, um, us. And, given the example of his displeasure we've all been living, I think we should keep the guy happy."

"So what do we do?"

"First we empty the hold of those casks the minute we're no longer afloat, just to finish the bargain I made with the man. I'll bet they'll be easy to break about two heartbeats after the keel is aground. And break them we will, fulfilling finally this long task. After that, I think we simply have to try. Try to do a little bit more than stay fed, dry, and knee deep in children (though all those things are also fine). I think we need to try to be nice to each other, whether we like it or not. And we need to treat each other with honor."

"What's honor?"

"Good question Raleph."

"That's Raphel," the daughter he assumed was married to the young man sternly noted.

"Good question Raphel," Noah said, "I'm not sure myself. It's sort of being nice to each other, or perhaps respecting each other, but without love or family needing to be the reason. You just treat everyone well, and in a way that simply feels right."

"That's a very dim definition, Dad."

"Sorry. It's all new right now. Someone will make it more clear later, I'm sure." Noah was rescued from a fall down the well of empty reasoning by a terrible scraping noise far below them, accompanied by the first motion they had felt in many cycles. The motion was violent, sending them all to the deck in an assortment of screams and gasps, but those cries carried joy, not fear. The disturbance continued for a few moments, and then all was still. Everyone froze in their sundry positions and looked at Noah, who was smiling.

"We're there." He said.

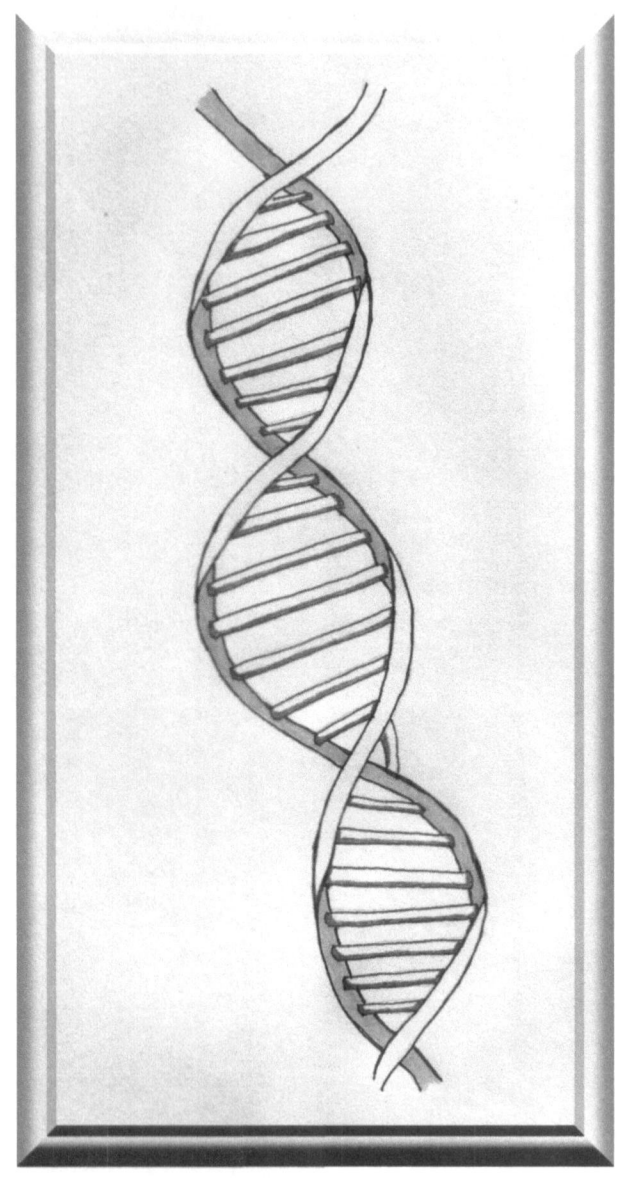

Litigating the Wind

"Your honor," Maxwell Wright III projected, sharing his perfect annunciation with the courtroom and the millions watching at home, "We have before us a young man whose life has been terribly, disastrously effected by his parents' gross negligence; parents who wish to continue that torture by denying the right of the boy to repair at least some of the damage while he can. Why, he --"

"Mr. Wright," Judge Warfield's low, precise voice interrupted the opening statement.

"Your honor?" Maxwell replied, refraining from turning away from the Jury Box.

"Mr. Wright, I understand the significance of this case, but, in light of the extreme public attention and your, um, interest in making an impact, I thought I should remind you that opening statements are limited to one minute."

"I understand the law, your honor," Max projected, still facing the Jury Box. He swept his hand in a dramatic flourish to it, continued: "but I was only interested in making clear to the jury the implications, the pain, of this monumental --"

"Mr. Wright?"

"Your honor?"

"The clock is ticking."

A light chuckle wandered the crowded gallery. Judge Warfield ignored it. He suspected he would have ample opportunities to censure the crowd later.

"Yes your honor," Max said softly. He held his gaze on the floor for a three count. Then he raised it smiled ruefully at the Jury Box, and resumed his original bluster.

"Young Simon Phillips," he pronounced, pointing without looking at the blond boy fidgeting at the plaintiff's table, "Nine-year-old Simon Phillips, feels that his life has been permanently damaged by his parents' -- Marjorie Corman and Brandon Phillips -- decision to omit DNA sampling and upgrades during his fetal stage, forcing him to be born at the mercy of nature."

"To compound the crime, the parents have denied young Simon opportunity to receive those post-natal upgrades available to him. They have no medical reason for this denial and time is running out, as we know that all DNA upgrades must be completed before puberty."

"And so, your honor, Mr. Simon Phillips will present his case before this jury, yourself, and the world. He will seek the right to choose his own future, to mold his own destiny."

"The amount of damages requested?" Judge Warfield asked, not looking up from his laptop.

"None, your honor," Max said, with profound dignity.

"None?" the judge squinted at him over ancient horn-rimmed glasses, clearly puzzled.

"The defendants are the boy's parents, your honor," Max said, palms up, "How could we?"

"So noted," Judge Warfield said, careful not to let his eyebrows rise. No damages, my ass, he thought. What the hell is this guy up to? He continued:

"Thank you Mr. Wright. Ms. Panther, your statement please." Max nodded to the judge and turned back toward his seat. His path was blocked by Clarissa Panther, a longtime adversary and occasionally close friend. She blocked it well, too. At over six feet tall with broad shoulders and exaggerated hourglass figure, she presented quite a case. Her perfect face and green eyes lost nothing as she smiled coldly at him, waiting for him to move. He returned the empty gesture and stepped aside. The scent of fresh roses enveloped her subtly.

Clarissa shouldered past Max, careful not to look up at his chiseled features framing soft blue eyes that consistently thawed her meticulously constructed persona. She stepped to the wooden podium centered between the bench, the Jury Box, and the gallery. She cleared her throat.

"Your honor," she said. Her soft, lilting voice heard clearly by everyone in the vast federal courtroom, "I represent Marjorie Corman and Brandon Phillips, and am honored to defend their actions and their deeply conscientious intentions. My clients have done nothing wrong, and love their son above all else in their lives. They simply do not believe, as so many still do not, that he needs any upgrades to his basic traits. Simon is a healthy, intelligent, sociable boy with great potential. His mother and father feel that God and nature have bestowed what was to be bestowed. Their child is fine as he is. They feel no changes are necessary, and he will appreciate more in life as a 'real' person.

"My clients feel that the media's glorification of upgrades, coupled with Mr. Wright's coaching, have confused their son. They know he is a strong child. Phillip will thank them for their actions in the future." Clarissa felt the murmur her last statement caused.

"Finally, your honor, since they are well within their rights to make decisions for their son while he is still so young, I ask that you dismiss this case on the grounds that nothing improper has happened."

"Ten seconds to spare, Ms. Panther," Judge Warfield allowed his craggy face to shape a minimal smile, "Thank you and forget the dismissal." Clarissa nodded and returned to her seat, not questioning Judge Warfield's flippant response to her request for an unlikely dismissal. She had to ask.

"Okay," the judge said, pushing back from his desk, "Now that opening statements are in, and we all know why we're here, let's break for lunch. Make it for, um, one hour. We will reconvene at 12:30. The jury is excused until then," He paused until the bailiff flipped the ornate switch that darkened the Jury Box, then said "Hopefully we'll finish this up by five. And remember, no contact with the press!" Without another word he rose to his full height of about five feet and raced out the door to his chambers before the bailiff could call "all rise."

The sound of his oak chambers door slamming shut triggered a cacophony of lively conversation. Everyone had an opinion to share or question to ask. Only the litigants remained silent as they filed out of the courtroom. Simon and Max ran the gauntlet of press, concerned citizens, and court ghouls first. Simon, numb to the attention, strode fearlessly down the narrow flesh-lined path without speaking to or making eye contact with anyone in the crowd.

His parents did about as well, though they did throw out a few "no comments" to the barrage of questions that flowed at them:

"Has the judge changed your mind yet? Is this a religious decision? Will you be having more children? Do you still love your son? Is Simon psychologically unstable? Do you feel you're making a statement? What did you have for breakfast? Do you think the trial will go both days? Are you upset with the judge?"

"Ms. Corman," A diminutive woman who had used her stature to wriggle between the couple, stretched up to Marjorie's ear, "Ms. Corman. Please. Tell me how you feel about your son's charges."

"We can't discuss anything with you, Elise, you know that," Clarissa boomed from behind Marjorie, "Now leave us alone."

The two groups made it through the old courthouse, down the steps and to their waiting cars without breaking under the considerable pressure of the media. After he deposited Simon in his car, Max edged through the crowd to a position beside Clarissa. He touched her elbow.

"Henry's?" he shouted in her ear. It could have been a whisper. Clarissa nodded almost imperceptibly and got in her group's car without turning. "Okay," he mouthed to his reflection in her closed tinted window, "See you there." He pushed his way back to his car. A rear door opened to his touch, he slid into the back seat and slammed the door to another barrage of unanswerable questions and the screech of a man who had left his fingers in the wrong place.

"We're out a here, Freddy," he said to his young, very large driver.

"Henry's?" Freddy asked his mirror as he left the curb.

"You got it."

Once the car was moving, Simon's catatonia broke. He knelt on the seat to get a better look out the back window. He gawked back at the people, many of whom were chasing them on foot and still shouting questions.

"They're pretty wild," he said, his alto voice clear, fresh. I can't wait to get that voice on the stand, Max thought.

"Who's wild?"

"Those people. Why do they still ask all those questions, even when Judge told us to shut up?"

"Got me. I guess they can get information from some people. People that aren't as tough as you."

"Yeah," Simon beamed, "Tough. Like my dad. He's real tough." He meant that in the most positive, admirable way, Max thought. This is a weird case, and it's gonna get weirder before tonight, I'm sure.

"Your parents are tough people, Simon. Tough in many ways," Max said, "I'm sorry you had to hear me say some bad things about them today."

"Oh, that's okay, Mr. Wright," Simon said, plopping back down into the plush back seat. He had to slouch a bit to get his feet to touch the floor. "We, my Mom and Dad and me, we had a talk about all this way back in the beginning. They told me there'll be bad things to say. I understand."

"You're still not angry with them, are you?"

"Nope."

"You just want to be able to have upgrades," Max asked for at least the hundredth time. This exchange had become routine.

"That's right. I want to be cool," Simon emphasized the last word, then folded his arms and smiled. The kid has a beautiful smile, Max thought, and those eyes. He'll have no trouble with the ladies when he grows up. He shook his head, forcing the blasphemy from his mind.

"Are you hungry Simon?" he asked, changing the subject.

"Oh yeah, I am. Are we going to Henry's?"

"Oh yeah we are."

"And I can have the sizzler burger?"

"Oh yeah, you can."

"Cool. And Mommy and Daddy will be there too, right?"

"Yes they will. And so will Ms. Panther."

"I know," Simon said. He furrowed his brow, continued in mock severity, "To keep us honest." He giggled, put out his hand for a high-five.

"You got it, kid," Max said, lightly slapping the child's palm with his, "And we're nothing if we're not honest, right?"

"Nothing at all," Simon answered, finishing the litany.

They sat in silence for the remainder of the short ride to lunch. Henry's was a small restaurant outside town that offered privacy and a decent menu. The ride would have been shorter, except that Freddy took a circuitous route to avoid the more intrepid of the press.

As Max had hoped, Henry's gravel parking lot was almost empty. He and Simon got out of the car and entered the dim wooden restaurant without waiting for Simon's parents, who hadn't shown up yet. They walked without pause through the main dining room and into the bar, which featured antique booths with seat backs that rose a full six feet. No one would see them. The waitress, Barbara, didn't care who they were. They took their seats and ordered drinks. Vodka on the rocks and a coke. Max sighed, relieved that all was in order.

They passed the two minute wait for the rest of the party in silence, playing with the ashtray and sugar packets. Also without fanfare, Simon's parents and lawyer slid into the other side of the booth. Their tight grins failed to mask the day's fundamental pressure. Max had considered making light of the clandestine meeting, but the emotion glistening in Marjorie's eyes restrained him.

"Simon," Marjorie said, her voice a sigh, "Are you doing okay?"

"Sure mom," Simon chimed, "I'm fine. Really. You mad at me yet?"

"No, dear, but we came close this morning, with the things Mr. Wright was saying about us."

"Hey. Hey now," Clarissa interrupted, palms extended, "You remember the agreement. We swore to the judge that we wouldn't discuss the case."

"Specifics," Max corrected, "We wouldn't discuss specifics."

"Well, we shouldn't be talking at all. I still can't believe Warfield let us do this."

"It's because he trusts us Clarissa. Well, you, anyway," Max paused for a heartbeat to absorb the rare smile she rewarded him with, then continued, "And he wasn't about to break up this happy family during the proceedings."

"Well enough, but we have to be careful. At this point none of us can afford to have this case trashed on a technicality."

"True," Brandon spoke, startling Max. Brandon never spoke. But then he did it again when he continued, "But I didn't realize how big this was."

"Scopes all over again," Clarissa said softly, eyes down.

"Huh?" Simon asked.

"Nothing. We don't have much time. We should order. Where's Barbara?"

The family of litigants ordered their lunches, which were on the table in three minutes. They ate in a nervous silence, broken only by an occasional empty comment about the weather and a short but lively argument about whether the NBA should raise the hoops to 20 feet to make the games and slam dunks more interesting. Not a word was breathed about the trial that would begin ripping into their souls in less than an hour. Clarissa had guessed that breaking the gag rule was Judge Warfield's real intent in allowing contact between Simon and his parents. If they discussed the problem once more, the judge must have hoped, then maybe they would resolve it themselves and avoid the circus back in the city. Plus, he would avoid a ruling that could potentially end his career. She could have told the judge the idea wouldn't work: these were good, honest, and amazingly strong willed people. Even, or especially, Simon. They were instructed not to discuss the case, so there was no chance the case would be discussed. An accidental resolution to this piece of human history was not happening.

In less than thirty minutes after their arrival, the table was littered with dirty plates waiting to be picked up, and enshrouded in a tangible gloom as the litigants began to fall into their own thoughts about the afternoon. Max's watch beeped.

Good timing, he thought. He put out his third cigarette and checked his watch for a message. The instrument's smooth chrome face loudly proclaimed, "You've only got fifteen minutes...get moving!" He looked around for the waitress.

"Where's Barbara? It's time we were on our way."

"Right here," the young waitress said, appearing beside the booth. She handed them the check.

"If I didn't know better," Clarissa said with a wink, "I'd say you've been keeping an eye on us."

"Hey, you never know," Barbara winked back without a trace of defensiveness. Good, Clarissa thought, I like Barbara.

"Okay, then," Marjorie said. She lifted the cloth napkin off her lap and carefully draped it on her plate, covering her untouched meal. She tried to relay a cheery demeanor across her thin, plain Midwestern features. The effort failed.

"I would have liked some coffee," Brandon grumbled, "But I guess we'd best go. The sooner we deal with this, the better."

"Yup," Simon said, doing his best imitation of an adult, "We should leave now." Everyone stood at the boy's amusing cue.

"You guys should leave first," Clarissa said, "Just to be consistent."

"Sounds good," Max said conspiratorially, already headed for the door, "Let's go, Simon."

Max turned when he didn't get a response from Simon. The boy's face was buried in his mother's bosom. Marjorie was fighting back tears as she hugged her son.

"It's okay, Simon," she managed. She squatted on her heels to face him. "You still don't have to go through with this if you don't want to." Simon gently pulled away from her, still holding her hands. He had been a bit less successful holding back tears, but was back in control. He cast his blurred eyes to her. They were awash in the emotional residue of the difficult moment, but they were resolute.

"I have to, Mom," he said, "You know it." He sounded far too serious, too much an adult, to Clarissa.

"Yes," Marjorie said, releasing her only son's hands, "That's my Simon."

"We won't wish you luck, you know," Brandon announced too loudly. His attempt at humor was overlooked by all.

"Nope. Me neither," Simon answered through a big straight-toothed smile. He reached for Max's hand and with no further ado led him from the restaurant.

Max's car was waiting near the entrance, engine running, rear door open.

"Hurry up," Freddy shouted from the driver's seat, "We're late."

"And we're ready," Max responded out of habit. He was well past ready, and just wanted the afternoon to be finished. He and his client climbed into the car and rode in silence back to the courthouse.

"Your honor," Max announced to the silent courtroom, "For my first witness, I would like to call Dr. Theodora Milky."

"She'll be your expert?"

"Yes your honor, and she has already been fully screened and approved by both myself and the defense."

"Good," the judge said, leaning back in his chair. He considered the design of the ceiling tiles for a moment, then looked sharply at Max, "So, where is she, Mr. Wright?"

"She's right next to you, your honor, on the screen," Max responded politely, pointing to the large flat screen that had risen behind the witness stand, presenting a full-sized image of Max's expert witness. Dr. Milky bit her lip and smiled sheepishly at Max.

"Oh," the judge grumbled, "I keep forgetting about that damn thing. Proceed."

"Thank you, your honor. Doctor Milky, please state for the court your professional qualifications."

"Well, I hold doctorates in Family Planning, Embryonic Development, and DNA Cartography. I have been in practice for over 20 years. I also..."

"I think," Judge Warfield interrupted, "That in the name of expediency we dispense with the rest of Dr. Milky's biography."

"But your honor," Max said, facing the jury, "We feel that it is imperative that the jury understand Dr. Milky's background, and that she is to be --" Judge Warfield held up a hand, stifling Max. He took off his horn-rimmed glasses, carefully set the irreplaceable antique on his desk, and leaned toward the Jury Box.

"Ladies and gentlemen, please be advised that Dr. Milky has been thoroughly screened by the bench -- that's me -- and can be considered a reliable source. Mr. Wright?"

"Thank you, your honor. Dr. Milky. Did you review this case?"

"Extensively."

"Good. Please share with us your reaction."

"I was disgusted," Dr. Milky said, her voice husky, her attitude superior, "In this age of advanced human technology and health, to think that anyone would be so backward as to deprive their child of even the most basic of preparatory DNA sampling. It's utterly amazing, unthinkable"

"So, you disagree with the defendants' decision?"

"Emphatically."

"Will depriving Simon of these common services have some effect on his life?"

"Absolutely. He will have difficulty in school, and undoubtedly his adult life will be challenged by his need to compete with people who are clearly superior to him."

"Compete?"

"In business, and socially."

"How so, socially?"

"Well, look around you. How can you expect him to find a mate in today's society? Why, he would have to move to Africa or South America just to mix with people of his own kind."

"Objection your honor!" Clarissa shouted, jumping to her feet, "Dr. Milky might be a DNA expert, but she certainly has no authority to cast judgment on American society."

"Sustained," Judge Warfield said, "And I would also like to suggest, Dr. Milky, that you mind your opinions. There are still a few of us pre-DNA upgrade Neanderthals around."

"Yes your honor," Dr. Milky murmured, visibly blushing, "I didn't realize those were opinions."

"Dr. Milky! Your honor!" Clarissa shouted, slamming her hands on her table. Oops, Max thought, that can't be good. At least the jury heard it. Judge Warfield put his glasses back on, gestured for Max and Clarissa to approach the bench. When they did, he signaled the bailiff to interrupt communications to Dr. Milky, shut off the Jury Box. The Bailiff leaned forward from his position near the bench and switched an ornate brass toggle switch to its 'off' position. The green light over the Jury Box went out, leaving the millions of viewers, and jurors, in the dark. Almost simultaneously, Dr. Milky disappeared. Max and Clarissa approached the bench.

"Mr. Wright," Judge Warfield spoke almost under his breath, wary of the stealth mics that may have been smuggled in by the press, "Don't you think that this case is volatile enough without sowing ethical seeds like this right out of the chute?"

"I had no idea she'd open like that your honor," Max said, dripping with piety, "My line of questioning was intended to cover clinical facts only."

"Mm hmm," Clarissa, arms folded, commented.

"Ms Panther? You have something to say?"

"Only that this woman is clearly a bigot, and should be excused immediately, before more damage is done."

"A bigot?" Judge Warfield folded his hands, "Now there's a word I've not heard in years. Mr. Wright? Will you be able to control her?"

"Control Ms Panther? I'd like to, but why?" His quip not only failed to elicit levity from the judge, it created an icy silence. Oops.

"Yes, your honor, I think I can. Besides, her ten minutes is almost up."

"True. Bailiff, switch the witness back on."

"Thanks, your honor," Max said. Clarissa said nothing, but returned gracefully to her seat, whispered a few notes to her lapelcom. Dr. Milky's voice and hearing were returned to her, unfortunately at the instant that she was blowing her nose. After the laughter settled, Max attempted to re-establish his line of questioning.

"Dr. Milky, in your own words, and as few of them as possible, please list for the court the positive aspects of DNA sampling."

"Sampling? But that's common –"

"Indulge me, Dr. Milky."

"Well," Dr. Milky said, rolling her eyes, then reciting her answer like a schoolgirl, "The primary purpose of DNA sampling, or screening, is to discover any traits or malevolent genes that could have a negative impact on the subject's life. It's the surest way to screen for birth defects, congenital cancer, criminal propensity, or other unwanted variables."

"And the positive aspects of fetal upgrades?"

Dr. Milky's stern face broke into a delighted grin, "Well, I could go on about that for hours –"

"You only have 3 minutes, Dr. Milky," Judge Warfield interjected. Dr. Milky frowned, betraying her distaste for the judge. Then she blushed when she remembered that she was being watched by millions. She adjusted back to her original, passive academic composure before she continued. Sheesh, Max thought, this is a mess.

"Yes your honor," Dr. Milky said, "I understand. Fetal upgrades are perhaps the greatest boon Mankind has ever bestowed upon itself. We are able, after exhaustive DNA sampling and testing, to re-code thousands of aspects of fetal potential; like growth, intelligence, demeanor, facial structure, ambition, athletic skills. Why, with modern applications, we can enhance even the most subtle nuance of the subject's physique and character, we can produce the most perfect child, and later, adult, possible."

"Can this process cause any harm to the fetus?" Max asked, careful to have his tone border between the sublime and sardonic, depending on who was listening.

"Why no," Dr. Milky said, waving her hand dismissively, "It's been years, perhaps a decade now, since a case of damage caused by an upgrade has been recorded. It's a perfectly safe procedure, done millions of times a year."

"Can you think of any reason why you would not recommend upgrades to a pregnant patient?"

"Not a one."

"Has DNA sampling ever produced a perfect readout; one that indicated that no upgrades were necessary?"

"Never. At least, not in my experience."

"Thank you, Dr. Milky. No further questions." Max returned to his seat, winked at his clearly impressed client, sat down. Judge Warfield nodded to Clarissa:

"Cross, Ms. Panther?"

"Yes, your honor," Clarissa answered, not getting up, "Dr. Milky. What I heard you just say is that all fetuses require, without question, upgrades. Do you feel this is true?"

"Yes. Absolutely."

"Did you have any fetal upgrades performed on you?"

"Why, no. I'm seventy years old. They hadn't perfected upgrades yet, when I was born."

"You've never been upgraded?"

"Well," Dr. Milky said, blushing and averting her eyes, "I might have had one or two cosmetic changes in the last 20 years." Dr. Milky's smooth olive complexion and bright eyes concealed decades of decay.

"We are not discussing skin tighteners today, Dr. Milky. So you have never had a DNA adjustment, of any kind?"

"No, I haven't. I don't understand what this has got –
"

"And yet, you're a successful doctor, with degrees littering your office walls. Have you ever been married?"

"Objection, your honor," Max said, "What relevance does this witness's marital status have on the case?"

"I'm not sure myself, but I'm going to allow the question. Dr. Milky?"

"Yes. Three times now. All quite happy and fruitful, I must say."

"And when did the third wedding happen?"

"Why, just six years ago, in the fall of '76."

"Wait a minute, Dr. Milky," Clarissa said. She ran her hand through her permanently clean blond tresses, trying to look as puzzled as possible. She faced the Jury Box, slit her eyes in apparent concentration, and continued: "You were able to find a husband, at the age of 64, with not one fetal upgrade in your life's resumé?"

"Well," Dr. Milky said, catching on to the line of questioning, "Yes. But this was different."

"How so? Was he from South America or Africa?"

"Your honor," Max shouted, "Please!"

"Please what? Was that an objection?" Judge Warfield asked, resting his chin on his fist as he glared at Max. Max considered for a moment. Finally, unwilling to define his objection to the jury, shook his head.

"Good," Judge Warfield said, "Dr. Milky?"

"No. He was from New Jersey."

"So," Clarissa said, clenching her fist to stay calm, "What you're telling me is that, with your inferior natural programming, you were able to assemble a successful career and successful marriages, including one that started just six years ago? Long after 'perfect' children had reached adulthood?"

"Well…"

"Objection," Max said, without much conviction.

"Mr. Wright?"

"Your honor, surely the court realizes that Dr. Milky was born before DNA upgrades were available. Clearly her success was based on competition with similarly handicapped contemporaries." Awe, shit, he thought.

"Excuse me?" Judge Warfield snapped, "Well, this handicapped judge is overruling your objection. Ms Panther, I'll allow you time for one more question."

"Thank you, your honor. Dr. Milky, in your honest opinion, and considering the careers and lives of people like yourself and Judge Warfield, do you believe that Simon's chances for a fruitful and happy life have been eliminated by his parents actions?"

"I, um," Dr. Milky cast a forlorn glance at Max, then averted her eyes and paused. C'mon, Max thought, say it like we practiced, you proud old bitch. As if she heard him, Dr. Milky's eyes flashed wide. She turned her head toward the Jury Box, and said, loudly, "Yes. Yes I do. My life, and the honorable judge's, cannot be included in this category since we're..." her voice trailed off the moment she realized that something had come out wrong. No! Max thought, fighting an impulse to bury his head in his arms. Dr. Milky continued, slightly apprehensive, "We are from a different time, a time when an individual could make do with less."

"So you consider yourself inferior to, say, Mr. Wright, then?" Clarissa threw in before Judge Warfield could stop her. Answer quick, lady, she thought as she stared directly at Dr. Milky.

"Well, I wouldn't say that," Dr. Milky started.

"The witness will please refrain from answering," Judge Warfield interrupted, a little red from his gaff, "Ms Panther, I said one more question, not two. The jury will disregard that last answer."

"Sorry, your honor," Clarissa said softly, satisfied that the jury got the message. If they didn't, she hoped that the murmurs from the gallery might help drive it home.

"I'm sure," the judge said sternly, "Mr. Wright, you have three minutes to redirect."

"No questions, your honor," Max said, not getting up, "However, plaintive requests to reserve that three minutes for examination of subsequent witnesses."

"Granted. Thank you, Dr. Milky. We'll be shutting you off now." The screen went blank, then dropped down behind the witness stand. "Next witness, Mr. Wright."

"Your honor, I would like to call the true expert in this case to the stand," Max said, pausing dramatically. He had another expert lined up, but he wasn't opening any more doors that he couldn't shut in the next three hours. He continued speaking right at the jury, "the one witness who truly understands Simon's needs --"

"Just call him, Mr. Wright." Judge Warfield interrupted.

"Sorry your honor. Plaintiff calls Simon Phillips to the stand."

Already? Clarissa thought. She leaned over to Marjorie, seated beside her, and whispered in her ear, "That's a good sign. Max had twenty minutes worth of expert witness time left before calling the primary. He's nervous." Marjorie nodded, but remained somber, lost in her own personal battle for control.

Simon jerked out of a consuming daydream when he heard his name called. He looked at his watch, then at Max, then at his watch again. Confused, he shook his head vigorously. A soft chuckle rose from the gallery. Max sighed. With a nod from the judge, he crossed to the plaintiff's table, leaned closely to Simon.

"It's okay Simon," he whispered, "We've just had a little change of plans."

"I thought you said there'd be more people on my side?" Simon whispered, too loudly. Damn, Max thought, the press will definitely pick that up! He put his finger to his mouth, then whispered, "It's okay, Simon. We just had to speed things up a bit. You ready to speak now?"

"Yeah, sure," Simon said, way too loudly, "I been ready for weeks!" That raised the volume of gallery amusement. Max struggled against the urge to laugh while he sternly instructed Simon in the softest of whispers to say only what they discussed.

"Is there a problem?" Judge Warfield interrupted, silencing the gallery. Shit, Max thought, how much trouble am I going to get into this time?

"No your honor," He said quickly, "We're set." At Max's gesture, Simon stood and crossed with great pomp to the witness stand. As rehearsed, he waited for the clerk to swear him in, proudly said "I do," then sat down. He swung his little legs as he waited for the first question. His perfect blue eyes glistened in the harsh courtroom lights as they scanned the delighted audience. Damn, Max thought, he looks too adorable. We shouldn't have gotten his hair cut last week, and he's not slouching like I told him to!

"Simon," Max asked softly, standing as close to the child as the rules allowed, "Tell us, in your own words, why you are here."

Simon bowed his head, played with his fingers. Shit, kid, Max thought, cut out the cuteness!

"I'm here," Simon said clearly, inserting a pregnant pause, "I'm here because I found out a while ago that my future could be much better if only I could have DNA upgrades, and when I asked my parents if I had them they said no, and when I asked if I could get some now, they said no. So, since my parents get to decide these things, and they don't want to change me, I decided to do it myself."

Max paused a moment to allow time for his audience to absorb Simon's diction, and to give Clarissa opportunity to object while he was ready. She didn't, so he started the prepared dialogue with Simon:

"How did you find out about upgrades?"

"From school. Kids told me about them years ago, but I didn't pay much attention."

"Why?"

"Because they weren't taller than me yet, and they were still working as hard as me to get the same grades."

"And now that's different?" Max asked wincing slightly in anticipation.

"Objection, your honor," Clarissa interrupted forcefully, "The plaintiff has not been determined to be an expert in establishing what is 'different' between his own development and that of his peers."

"Mr. Wright," Judge Warfield said, his gray-bearded chin resting on a puffy fist, "Have you prepared proof to support Simon as an expert witness?"

"Of course not, your honor, but --"

"Objection sustained. Please adjust your line of questioning."

"Yes your honor," Max said, trying to keep his tone steady. Damn, he thought, I was hoping he wouldn't go that way. Now Simon has to get through Plan B. He took a breath, reminded himself that Simon was a smart kid and could handle the switch, and said, "Okay Simon. When did you first feel that you weren't the same as other kids?" He saw Simon smirk when he recognized the contingency.

"Well, probably around a year ago. Other kids, my friends then, started teasing me because I wasn't as tall or dark as them. They were calling me Nature-Boy."

"Did you tell your parents about this?"

"Yes I did."

"What did they say?"

"They told me not to worry, that this is part of growing up, that real friends don't talk like that."

"Did they tell you then that they could help you?"

"Nope."

"I see," Max said, pensively rubbing his chin, "So your parents kept you unaware of upgrades, ways to make you change like the other kids?"

"Yup. I guess they did."

"Then how did you learn about upgrades?"

"I found out later, after one kid, Jerry Disnel, got an upgrade."

"How did you know he got an upgrade?"

"He told me," Simon said. Max raised an eyebrow. Simon caught the gesture, nodded, and continued, "Oh. And he suddenly seemed happier, more smart. And he got picked for teams sooner." Max shot a glance over to Clarissa. She was hissing furiously into her blouse. That's going to hurt, he thought.

"Did this bother you?"

"Yes it did, because I already was getting picked almost last for teams."

"What did you do?"

"I asked my mom and dad. They said I didn't have any upgrades, and that I could never get them." A hint of a tear sparkled in Simon's left eye. Perfect, Max thought.

"Did you tell them how much you wanted to be changed?"

"Yes. And I told them that I needed it, so I could be as good as the other kids."

"And they still wouldn't allow the upgrades?"

"Nope."

"Even though you needed it?"

"Objection your honor," Clarissa said without looking up, "The witness is not qualified to judge what he needs."

"Isn't that what this is all about?" Max interjected, careful to sound prosaic.

"Not in this respect," Clarissa said to the judge, "Your honor, can we discuss this before you rule on the objection?"

"Well, Ms Panther, as much as I hate letting counsel make decisions for me, yes, we should. Bailiff, please shut off the jury." The Bailiff hit the brass toggle and paused, his empty gray gaze directed at the bench. Then Judge Warfield nodded again to the Bailiff, and the oversized guard flipped an equally ornate switch near the jury controller to its 'on' position. Max sensed no discernible change, but he knew that the courts anti-mic system had been activated. No sound made by the judge or litigants could be heard by the witness or anyone in the courtroom. They were completely alone.

"This seemed like a good time for privacy," Judge Warfield said. He cast an encouraging smile to Simon, who showed some panic at his sudden deafness. Simon calmed down, remembering Max's earlier warning and explanation. The judge continued, "Ms Panther, please tell me why the boy should not answer."

"It's quite obvious your honor."

"Humor me."

"Fine," Clarissa said pleasantly, "Mr. Phillips, though he is certainly the most important person in this case, is not an expert in DNA upgrades. His opinions about the subject, though paramount to him, can't possibly be considered valid proofs for upgrades."

"Okay. Mr. Wright?"

"Your honor," Max said, drawing a breath, and grateful the judge had used the masks for this, "Simon might be a child, with no schooling in the subject, but surely he's the one to ask. He must live with his parents' decision for the rest of his life. He's the one that sees perfect children growing up around him, moving ahead of him --"

"And he's the one offering pure conjecture your honor," Clarissa interrupted, rolling her eyes and shaking a titanium fingernail at Max, "He's proven none of this."

"Right you are," Judge Warfield said. He leaned back in his chair, hands behind his head, and appeared to be regarding the decision all three of them knew he had already made. Eventually he leaned forward, tapped something into his notebook, and said, "Mr. Wright. I am going to overrule Ms. Panther's objection, but with a caveat."

"But your honor!" Clarissa exclaimed, risking the famous wrath of Judge Warfield. Her interruption was expected, however, and the judge merely lifted his gnarled little hand and continued.

"That caveat being that you will in no way present this lad's opinion as anything but a boy's wishes and dreams. He is in no way an expert. Remember, you had one of those."

"Yes your honor," Max said, "I had intended nothing more."

"Good. Then this will be easy. Bailiff, please bring everybody back."

The bailiff flipped both switches back on. The gallery had broken into animated conversation while they were locked out, and the sound of a hundred different conversations hit the lawyers as if they had been dropped into a boxing arena. Max jumped, but managed to suppress a yelp of surprise. I'll never get used to that, he thought. The only one that spotted his reaction was Simon, who was delighted. Judge Warfield slammed his gavel three times. He didn't need to say anything. The gallery, aware of the routine, was silent immediately.

"We are back, with answers," the judge said, "I am overruling Ms Panther's objection. You may proceed, cautiously, Mr. Wright."

"Thank you, your honor," Max said. He turned once more to Simon.

"Did you miss us, Simon?"

"Nah. But my ears were ringing big time!" The gallery burst into laughter. Even Judge Warfield grinned. God bless cute witnesses! Max thought.

"As well they should have, Simon. Now, where were we? Oh, yes, I was asking if your parents would allow you to have upgrades, and you confirmed that they would not. Correct?"

"Correct!" Simon shot back, sitting upright and feeling very important.

"Thank you," Max said, shaking his head at the boy's enthusiasm. Don't look too happy, kid, he thought, this isn't a game. "Now. Are these upgrades important to you?"

"Oh, yeah, the most important thing I could imagine."

"Do you feel, in your own opinion, that upgrades would make your life better?" Max cringed involuntarily.

"Objection!"

"Overruled. However, the jury is advised that Mr. Phillips is not an expert in this field, and his opinion is untrained and very much his own. You may answer now, Mr. Phillips."

"Thanks man," Simon said, to the judge. Then he turned back to face Max, who stood before the Jury Box, drew a breath and spoke in his most serious tone:

"I understand that I'm real young, and might not get it yet, but I see kids growing up around me. I hear them talk.

They're all going to be tall, and smart. They know exactly how tall and smart too. Me, I'm alone. I'm short now, and not as bright, and I just don't know if any of that is going to change for me. It's a scary thing." His speech finished, Simon folded his little arms and settled back in his seat, legs swinging. Max's mind raced to remember what Simon had left out.

"Is there anything else those upgrades might help you with, Simon? Maybe when you're an adult?" Max asked. Simon looked startled for an instant, realizing he had forgotten part of his well-rehearsed speech. He sighed and continued:

"Sure, there's lots of things. What if I'm supposed to go bald? Or blind? What if there's some disease..."

"Objection, your honor. There are no known diseases that cannot be treated when they occur, regardless of a subject's genetic makeup."

"Sustained," Judge Warfield said. Then he leaned down to Simon, and said softly, "Don't worry, son, you won't get sick because of all this. Now go on."

"Thanks your honor," Simon said, "Of course she did say `no known diseases' -- "

"That's enough of that, Mr. Phillips," Judge Warfield snapped, feeling like he was set up. All right, Max exclaimed to himself, beaming at Simon.

"Sorry Judge," Simon said, honestly apologetic, "Anyway, there's lots of things I could get done to me that my Mom and Dad are keeping away. I could get a bigger heart and lungs, like Freddy and James, and be great at sports. Maybe get a cortex extension, and be a better engineer (I want to be an engineer, you know). There's so many things that all the kids I know are getting, I couldn't begin to list."

"Then you don't need to," Max said softly, "Just tell us how you feel about your parents holding your upgrades back."

"Awful. I thought they loved me," Simon paused, choking a bit. He had rehearsed the answer many times, but this was the first time it touched his consciousness. He continued, "I really did. They say they still do, but I just don't see it. I mean, don't they want me to be great?"

"No further questions, your honor," Max proclaimed, with studied gravity. He crossed back to his seat and fell into it as if the weight of the examination had drained him of all energy. God, what a ham, Clarissa thought.

"Ms Panther?"

"Thank you, your honor," Clarissa said. She stood, crossed to the witness stand, and leaned gently on its rail. She gazed carefully into Simon's eyes, as if to remind him that he was in a very serious seat.

"Hello Simon. Are you comfortable?"

"Well I was. Now I'm scared."

Clarissa smiled, said, "There's no need to be, Simon. We all want to be friends here. You understand that, don't you? That your parents love you deeply and want above all else to keep your love and respect?"

"Yeah, I guess," Simon responded softly, aware of the contradiction. Well then, Clarissa thought, let's see what the jury does with that. She cast a furtive glance to Max. He was staring, pleasantly, at her.

"Good," she said, "Now tell us all again that you understand that upgrades are different from cures."

"Sure I do," Simon said, pursing his lips with his fingers, "An upgrade makes you better, and a cure makes you *better*." Clarissa bowed her head, waited for the titters and 'so cute's' behind her to die out, then folded her arms and looked at Simon again.

"Could you be a little more specific, Simon? What does each 'better' do?"

"Well," Simon said, tugging a finger after each point, "An upgrade makes you taller, or smarter, or good at basketball, or smooth with people. A cure makes cancer and other things that can make you sick go away."

"Is that all a cure can do?"

"S'far as I know?"

"Are you sure? Did you know baldness can be cured?"

Oh, shit, Max thought. "Objection, your honor!" He shouted while he recalled previous testimony from his watch.

"Mr. Wright?" Judge Warfield asked over his spectacles.

"We have already established that Mr. Phillips is not an expert in determining options and results of upgrades."

"I believe the witness is simply stating his opinion, which is what we're all here for in the first place. Overruled."

"Yes, your honor," Max said. He expected to be overruled, but the jury needed to be led off the track a bit. He hoped that worked.

"You can continue, Mr. Phillips," the judge said gently to Simon.

"Thanks man," Simon said, "Anyway, yeah, I did know that baldness can be cured. It's a pill you can buy. My dad's got a jar at home-- oops! Sorry Dad!" More laughter. Brandon was not amused, but affected a feeble grin through spreading blush.

"Then why did you list not being bald as one of the things upgrades could do for you."

"'Cause it is."

"That's true, but if a cure is as easy as a little pill, then why get an upgrade?"

"Don't know. 'Cause it would be cool, I guess."

"And what about being smart? Do you think you're smart?"

"Not smart *enough*," Simon said quickly.

"Do you get good grades at school?"

"Almost the best in my class!"

"Do your parents think your grades are good?"

"Well, they say so, but I know they always want me to try harder."

"Do you remember if the teacher ever has to stop her class for you, so she can explain something to you that the rest of the class understands?"

"No way, never!"

Fine, Max thought. There goes the pathos. Looks like we'll have to move on to plan "C".

"So let me get this straight," Clarissa said good-naturedly, one finger on her lower lip, "You're doing better than most of kids at your school, you feel you're pretty smart, your parents feel you're even smarter, and you know you have no health or appearance fears. Why do you need an upgrade?"

"Your honor," Max interrupted, "I fear this question verges on a need for expertise again."

"Fear not, Mr. Wright, but I will remind the jury that Mr. Phillips is only expressing his opinion."

"Thank you your honor," Max said. He knew what the response would be, but also knew that, by interjecting, he bought a few precious seconds for Simon to formulate an answer and still make it appear spontaneous.

"Simon?" The judge said softly, "Please answer Ms Panther's question."

"Sure," Simon said. His soft eyes closed as he concentrated for a moment, then they snapped open and he said with a sigh, "Ms Panther, you don't understand. It doesn't matter how perfect I started out. I have to change something. Anything."

"Why?"

Simon bowed his head, sorting out his response. Max crossed his fingers. Clarissa had already shot down all the answers they had rehearsed. He hoped that repetition of the boy's dreams would go well with the jury. Simon lifted his head, swept his glassy gaze around the room, stopped at his parents, and blurted out, in a rush, directly at them:

"Because if I don't, none of the other kids will talk to me. Unless to call me cro-man, or nature-boy. I won't have any friends, ever, and they'll all treat me like a monster. I'll be alone." He paused, rubbed his button nose, then finished in a near whisper:

"I don't want to be alone."

Whoa, Max thought, where did that come from?

Clarissa paused, eyes down. Her delay was allowing Simon's response to ricochet around the jury, forming irreparable opinions, but she didn't want to pose a follow-up question. Memories of her own youth and college career crowded into her mind; what she had done to and how she had felt about the 'normals.' The kid's right, she thought. She shook her head as imperceptibly as possible, regrouped. He may be right, she corrected herself. Right in his heart, in reality, and socially, but not legally. She raised her head, then faced the Jury Box while she asked the next question.

"Simon," She said, "We all understand that you feel very deeply about this, and you might think other kids --"

"I don't think it," Simon interrupted, shouting at her back, "I live it. It's true!"

"Okay, Simon," Clarissa said, turning back to Simon with palms up, "I know you feel strongly about this. But are you aware that it is illegal to discriminate against anybody in this country, no matter who they are, or what their genetic makeup is?"

"I don't know," Simon said, fighting back a tear, "I guess."

"Your honor!" Max shouted from his seat, "Ms Panther is debating constitutional law with a nine year old. My client is distraught; we respectfully would like a recess."

"I would hardly call it a legal debate, Mr. Wright, but perhaps we should take a break."

"That's all right, your honor," Clarissa said, "Defense has no further questions." A perceptible sigh rose from the gallery.

"Fine," Judge Warfield said, "Redirect?"

"Just one question, your honor," Max said. He referred to his watch for the question he had whispered seconds earlier. A question that seemed irrelevant during preparation of the case, but begged now to be asked. He stood up, crossed to Simon without a glance at Clarissa, and leaned his hands on the polished wooden rail in front of the boy.

"Simon," He said softly, "In light of your true feelings about upgrades, tell us what you really believe will happen to you without them."

"But we never practiced --" Simon whispered. Max put a finger to his lips, nodded to Simon to continue. Simon grimaced, but he did go on:

"Well, I don't know much about it, but I do hear the bigger kids talking about the naturals, and how they're all losers, and easy to beat up, and should all be dropped on an island somewhere so they can be natural together. I don't want to get dropped on an Island."

"Do you believe," Max asked, slowly, "Do you believe that this will happen to you?"

"It's already started. My friends -- Billy, Julian, Michael, Brittany, everyone -- don't play with me anymore, now that they know. They don't even talk to me or say "Hi" or anything. I'm alone all the time. Miss Walkill, my teacher, she tries to help by telling me everything will be fine once I get the upgrades. I'm alone already, and I'm not even in high school yet." Simon's voice began to shake. Still staring directly at his parents, who he felt would never understand, he managed one more sentence before his emotions stifled words, "What will happen then?" He dropped his chin into his hands, stared at nothing at the back of the courtroom.

Silence ruled the room for a minute before Max remembered that he was supposed to say something. He stopped trying to list his own 'natural' friends -- he had none -- and cleared his throat. The sound was obscenely loud in the static atmosphere, but there was no chuckle, nervous or not, from the gallery this time.

"No further questions, your honor."

"Ms. Panther?"

"No questions, your honor."

The judge, peering over his glasses, tapped at his blottercom for a moment, then folded his hands in front of him. "You may step down, Mr. Phillips."

Simon didn't hear the instruction. Max came around to the entrance to the witness box, gently tapped Simon on the shoulder.

"Simon," he whispered, "You're done."

Simon wiped his eyes with untrained subtlety, then, glaring at Max, said, "I sure am, aren't I?"

"C'mon," was all Max could manage. He gently helped Simon to his feet, led him back to the table. They both sat, and Max let his arm stay around Simon's tiny shoulders. His training and carefully coded instincts were screaming "this is great!" but Max found no joy in the future Simon faced. He still could not name one natural from his generation with whom he was close, or consciously aware of.

It was then Judge Warfield's turn to clear his throat.

"Mr. Wright. Given the circumstances, I have allowed you to exceed the legal time limit for this witness. Unfortunately, I must keep us on schedule. You have five minutes to present your next, and I would assume final, witness testimony."

Five minutes, Max thought, holy shit. His mind sprang into action as quickly as he rose to his feet. The clock was ticking, but he ran the request he just thought of through his head once more before presenting it to the judge.

"Your honor, I do not yet know who my final witness will be."

"Oh?" Judge Warfield said, removing his glasses, "And when exactly will you?"

"Momentarily. Plaintiff requests that you allow me to draw one witness, one volunteer, one "natural", from the gallery for a few questions."

"Your honor, this is silly!" Clarissa exclaimed. And it must not happen either, she said to herself.

"Perhaps," Judge Warfield said, "Mr. Wright, please explain carefully why you would call a stranger, unrehearsed and unprepared, to the stand. "

"I feel that Simon has struck an unanticipated chord, and we must spend a moment discussing it. We assumed that our case's primary purpose was to enable Simon to better himself and secure his future. However, maybe there is something else, something deeper; a human attitude we thought we had left in the last century."

"Save your closing arguments for the end, Mr. Wright. Who would you like to call?"

"I don't know," Max said.

"Your honor! Please stop this farce!"

"Quiet, Ms Panther. I'm going to indulge Mr. Wright."

"Exception, your honor."

"Exception noted. Mr. Wright?"

"Thank you, your honor," Max said. He turned to face the gallery, raised his voice to a boom that bounced easily off distant walls, "I would like to request that a special witness step forward to be sworn in. This witness must be between 20 & 30 years old, and must not have had any upgrades performed at any time in his or her life, including prenatal. I know this is sudden, and may be difficult or embarrassing. Please be assured it is of the utmost importance, both to the future of Simon Phillips, and the future of the natural human race. Now, please. Is there anyone who will speak?"

A surprised restlessness vibrated the gallery, followed by silence. The litigants rotated their heads and shoulders, scanned the thousand startled faces. The fidgeting and mumbling subsided as everyone did their best to become invisible. Max allowed the expected silence to continue for a few seconds, then asked, "Nobody will speak? I see many faces in the room that are most certainly younger than twenty. You've all had upgrades?" A few nodded vigorously; most stayed as still as possible.

"Well," Clarissa said, trying to hide her deep relief behind a sardonic tone, "I guess that ends your strange experiment." Max raised his hand.

"Not quite, your honor. Given the small representation of the American people in the room, I had expected we might have difficulty finding a witness. I would like to consult one more pool of potential witnesses, if you would allow it."

"Oh? And what pool would that be?" Judge Warfield asked, fully aware, and completely apprehensive of, the pool Max would request.

"The Jury Box, your honor."

"No way!" Clarissa exclaimed, furious, "You can't allow that, Judge Warfield."

"Please stop instructing me in jurisprudence, Ms Panther. I understand that you are bred to the law and may indeed have a higher awareness of its many words than a pitiful 'natural' like myself, but this is still my courtroom."

"And this is still wrong! You're tampering with the Jury Box!"

"Ms Panther, please! Sit down and bear with the court's senility."

"But --"

"Now, Ms Panther," Judge Warfield snapped. Clarissa sat obediently, dejected. She could feel the blood swirling in her cheeks, and dared not glance at her clients, lest they see her fear. The judge continued, "Now Mr. Wright, please be advised that I too share much of Ms Panther's apprehension. How do you plan to find this witness?"

"Quite simply, your honor. I propose that we ask the National Human Resources Center to download a list of all citizens who fit my previous description. We then target a connection to those jurors only, and ask anyone who wishes to come forth to click 'not guilty'. Then we can quickly contact one of those respondees at random, and bring the entire jury back. That witness will, of course, not have a say in the verdict." Shit, Clarissa thought, he can do this.

"How long will this process take? Remember you only have five minutes allotted for this witness."

"Best guess, your honor? If we run it through your chamber's computer, about two minutes."

"Sounds fair. Any objections? Ms Panther?"

Clarissa shook her head. The recorder would note her dejected gesture as a no.

"Good," Judge Warfield said. He tapped his notebook, placed his palms on the desk before him, leaned forward, "Mr. Wright, you now have access to my security clearance, and two minutes to find a witness."

"Thank you, your honor," Max said. He was already whispering instructions into his watch. In about thirty seconds it acknowledged acquisition of a list of 1,627,341 Americans between ages 20 & 30 that never had upgrades. He downloaded that list into the Jury Box monitor program, and asked for two-way communications. He got it, with fifteen seconds to spare. He looked over at Clarissa -- who had regained her composure by becoming rigid -- winked, then nodded to the judge.

"Okay, your honor, we're ready. There are currently 25,569 potential witnesses. We now simply have to --"

"Your honor," Clarissa snapped, "I respectfully request that you choose the witness personally, to guarantee a random choice. Not that I don't trust Mr. Wright, of course."

"Of course. That is a most unusual request, Ms Panther, one that I would normally and quite summarily deny. However, given the generally bizarre nature of this activity and the precedents it will surely set, I will accede to your request."

"Thank you your honor."

"You are welcome. Mr. Wright, please allow me access into your window."

"Already done, your honor. Just click on 'natwit' in your own chamber files, and the routine query will present itself."

"Thank you." Judge Warfield had a witness on-line in another minute. After a moment of muted introduction and consultation with the witness, the judge addressed the litigants.

"I'm pleased and somewhat surprised to say that we have a witness. The witness has requested to remain anonymous, and the court will honor that request. Any objections?"

There were no objections. Clarissa was whispering furiously into her lapel, desperately trying to develop a line of questioning. She glanced over at her clients, who seemed strangely amused by the sideshow.

"I thought not," Judge Warfield said, "You may question the witness, Mr. Wright." The usual androgynous 3-D privacy image appeared in the witness stand, in place of an actual video feed.

"Thank you, your honor," Max said, "Greetings, witness, and thank you for your support. I hope you will have no problem with the questions I will ask."

"Me too," the witness's electronic voice chimed, its image smoothly generating a concerned expression.

"Good. First, please let the court know your basic feelings about upgrades."

"I missed out on them, but am doing what I can to get by without them."

"Are you in dire straits financially?"

"Dire straits? No. I do all right, thanks. Who doesn't these days?"

"Socially?"

"If I had a social life, I could answer that." The gallery laughed loudly at the response, and the witness image smiled, but Clarissa found no joy in the portent of the response. The witness continued, "Seriously, though, I've always felt alone, like an outcast."

"Can you provide any examples?"

"Ever try to join a health club? You know that line on the application that asks you to list the enhancements you've had? Well, leaving it blank guarantees you'll never get in."

"Are these exclusive health clubs?"

"Not when you ask them. Not just health clubs, either. That one line was the kiss of death at about a dozen of the colleges I applied to, in spite of my great grades. I attended a small, yet more traditional, Catholic University. It really sucked. Not the school, of course, but the treatment."

"Do you feel you've been discriminated against?"

"Well I don't know, really. When I push for explanations I'm always told, with clear examples, that someone else, someone more qualified, got in ahead of me. I can't do much about upgrades making people appear better. Even if they're not."

"Back to your social life, if you please --"

"Damn. I thought I changed that subject." The gallery forced a chuckle again, but too many minds were working, making connections that overshadowed amusement.

"No such luck," Max said, "Are you married?"

"No such luck, sir. I haven't found anyone yet. but I'm hopeful."

"Do you date?"

"I try."

"Do you date people with upgrades?"

"I wish. Nope, I'm afraid I don't get to run with that crowd."

"Mr. Wright," Judge Warfield interrupted, "You are down to your last thirty seconds."

"Thanks for the reminder, your honor," Max said, then turned back to the witness stand, "I have one last question. Do you feel that you are a second-class citizen because you have no upgrades?"

The image froze for a few seconds, eyes closed. Max fretted about the connection until the electronic eyes flashed open and the witness responded tentatively:

"Of course. Aren't I?"

"No further questions, your honor."

"Thank you, Mr. Wright. Cross, Ms Panther?"

"Yes, your honor," Clarissa said. Cross isn't the word for how I feel, she thought. She faced the witness box.

"Have you been following the proceedings today?"

"Matter of fact, yes. I don't usually get into court stuff, but this case kept drawing me back."

"Ms Panther," Judge Warfield said "I'm not sure where you're going with this, but might I remind you that the witness is completely within his or her rights to view the case at hand, and has been for over twenty years?"

"Sorry, your honor. It slipped out," Clarissa said. She faced the witness box, smiled. The image smiled back.

"Good afternoon," she said, her tone radically improved.

"Afternoon."

"How are you?"

"Fine."

"I see. If I may ask, what is your profession?"

"I'm studying to be a doctor."

"Well," Clarissa smiled, "That's quite a goal. But wait. Don't you need to be admitted into medical school for that? I would have thought that, given your professed class problems --"

"I'm sorry, I wasn't totally clear. I'm going to be a doctor of Philosophy, not an MD."

"Oh. No further questions," Clarissa said, backing away quickly.

"I did try to be an MD," the witness volunteered, "But after applying to over thirty schools without so much as a response from them, I gave up. Philosophy was really--"

"Your honor. I said no further questions," Clarissa interrupted the damning flood.

"So you did. I ask the jury to disregard the witness's last sentence," Judge Warfield sighed, "Mr. Wright. Defense council has left you two minutes to redirect."

"Thank you, your honor, I'll need much less. I have just one additional question for the witness," Max said, facing the witness box, "If you could do it all over again, do you wish that you had been upgraded, both prenatally and in your youth?"

"Are you kidding? Of course I would. You don't know how much this condition sucks unless you have it."

"Thank you. No further questions."

"That ends our need of this witness," the judge said. He turned to the witness, said, "Special thanks to you, witness, for coming forth so readily to assist in this case."

"Hey, no problem," the witness chirped before its image disappeared. Max continued to stare at the blank screen, not sure yet what strange gift to society he had unwrapped. The judge broke his reverie:

"Any more witnesses, Mr. Wright?" he asked loudly, his voice shattering the tense silence, "Any more theatrics?"

"No your honor, on both counts," Max said somber, "Plaintiff rests." He returned to his seat, next to a beaming Simon. They slapped each other's palms under the table.

"Very well. Let's keep this moving. Ms Panther, you may present your defense now.

"Thank you, your honor," Clarissa said, bowing her head and turning on her sincerity afterburners, "But, in light of the unusual testimony just given, I would like a recess to discuss options with my clients." She held her breath; time was without question the most difficult request to make of a judge.

"Fine," Judge Warfield said immediately, "Court's adjourned for ten minutes." He slammed his gavel once, checked that the Jury Box was shut off, and rushed to his chambers. Guess he had to pee, Clarissa thought as she turned to face Simon's parents. They did not look happy. Shit, she thought.

"Okay, I didn't expect him to give us that much time, so let's make the best of it. First, I have to ask you both: did Simon or the computer witness change your mind about anything?"

"No, not at all," Marjorie said, "Except that I guess I never listened, or cared for, how deeply Simon feels about this. I didn't think he'd take it this far."

"Good. I'm not sure we should present a defense."

"Why not?" Brandon hissed, "We're right about this. Especially now. The world needs to know that naturals won't be shit on."

"Jeez Brandon," Clarissa said, "Ease up. If you've noticed, everything we do just buries us deeper. Max's case has jumped the boundaries, on many levels. We can't fight him today, but I think his actions, and the judge's, will leave room for an appeal."

"Appeal!" Brandon whispered too loudly, slamming his fist on the table, "What the hell are you talking about?"

"What she's talking about, Brandon dear," Marjorie said softly touching her husband's tense upper arm, "Is that she feels our son is right. That we naturals are inferior and have no case. In a court of law, or in life."

"Now wait just a minute," Clarissa hissed, her sudden anger nearly gagging her, "That is not fair. I've done everything I can for you. I hadn't anticipating Max turning this into a social issue, though. Frankly neither did he."

"That's because neither of you perfect people realized there is an issue at all," Brandon snarled. Clarissa, head bowed, didn't respond.

Brandon lowered his head, mumbled through his clenched, square jaw, "Please don't give up on us Clarissa." He looked up, regarded her with wet eyes. Clarissa took his hands.

"Brandon," she said gently, earnestly, to the frightened father, "You know I would never do that." Brandon only nodded.

"So what do we do now?" Marjorie asked, her cool tone injecting reassurance into the moment. Clarissa took the cue, gathered her thoughts in an instant, went back to work.

"Our experts are useless now," she said, "Because the subject's been changed. I can't play Max's jury roulette game because the chances are too good that we'll have a reverse Dr. Milky on our hands. The best we can do is call Marjorie to the stand and use the emotional line of questioning we worked on, and hope that someone is listening."

"Yeah right," Brandon said, still smoldering, "What about me? Shouldn't I be testifying?"

"I don't think so, Brandon."

"Why the hell not?" He demanded, rage and red returning. He set his face a few inches from Clarissa's.

"Because," Marjorie said sticking her arms between the two to separate them, "You're exactly what Simon doesn't want to be."

"Huh?" Brandon asked.

"You're angry. You're hurt at being second rate no matter how much you achieve, and you'd only solidify Max's 'second class citizen' scenario."

Brandon opened his mouth to rebut, then shut it. He lowered his head into his hands.

"I'm sorry, Brandon," Clarissa said, "But I couldn't agree more. Now. Hate me or not, you're paying me good money to defend you, and I'm giving you the best choice I can offer in this situation. We've only got two minutes to decide. What do you want to do?"

"You really think our prepared stuff is worthless?" Marjorie asked.

"Absolutely."

"Even my testimony?"

"Your testimony is safe enough, because it irrefutably states your love for Simon, and that you would never do anything to hurt him, but I'm concerned about cross. Max is riding a wave, and he might twist anything you say into this whole class repression thing."

"I'd like to take that chance."

"Hey, it's your money."

"Yes it is. Brandon?"

"Yeah?" Brandon looked up at his wife. His eyes were red, wet.

"You're not testifying. Okay?" Marjorie said, firm.

"Yeah, I know. And I'll sit here and shut up until it's over. But I won't like it."

"Great," Clarissa said, "The judge will be out in a minute. Stay calm, cross your fingers, smile at your son a lot, and hope for the best."

Judge Warfield reentered the courtroom with no fanfare. He sat and signaled that the Jury Box be switched back on. When it was, he looked at Clarissa, said, "Ms Panther?"

"Defense wishes to call one witness your honor," Clarissa said.

Hot damn, Max thought. He nudged Simon, flashed him the `OK' sign with his left hand. Simon absently returned the signal. He had been unusually quiet since his testimony. Max had not been able to coax a word from him during the break. Oh well, he thought. This is rough stuff; he'll be happy later.

"Very well," Judge Warfield said, gruffly, "Begin."

"Defense calls Marjorie Corman to the stand."

Marjorie stood, adjusted her loose print dress, and crossed to the witness stand. She stood, poised and calm, by the mahogany rail as she was sworn in.

"Raise your right hand," the stand said. She did, a little startled that there was no human clerk to swear her in.

"Do you swear to tell the truth, the whole truth, and nothing but the truth?"

"I do," she said, then added loudly, "So help me God."

Marjorie sat gracefully, folded her hands on her lap and waited for Clarissa's questions with a tight smile. Clarissa admired her vintage beauty: Marjorie's classic midwestern lines -- long sandy hair, faded, almost gray eyes, and short stature -- were a rarity these days. She smiled at Simon's mother, double-checked the notes floating in her retinas, and said:

"Hi Marjorie. We'll be sure to make this as painless as possible. First, are you affiliated with any religion?"

"Yes. My family is Christian - Baptists, actually."

"Practicing Baptists?"

"Yes."

"Is there any rule in your church's organization, or commandment maybe, that forbids genetic upgrades?"

"No," Marjorie said, frowning, "We're not Catholics, you know."

Clarissa lowered her head, waited for the scattered burst of laughter behind her to subside before continuing, "So basically you have no religious reason to deny your son, Simon, upgrades?"

"Not a one."

"And no medical reason? Your doctor never indicated a history in Simon's DNA that would preclude upgrades?"

"No, he never even brought up the subject," Marjorie said.

"And you can afford the procedures?"

"Afford? They practically give upgrades away these days, what with all the subsidies."

"So," Clarissa said, facing the Jury Box, "What you're really telling me is that there was no outside source or institution, no issue of faith, or cost barriers that led you to forego upgrades?"

"None at all."

"How did you make the decision?"

"We didn't. Well, I guess we did, in that we chose not to decide. We knew Simon (and we didn't even know his sex before he was born) would turn out just fine, like we did. We knew he would grow up to be as handsome, strong, smart, and successful as God meant him to be."

"Do you still think you made the right decision?"

"Absolutely," Marjorie said, her pride animating her speech, "You can see that Simon is a wonderful, flawless boy, with a bright future. We know that whatever happens to him, wherever his life leads him, will come from him, and from us. He can live knowing everything he is was always in him; he has no aftermarket boosters to mar his perfection." Marjorie was positively glowing. Perfect, Clarissa thought, now to shift the mood a bit.

"How do you feel about this lawsuit?"

"I'm very hurt, occasionally furious, but in the end I guess I'm a little confused about why it happened at all." Judge Warfield waited for Max's objection, but it never came. Max sat, elbows on the table before him, looking almost wistful. Clarissa noticed his attitude as well, and decided that it was time to ask the question this trial was leading to:

"Do you feel that you and your husband withheld upgrades to make a political statement?" she asked quickly, hoping for an instant response from Marjorie.

"Not in any way, shape or form," Marjorie snapped back, raising her voice over Max, who had risen to his feet a second too late to stop her answer.

"Objection!" Max shouted as he stood, "Politics was never a part of the plaintiff's case!" He knew he was too late.

"Oh?" Clarissa said to Max before the judge, who was banging his gavel to quiet the din of shocked discussion emanating from the gallery, could speak, "Isn't that exactly what you have turned to?"

"That's enough, Ms Panther," Judge Warfield snarled, slamming his gavel one more time, "Please allow me to do my job!" He paused for a moment, waiting for the last of the whispers to die out and his breath to return. When they did, he continued, "Mr. Wright may have a valid objection. Bailiff, please disconnect the jury." He waited for the switch to be flipped, then leaned forward, stretching across his desk toward Clarissa. Here we go, he thought.

"I don't believe politics were mentioned at any time during his presentation."

"That's correct. The word was not mentioned, your honor," Clarissa said, pointing to Simon, "But the plaintiff's testimony was bathed in its definition. We are merely clarifying."

"I don't think so, your honor," Max said angrily.

"Then it's a good thing thinking is what they pay me for, huh? Ms Panther, please explain yourself before I decide on Mr. Wright's objection."

"Your honor, please look back to Simon's testimony. It is fraught with statements that could be best termed racist. I know we haven't heard that word in decades, but a child's fears of oppression and his blind distaste for what he is because he is not like everyone else betrays a racist attitude on his part."

"I think you have slightly twisted that definition, Ms Panther, but let's assume racism. Where are the politics?"

"Politics are the tool for society's correction of racism. Any reaction to it must be termed political."

"Okay. Let's say I give you that -- Why have you brought it up if Ms Corman does not believe she was making a political statement?"

"The question was begged. We needed to respond."

"Mr. Wright? Your objection?"

"Withdrawn, your honor, as long as I can consider this a line of questioning to be pursued in my cross."

"Of course. Continue, Ms Panther."

"Thank you, your honor," Clarissa said softly, grabbing the witness stand rail and squeezing it hard to suppress her joy, "Ms Corman. I'd like to clarify once more. If you weren't making a statement, your church allows it, there was no medical reason, and you can afford them, then why did you withhold upgrades from your son?"

Marjorie's voice was shaking, her eyes glassy, and her hands wrestled each other, but she got her statement out with the kind of conviction about which Clarissa could only dream.

"Because we believe that God, fate, and perhaps luck are far more powerful shapers than any scientist can be, and we would rather rely on them than a hypodermic filled with mail-order genes."

Her answer was met by silence as her words drifted into a courtroom filled with softening, mostly upgraded, minds. Clarissa stepped back, satisfied, and decided not to open any more doors.

"No further questions, your honor, but I would like to reserve the --" she referred briefly to her lapelcom, "Three remaining minutes of Ms Corman's testimony for possible redirect."

"Granted. Mr. Wright?" Judge Warfield said, looking over his glasses at Max. Max patted Simon's hand and stood.

Simon acknowledge the tap blandly. He appeared lost in his mother's words. Or just bored.

"Ms Corman," Max said, "Thank you for your answers; I know this must be very hard for you." He paused for a moment, feigning to surf through his notes for some lost reference. He wanted to be sure that Marjorie had had enough time to calm down before he asked his first question. Max didn't want any unnecessary and damaging emotion from the boy's mother. He continued:

"Ms Corman. You mentioned that you felt no religious pressure to deny upgrades to your son. Yet throughout your testimony God was referenced. Can you explain this?"

"I don't think that mentioning God, Who I believe in, in the same sentence with fate and luck is a sign of religious pressure," Marjorie said, checking the status of her fingernails as she spoke. Oh my, Max thought, better get out of this one quick.

"You referenced God more than once, Ms Corman. In any event, would you agree that God, fate, and luck could also refer to nature?"

Marjorie's eyebrows rose slightly. She thought for a moment, still inspecting her nails, then looked up. "I suppose you could define nature that way. Sure."

"And you understand that, in its vast complexity, there is a high level of randomness in nature?"

"I think you just contradicted yourself, Mr. Wright," Marjorie said, smiling, "Should I agree that nature is complex, or random?"

"You tell me," Max said sternly, stifling loose chuckles from the gallery.

"I'll tell you what I believe to be true. I believe that nature may appear random, even chaotic, or destructive. But I think there is an order to it; a pattern that has been in design for four billion years. That pattern defines all life, for better or worse. Who is man, with his 200 years of practice, to say he can produce a better product than nature?"

Max scrambled for a response before Marjorie's profundity sunk into the jury, but he couldn't find the right words fast enough. Too late to stop the effect, he countered anyway:

"You asked me a question, and I'll answer it, Marjorie. Man is the result of nature's epochal development. Through man's intercession, nature can achieve perfection at a far faster pace.

"No further questions," Max finished, dramatically. Damn, he thought, now I have to come up with a different zinger for closing.

Judge Warfield sat, pensive, for a moment, then gestured to Clarissa, "Redirect, Ms Panther?"

"N-no. No thank you, your honor," Clarissa said, moved, "I believe my client has done a fine job on her own."

"Fine. Any more witnesses?"

"No, your honor."

"No experts?"

"I think we just had one, your honor."

"Objection," Max mumbled automatically.

"Sustained," Warfield said, "The jury will disregard Ms Panther's obviously personal opinion of her witness's status. So, I may assume the defense rests?"

"It does, your honor. We do, however, request the three minutes held for redirect of Ms Corman be added to our closing arguments."

"Denied. You had your chance for that time."

"Exception, your honor."

"Noted. Are you done?"

"Yes," Clarissa said, not particularly upset at losing the three minutes. She knew the judge would deny the request, but figured it was worth a shot.

"Good," Warfield said, looking at his watch, "And what do you know? We're ahead of schedule. That gives us time for a ten minute break before closing statements." He stood and retired to his chambers before the gallery had a chance to rise. The bailiff rushed to toggle the jury out. Max glanced at Simon, who was still silent, carefully studying the grain of the table that supported his thin white elbows. He leaned over, gently pulled a tiny hand from the boy's ear.

"The judge must have to pee real bad," he whispered. Simon broke from his dismal reverie to produce one toothy grin for Max, then returned to his thoughts. Max patted him on the shoulder, said, "Don't worry, kid. Everything will work itself out." He then set about reviewing his closing statement. He had already dumped his original arguments, which had been rendered obsolete by the sharp turn of events on the stand. He was not sure what he could come up with in the nine minutes he had to work, but he did not panic. This kind of rush work was common, and he was sure he would wrap things up nicely, even if he had to improvise his entire speech.

Clarissa was more confident. She was able to leave her closing argument intact. She always felt a higher level of confidence when closing arguments that she wrote days before the court date still had something to do with the case. After confirming that she had committed her statement to memory, she leaned over to Marjorie. Her pale client was visibly shaking. Clarissa gently laid a hand on her wrist. Brandon had her other hand firmly clasped in his. His eyes were closed. Clarissa wondered if they were praying.

"Don't worry," Clarissa whispered to the tense couple, "I think things went really well. Hopefully I can convince some more of the jury with our closing statement, but this might turn out okay." Marjorie turned to face Clarissa, her visage a vague facsimile of confidence.

"Turn out okay," Marjorie repeated, struggling to keep her voice low, "Your only son's not being permanently damaged by this twisted society, is he? Nothing will ever be okay. Especially if we win." Clarissa didn't withdraw her hand, but did choose not to offer any platitudes, or respond to her client's rejection of the case. Instead, she attempted in vain to shelve her personal thoughts. This cause stuff is out of my league, she thought. Better to just shut up and do my job than try to understand this family's love and conviction. She cast a furtive glance at Max, who was whispering rapidly to his watch. She smiled, knowing that he wouldn't even refer to the notes he was spouting; he never did. He appeared oblivious to the door this case was opening, even to Marjorie's outburst. She tried to sneak a peak at Simon, but he was effectively concealed behind Max's thick profile. She closed her notebook, folded her hands on it, and waited for the judge to return. Beneath her usual air of affected confidence, Clarissa was a quivering twig, ready to snap.

The two groups were ready three minutes early. They waited with no further exchange for Judge Warfield's return. Their silence was contagious, spreading through the gallery like an ominous cloud.

When Judge Warfield returned to the courtroom he paused at the doorway and did a classic double-take. He thought for a second that he had walked into the wrong courtroom. Everyone had risen at the bailiff's instruction, but they were impossibly silent. Their palpable anticipation shook him slightly. Well, he thought, they're all waiting for me to offer them reason to hate again. He sat at his bench, reached automatically for his gavel, then realized it wasn't, for the first time in his memory, necessary. Max Wright remained standing after everyone else sat slowly. He was smiling. Odd, the judge thought. He put on his glasses, nodded to Max.

"Okay, Mr. Wright," he said, "You know the rules. You have two minutes to present closing arguments."

"Thank you, your honor," Max said as he crossed to face the Jury Box, "And special thanks to those jury members who have been with us all day." Max hated wasting seven seconds on gratuities, but the votes from full-day jurors were the only ones that counted, so he made a practice of singling them out. He continued:

"First I will tell you what was not brought forth in this trial: greed. The plaintiff seeks no monetary sum from his parents. Animosity. Simon makes his requests on the friendliest of levels. And, as you have seen by the testimony today, we do not, under any circumstances, have a trivial case pursuing casual, even cosmetic ends. No. None of that is evident today.

"What is evident," He said, initially invoking a clandestine tone that would crescendo into a noisy bluster, impressing the jurors on levels they were not aware of, regardless of content, "Is that Simon has rustled the embers of a powerful societal torch thought long since extinguished. This 'discrimination' is appearing because a stubborn few refuse to accept the changes the modern world offers, and risk being ostracized by once potential peers. If you ignore his cause, you imperil millions to his fate. You must not let the spark die!"

When he finished, he shifted his weight forward slightly. The Jury Box rail groaned under his weight. Max was surprised that he sought its support, but had the sense to capitalize on the effect. He paused for several precious seconds before he continued with a sincerity he did not, for a change, need to invent.

"What we have witnessed together today was a revelation," he said, resuming a conversational tone, "A primordial public display of a social phenomenon that has been etched into the public psyche by the powers of science. Now that this non-parity has been discovered, and described, we are able to prove that, without enhancements, Simon Phillips will fall prey to discrimination and rejection for the rest of his life. He will not be able to compete in a world beset with unnaturally high standards. He will likely suffer lifelong depression, and a hopeless yearning for things left out of his grasp. This because of parents that cling to their past, and refuse to accept the norms of the present."

"We request, in the name of decency, that you the jury find in favor of young Mr. Phillips, and allow him the enhancements he desires. The life he deserves."

"Thank you." He leaned on the rail again, looking down, emotionally drained. He turned to face Simon. The boy was staring at him, silent, either lost in his own thoughts or deeply confused. Fine, Max thought, I couldn't even keep the kid interested. And he's smarter than most of the jurors. Then he looked up and noticed that the entire gallery shared the boy's pensive blankness. Furtive glances as he approached his seat revealed that only Clarissa and the judge were shaking their heads cynically. Well, they know me, he thought, I guess I can't blame them. As he slumped into his chair it squealed violently (though no more loudly than any other time that day). Judge Warfield cleared his throat.

"Thank you, Mr. Wright. Ms Panther?"

Shit shit shit, Clarissa thought, trying to shake off the lingering energy of Max's summation. She felt a hand on her wrist as she prepared to stand, looked over at Marjorie. Her moist gray eyes seemed to say 'whatever.'

"Well, here we go," Clarissa said softly as she lifted Marjorie's warm hand, gave it a squeeze. She stood, drew her breath, gathered her thoughts and her courage, and crossed to the Jury Box.

"Thank you, your honor," she said, focusing sharply on empty space about three feet in front of her eyes, "Mr. Wright is correct. We may indeed be witness to a revelation, a harbinger of a biological sea change that could affect millions in the future by fueling fears thought left to the past."

"This revelation, this premiere of a new discrimination, is very, very dangerous. You, good jurors, are our front line. You are our strength to fend off, maybe even prevent, a hazardous era in human history. You can become a milestone in our history, our way of life. Simply vote in favor of the pure, human beliefs that Brandon and Marjorie struggle, possibly at the cost of their own son's allegiance, to uphold."

"If their belief (and that of some stockinged gentlemen some 300 years ago) that all men are created equal survives the day, perhaps it will spread among the new human race we are fabricating. Spread as a reminder that, though we might be fixing a few leaks and adding some springs and gears, the human spirit has not been effected. It alone carries all our days, regardless of synthetic upgrades." It was her turn to pause, head bowed. She carefully avoided leaning on the rail, though. That would be too much. After a few seconds her eyes shot up again, wet but wide with sincerity. She continued, softly:

"Please don't foster divisions today. Vote down Simon's heartfelt plea. Don't let your empathy for his pain, his fears, betray a victory for the collective human soul." Clarissa held her eyes to the Jury Box screen for about five seconds, giving all viewers a clear image of her watery eyes, then closed them and finished:

"Please," she said, then turned away. She whispered "Thank you, your honor," to Judge Warfield as she passed the bench on her way back to her seat. She was met by the same silence that Max witnessed, but was not confused. She had anticipated the silence. Now she wondered whether it was out of respect, awe, or repetition. She assumed the latter, but hoped that she had an impact anyway. Marjorie and Brandon nodded as she sat, but Clarissa knew she was alone.

"Thank you, Ms Panther," The judge's voice boomed through the silence, "Five seconds to spare." He turned to address the Jury Box:

"I too wish to thank the jury for its support today, and advise you of the following rules. I'm sure you heard this before, but please bear with me; they must be stated." He lifted an archaic index card closer to his eyes and read its fading contents to the jury.

"Qualification for valid votes are as follows: first, you must have witnessed at least 90% of today's proceedings; second, you must register your vote within ten minutes of the conclusion of these instructions; third, you may vote only once; and fourth, you must vote your opinion as a result of the testimony presented today, with no outside help. The first three rules will be checked by the Jury Box system, the fourth relies upon your own integrity and support of the American judicial system."

After a brief, significant pause, Judge Warfield tossed the card onto his desk and said, "These instructions are concluded. You have ten minutes from.... now. Please vote wisely." He pressed a few keys on his desk, then stood. He looked down at the litigants, said, "That's it. We'll know in ten minutes. Court is adjourned until then."

Judge Warfield again stepped into his chambers before anyone could stand to register his exit. Everyone remained silent until his door closed, then burst into a cacophony of animated conversation, phone dialing, and exited whispers into coms. Max glanced down at his client. Simon was staring over at his parents, who returned his gaze with a warmth that, even at this point, surprised him. He stood, tousled Simon's soft hair, leaned over so his face was inches from the boy's.

"Only a few minutes left, Simon," He said, "Then we're all done."

"Yeah," Simon said, his eyes straying from Max, toward his parents, "Just a few minutes."

"Win or lose, Simon, you did real good."

"Thanks Max, but I don't know anymore. What I do know is that my mom did great." With no warning, Simon left Max to join his parents, who stood behind their seats as if to rise above the rabble. Simon was tentative, but they accepted him warmly, sharing a tearful hug with the boy.

The family then collapsed into a private conversation that the media was too busy to notice. Clarissa did.

"They always miss the real story, don't they?" she asked Max, surprising him. It wasn't like her to speak to him until after the verdict, and only then in response to his shallow gestures.

"S'true," he said, "What do you suppose they'll report?"

"It depends on the verdict, but I'll bet they'll miss the point."

"Which is?"

"We, upgraded as we are, may never know."

"Clarissa, in about six months I'll wake up at three in the morning and say 'you know, she was right.' For now though, I believe I do understand. Look at them. Those are the only brackets we need to surround this case."

"I hear you," Clarissa said, sighing at the family, still clutching all they really had. She looked around the courtroom. The din had not died down as the world learned that the decision was coming. She noticed a few circles of bettors gathered at the back of the room, closely following the Hackers' real-time tracking of the voting, and the resulting odds changes that appeared on insets of the same screens. My God, she thought, last week nobody even knew about this trial. How had it been 'juiced' to such a level? She shook her head and rolled her eyes.

"Can you believe it?" Max said "Too bad we can't write books anymore, huh?"

"Max, please," Clarissa whined.

"I know, I know," he said, then he touched her elbow, moved in close to her ear, "Hey, notice how none of them are talking to the family? How unusual is that?"

"Huh?" Clarissa said, turning back to her clients, then scanning the room. He was right; though the crowded room was alive with activity and the press had every chance to invade, still not a soul disturbed the family. They did not even notice that the plaintiff was hugging the defendants before the decision.

"Wow," she said, "I guess they're just not important anymore."

"The show has eclipsed the players. What has this little boy started?"

"Started? He didn't start anything, Max. Simon's just a bump in the road science paved a long time ago." Max stared blankly at her for a moment, then said:

"Damn. I wish we could still write books."

"Oh, Max," Clarissa said, lowering her head onto his shoulder, "What am I going to do with you?"

"I'll hold my response until after the decision, thank you," Max said, smiling. She punched his upper arm. The friendly gesture seemed to pack a little more force than usual.

The judge's door opened.

The room was silent before the doorway was wide enough to frame him. He bowed his head and scurried to the bench. The gallery sat immediately, with no instruction. Judge Warfield rested his glasses low on his nose, looked over them at the litigants.

"We," he said quietly, "Have a decision."

Max leaned forward, reached over to clutch Simon's hand, but found Clarissa's supple wrist instead. Not speaking, he squeezed it. When she turned to him, he furrowed his brow. Clarissa leaned very close.

"I guess we're not important anymore either," she whispered, almost imperceptibly. The judge noticed as well.

"Excuse me," he said, "Are we all in our proper seats?"

"Yes we are, your honor!" Simon called from between his parents. Clarissa could barely see him. Judge Warfield smiled hugely, and nodded.

"Well then, I suppose we are. Let's get to the decision then."

He opened his notebook, pressed some keys, then hrummphed. He adjusted his glasses, reread the short note before him, and looked up.

"Will the litigants please stand? For the record, the plaintiff has changed his position to that of the defendant's counsel, and said counsel is now beside counsel for plaintiff. I do not want to confuse the recorders."

C'mon c'mon c'mon, Max thought, get on with it. Weakly muted tsks and groans behind him reflected his impatience. He glanced at Clarissa, who appeared anxious as well; her lower lip was slightly pursed. Her pale eyes were also flashing on him, but both sets snapped back on the judge when they met.

Judge Warfield continued, "A record number of qualified jurors have cast their votes. They find, as does this court, in favor of the plaintiff." The room erupted. The judge waited. Marjorie showed no emotion, Brandon's shoulders slumped slightly, and Simon was visibly absent. He was unaware of his victory, lost in his thoughts, careless of the door he had opened. Max pushed Clarissa aside gently, then gathered Simon into his arms, picking him up off the floor.

"We did it!" Max shouted.

Simon reacted vaguely, as if something like a strong wind was shaking his body; something that would soon pass. Max set him back down, choosing to retain his victory speech until Simon was more coherent. Must be shock, he thought. Max then turned to Clarissa, hand extended.

Clarissa took it, amused. She had been watching Simon's response to his victory, her loss, with growing interest. She tightened her grip and pulled Max close, until her lips gently brushed his ear.

"Congratulations, Max," she whispered, "I think."

He loosened his grip, and, though his knees quivered from the brush of her lips, he responded tersely, offended, "What the hell's that supposed to mean?"

"Chill, Max" she said, smiling into his eyes, "You did great. Hell, you'll make the history books. Maybe you'll even change a few things. But I wonder if history will record any changes to your misty-eyed client."

"Huh? What are you talking about?" Max asked.

"That had better be rhetoric, counselor," she said, "Or I won't respect you at dinner tonight."

"I don't know what you're talking about," Max lied, "But hey, I'm willing to reconsider."

Clarissa let go of his hand, mouthed "later," and turned to her erstwhile clients.

"Well," she said, "I think we lost."

"Did we?" Marjorie said, her tone more condescending than angry, "I think the jury might still be out on that one."

"We can talk about appeal options next week," Clarissa heard herself say, "We have several--"

"Save it," Brandon said, squeezing Clarissa's upper arm, "Decision's been made. This chapter is closed."

"Yes," Marjorie affirmed, threading an arm around her husband's waste, resting her other hand on Simon's shoulder, "This one is. Can we go now, Clarissa?"

"No. Judge Warfield hasn't wrapped things up yet."

"Okay," Marjorie said. She tilted her head to the judge, stared at her son, and waited. Simon reached up and touched her fingers, still apparently unaware of the din around him.

The litigants waited for the waves of discussion, reporting, and congratulations to fade.

"Well," judge Warfield said after the rabble had settled a bit, "That should change a few things. Mr. Phillips, you have won the right to any upgrades or enhancements you so desire, and you have quite possibly concluded an epoch of human development. Congratulations, and choose wisely."

"Thank you, your honor," Simon shouted, "I'll try." He turned to face his parents, prepared to apologize to them for the pain he caused, the pain he knew he was many years from understanding. Then he turned back, winked at the judge.

"Then again," he said, his innocent grin back, alive, and well, "Maybe I won't choose anything."

Anniversary Day

Ed's alarm clock sounded its fifth round of angry buzzing for several seconds before his hand found that huge happy snooze button and silenced the electric harpy once more. Six was it, he knew, and then the patient machine would surrender to his sloth. With only guilt and entrenched routine available to flex his muscles, Ed slid slowly from his toasty sheets.

Ed was 47, balding, married, lonely, and tired, tired, tired. After confirming that his eyes were open in the predawn blackness, his first thought was that that cold morning marked a milestone: the 20th anniversary of the day he accepted his job, his security, his life in a cubicle. The job was okay, his coworkers tolerable, and the salary had bought much of his house. But its execution was hell, mired as it was in his commute, purgatorial down time, and his daily remembrance of long-buried ideals and forsaken goals. He didn't want to face all that; not today; not on his anniversary. But he had an important meeting at nine and he couldn't risk blowing off another day – he had taken a mental health day just one week ago.

So he donned his tattered robe and felt his way barefoot across the freezing floor to the bathroom. While his eyes adjusted to the cold fluorescent light he stood in front of the mirror and stared, hoping to awaken from a very tedious dream. When he did not, he sighed. While shaving he thought about the things he would not be doing at home that day.

The time allotted to mixing his liquid breakfast, finding some clothes, dressing, and kissing his sleeping wife goodbye passed instantly. Suddenly, to Ed, his fingers held the cold front doorknob waiting for his pale wrist to gather the strength to twist. My God, Ed thought, I need a nap, not a meeting; I need to waste my own time, especially today, and not have it wasted for me. It's just going to hurt too much today to shut my damn brain off for twelve hours. But his work ethic won, and Ed turned the knob.

The door stuck for a second, then swung inward toward him, open. Ed pushed against the rickety screen door next, but it was jammed. While he lamented his lack of time to fix even a simple door, Ed noticed that it wasn't broken: it was held fast by no less than two feet of snow that had gathered on his porch overnight. And the beautiful white stuff was still blanketing his dark silent neighborhood in its impassable cold gauze.

Ed sighed as he hadn't sighed in years. He stared for a moment, smiled, and then shut the door. Later he would waste some serious quality time, on his own, with his wife. But first, he would go back to bed.

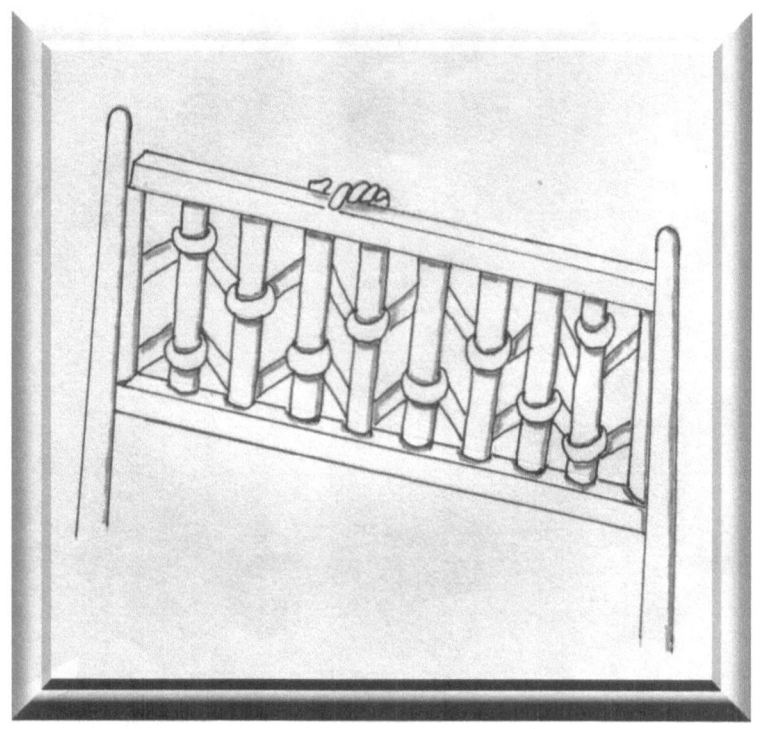

Sid's Cause

The Breath Taker's ironically sterile funnel glistened in the moonlight as it orbited Julia's gloved fingers. Its movement lent a pleasant moan to the cool, still air. She admired the arcs that flashed above her wrist. Simple beauty emanating from the Breath Taker, she thought. More irony. She was aware that the little spectacle that she had created was not prescribed in the manual under "doing the job right." Even this quiet distraction had potential to wake the baby; anything could. Remember why you're here, she nudged her worn psyche, you've wasted enough time already. Cursing herself for being so easily distracted, Julia stilled her fidgeting fingers.

Though fully cognizant of the damage she may have done, Julia waited patiently while the funnel wobbled to a stop below her thin wrist. After interminable seconds, its velocity had eased enough to permit a careful pinch of the thin surgical tube that tethered the funnel to the Breath Taker. Once it was in her grasp, she drew her hand back into secure shadows. She then froze, daring not even to breathe. She refrained from any movement or sound until she was sure that the infant nestled in the nearby crib was still asleep. The event of her casual indiscretion had consumed maybe twenty seconds, but it could still have been enough.

Can't wake the baby, she thought.

A sudden eruption by the slumbering mound of carefully swaddled human flesh would be sure to summon concerned parents and force Julia to abort her assignment. One failure and she would be out of the Service for good. Nope, she thought, can't wake the baby. Ever. She hid behind soft, freshly cleaned drapes -- who uses fabric softener on curtains? she mused -- and began the habitual, careful, review of her training. Scanning her mind for the rules powerfully installed there helped renew her resolve, to steady her unusually frayed nerves. And you'd better resolve quick, girl, she thought. The import of the moment, or lack of an available one, physically held her. More irony, she thought. After another long risky pause she was willing to move. The muted click of the working Breath Taker in her palm stopped stabbing her chest in time with her own heartbeat. She overcame preoccupation with the smell of her own sweat at about the same time that her hands lost interest in passing the time she wasted independent of her wishes – as suddenly as deeply buried misgivings had nearly ended her, Julie was back at work. She smiled. Her reverie, her slip, was a memory. Her control had returned. Exhausted nerves bundled again into compliant little clusters. She was strong, almost immune to the instinctive, frantic waving of tiny helpless hands and feet that would begin with the initiation of her assignment.

Almost.

My my, she thought, it looks like I could use a touch more resolve. She paused to wonder at the outdoor-fresh curtains behind which she hid. Her regard was, she knew, more one of delay than admiration. In time she shook her head and scowled at nothing. I must do this, she reminded herself, just like I did the last 300. It is for a cause. A good cause. The Service had convinced her of that. The training was thorough. She had emerged from her half-decade of conditioning at the top of her class. She understood the Service's mission. She had faith in the delphic calculations of its machines.

"It's true, Julia," Sid Simpson, her last and most personal personal instructor had insisted when they concluded her laudatory tour of the Service's planning center, "What the machines tell us makes it right; makes it necessary."

Necessary. Huh. She had borne that cynical mantra throughout her training. For years it rang true, but the assignments had become too regular. The Service had strung her deadly jaunts too close together for her to maintain the stoicism impressed upon her by intense rationale training. Julia roughly smacked her forehead, a flog not easily delivered in complete silence. What fleeting resolve she had just reined in was fading and she needed to act quickly. Though she ruefully sighed and began her task by the book, Julia's hand quivered when she examined the Breath Taker's LED preliminary readouts.

The small green numbers danced to the cadence of her shaking hand, their information blurred and unavailable. She lifted her head, closed her eyes, and reached deep inside herself to recover and repeat Sid's chant. Her struggle to remember it squandered yet another precious minute behind the curtain. The visceral fear of wasted time, of discovery, strengthened her. She summoned the will that the Service believed was permanently embedded in her. In time the readouts steadied. She forced a company smile. Necessary, she thought. Now where was I? The nasty little machine was ready. All its settings were correct -- deadly accurate. A clever instrument it was, too: painless, quick, silent, and subtle.

She took two long, irreversible paces into the room, stopped on the balls of her slippered feet. Like the commando she was, she reconnoitered the cozy battleground. The lightly ruffling satin she left behind encouraged sweet baby odors to waft around her: fresh linen, talc, and cleansing chemicals. The walls were festooned with plump elephants and fluffy bunnies. Their wide cartoon eyes glowed silver in the cold light of the midnight moon. They were cute, she thought. Happy. They watched her cross the room, and she absently thanked them for not trumpeting a cuddly hieroglyphic warning.

She reached the nursery's only door. It hung slightly ajar so loving parents could detect any discomfort or danger during their only child's hours of solitude. She carefully eased it closed, then turned and rested her back against it. She blew a puff of air up to her loose brown bangs, relieved that she had completed the second hardest phase of the mission. Confident that she would remain unnoticed, she unclipped the night vision goggles from her belt and donned them. She flipped the muffled toggle and waited. The goggles powered up, providing her with the detail of daylight in shades of green.

The elephants and bunnies came to life in the cold green light. Their eyes, now pale white orbs instead of imagined Disney cuteness, followed her, sinister without content. She shivered, tried to ignore them. The subtle whine of her electric eyes coupled with the rapid vibration of the Breath Taker comforted her. Their hi-tech presence re-ignited the cold confidence that her calling demanded. They forced the walls of recriminating white eyes to kneel before rational, scientific explanation. They helped blanket her apprehensions about approaching the mahogany crib a few feet away with a warm sense of technical superiority; knowledge wielded as power.

Mahogany. Carved mahogany. You don't see cribs like that anymore, Julia thought. Of course, her night-vision didn't permit her to see wood grain in the black outline of the crib at all; she remembered the detail from the infant's dossier. A handcrafted crib deposited in a nursery bigger than Julia's apartment, its walls lined with cute & cuddly critters. A traditional mobile of cloth butterflies, agitated by her presence, rotated above the crib. Bathed in the soft glow of the baby monitor, it was a death dance performed in slow motion by a dozen moths that had ventured too close to their flames.

Julia smiled in respect for this baby's rich, loving, and intelligent parents; perfect by any social measure. But she had read the file.

The parents *were* perfect, and they would be devastated. Unfortunately for them, their baby had been deemed evil in the most scientific and statistical of manners. Well, maybe not evil right now, while it wiggled merrily on its back, extending its chubby little arms to her. In a gesture of quintessential trust, he sought Julia's attention in spite of the monstrous mask she wore. Such innocence could not be evil, a once distant part of her argued angrily from the pit of her soul. Not now, Julia's training agreed, but the potential existed. The file said so. The file said the infant had to go. The file, the edict, was generated by the machines at the Planning Center. They knew at the Planning Center. They could in a heartbeat track the lives of every first world human on the planet. They could, and did, define them, examine their past, their present, their environment. In another heartbeat they can statistically judge every path any person's future might follow. They find, effortlessly, the most likely route a subject's future would take.

And it worked. Consistently. At least, that was the law she had been trained to believe without question: the same machines, with the same statistics, prove without evidence their infallibility. Still, she believed that the system worked. It had to.

She knew that generally the futures were passive. Most reviews, indeed most people, were ignored by the system as inconsequential, even if they showed some proclivity for crime, or perhaps damaging social behavior. The Service was not interested in modifying culture, only preventing disasters caused by massively evil individuals. And the machines occasionally revealed a threat -- a Hitler, a Geoffrey Daumer, a civil litigator that had to be dealt with. Eliminated. The terminal solution, the only one known, was summarily applied to all people previewed, including babies. Primarily babies. Even the round cuddly ones that could remain beautiful in the green wash of night-vision, eyes open wide; happy.

Julia stepped back, away from the crib. She closed her eyes. The backs of her lids glowed green as residual artificial light clung briefly to her retina. She reminded herself repeatedly of this child's destiny, its guaranteed future in politics, and its aspiration to rise to inhuman heights of despotic power. It was a potential monster, in spite of the baby powder fresh scents that tapped, insistent, at her nose, begging to differ. She clenched her free fist, feeling her nails dig into her palm. The pain brought her back, helped her reject the perceived purity. Then she opened her eyes. The baby was still there, wet gums flashing between smiling lips, eyes reflecting the baby monitor's soft glow.

"It's just a few pounds of meat," Sid always said, "See it as that, ignore your instinct, and remember what this pound of flesh will become." Yeah, she thought, just meat -- evil, festering meat.

Julia leaned over the crib's rail, careful not to disturb it. She looked directly at the baby. It had stopped smiling, but its emotions were difficult to judge with its face washed in cold green enhancement. Why the hell do I care how the monster feels, she wondered. It was fidgeting, still restless. Julia frowned and drew a thick foam mitten-shaped object from her vest. She dropped it over the monitor in an easy motion, and then re-addressed the infant. It was regarding her now with a confused, perhaps thoughtful visage; emotion was not easy to discern in harsh green electronic light. Time to go to work, she thought.

"Never waste an instant," Sid had repeatedly warned, "Moments lost to regard or introspection are time surrendered to discovery. We cannot be discovered; we cannot fail in our services. Ever."

Her hands no longer shaking, her glowing green eyes focused on blue (she assumed) Dr. Denton's, Julia withdrew the slender funnel from the body of the Breath Taker. Its umbilical unwound from inside the metal case without a sound. She held it, one component in each hand, for a moment of either apprehension or respect for its power; she was not sure. She then surreptitiously moved the funnel into position over the tiny mouth and nose. She kept her movements smooth and simple, so as not to alarm young Christopher Michael.

Whoops, she thought, where'd that come from?

"Never, never let the meat keep its name," Sid had said, "There's nothing more dangerous. Remember, it's just flesh. Evil, dangerous flesh."

Evil flesh, she reminded herself. She laid the warmed plastic funnel gently over the infant's mouth and nose. It wriggled a bit, but luckily didn't know to defend itself from her mortal gesture. She re-checked the Breath Taker's readouts, touched the green buttons. In less than a minute, it would be over.

Even an advanced device like the Breath Taker had a fault -- it needed time. Its cycle of peaceful death dealing was complete in just one minute, but that was time enough for young Christopher to grow aware of his circumstances. His eyes bulged, and his little arms and legs flailed wildly. By its very nature the Breath Taker prevented its victim from crying out, but a struggling subject could become a nuisance.

Julia was trained for this and focused solely on the changing readouts of the Breath Taker while she held the funnel firmly in place. The numbers on the 3-digit completion readout crept past fifty. When they reached 100 her job would be finished. Christopher would no longer be a threat.

Christopher.

With her free hand, Julia switched off her night vision, lowered the goggles to her neck. She waited in the darkness until her natural vision adjusted to reality. She passed the long seconds wondering what it was she would see.

Irises finally wide, she saw Christopher. His wide eyes glistened in the soft moonlight. Julia hesitated. She was made conscious of her unforgivable break from routine by the almost inaudible alarm that announced the Breath Taker's premature separation from its victim's mouth. She refocused passively on the Breath Taker and the baby, taking another moment and five more persistent beeps from the alarm to register what she had done. Her quivering hand was hovering several inches above the proscribed position, freeing the funnel from Christopher's mouth and nose; ending the process. The baby was gasping mutely for air to fuel his forthcoming scream.

"Never stop," Sid had warned, "One slip, one moment of empathy for the damned, and they'll scream their evil heads off. Someone will hear, the Breath Taker will self-destruct, and the Service will forget you ever existed."

Julia raised her gaze from her target. She stared at the wall (not the bunnies), stopped breathing to avoid sadistic scents. Sid's was a strong warning, she thought, feeling the stifling power of the strange invading emotion being siphoned off by visions of epic failure. She wondered briefly at her lapse. Two in one night! Sid might kill me anyway.

"Oh well," she whispered to herself, "Back to work."

She shrugged and, neglecting to replace her night-vision goggles, replaced the funnel over young Christopher's mouth with trained, mechanical precision. Perhaps guessing that she was helping, the trusting infant was calmed by her action. He watched Julia peacefully, as if waiting for her next motherly ministration. His doe eyes shimmered in the moonlight, utterly innocent. They locked on Julia's naked gaze. An unexpected flash of introspection suddenly raced through her. The speed with which it entered her soul left it barely perceived; its power changed her forever. This time under her control, her hand lifted once more, and finally.

Christopher's innocence enveloped her, turning her years of training into a midnight dream. Julia felt her body enveloped by warm waves of compassion, the Service's cardinal sin. She did not even attempt invocation of the well-rehearsed tantric response to this dreaded though occasionally unavoidable natural event. Instead, she welcomed the warmth.

Julia pulled the machine's tiny, shrilling speaker from her ear. She calmly rubbed it between her thumb and forefinger somewhere below her in the darkness. It was barely audible, but still hissed angrily. She dropped it into her hip pocket, then switched off the Breath Taker and secured it to her belt. She didn't notice that it had already begun to transform into a mass of black gelatin. She pulled the goggles from her neck, placing them gently on the quilted cushion of the mother's antique rocker. She soundlessly peeled off her surgical gloves, dropped them on the floor. She reached into the crib and gently ran a hand through Christopher's thin matte of hair. Its gossamer softness returned her caress, sending a wave of warmth through her body that surprised her, wringing a dangerously audible sigh of pleasure from her lungs. She leaned over the crib and carefully lifted Christopher to her shoulder. He rested his head there, quiet, content.

"That's right, Chris," She whispered into his ear, "They sent me on one too many assignments this month, and you are the happy result of my failure."

She padded silently around the room with the baby, instinctively avoiding furniture and noise in the dark. She aimlessly shuffled in a tight circle, still absorbed by the torrent of compassion that had defeated her. She wondered about her future. What does the service do with their failures? She had asked once.

"Hell, I don't know," Sid had said, eyes cast to the floor, "I never met anyone who blew a mission."

"So no one has?"

"Not that I know of."

Well, now you do, she thought as she smiled down at the infant cradled in her arms. She would assume the worst, of course -- that the Service would ostracize her and make another attempt at Christopher.

"Don't worry, little man," she said, tickling Christopher's chubby chin, eliciting a squeal of delight, "That won't happen. I know you're not evil. You can't be. I'll protect you. Your parents will protect you. They're rich and powerful. We'll tell them all about me, and about this sick service I just quit."

Julia's hand whipped to the wall and switched on the overhead light. Warm incandescence softened the nursery. The elephants and bunnies on the wall became cute and fluffy once more. She was surprised at the ease with which she had made her decision. She had decided, even as her hand hit the switch, that she knew the Service was wrong. The fresh realization of her long-held but previously denied confidence in the Service's error held power for Julia. She was able with the flick of a switch to flush the Service and all its training from her system. A strong dose of those wide blue eyes was simply a spoonful of sugar to her. Julia returned the baby's smile.

"Oh, Christopher," she said, reaching for the brass doorknob that led to the hall, the parents, and resolution, "I'm so glad you were able to stop me, stop the madness that I had let consume me. Now, let's go get your parents."

A gloved hand dropped from nowhere onto hers. It gently applied enough force to prevent her from turning the knob. Julia gasped, but was not surprised. She was on first-name terms with everyone on the planet able to sneak up on her like that. She let him control her hand, but wouldn't remove it from the knob.

"Let's not, Julia," a tired, pained voice whispered from an inch behind her ear. It was Sid. Thank God, she thought; Sid'll understand. She felt a pin prick the base of her neck.

Or not.

"Sid. No," was all she could manage before paralysis set in. She had used that needle in the past. She would be dead in just a click under 3 minutes. Quite silently, of course. Sid had shut off the light.

Her limp body fell into Sid's waiting arms. Her back was snug against his chest. His thick arms enveloped her. She would have, and had, welcomed that embrace in another time. He turned her away from the door. She faced the empty crib, and remembered Christopher, the baby in her distant arms. Her eyes still worked, and she watched, helpless, as another serviceman gently snatched Christopher as he tumbled from her flaccid grasp. Cooing softly to the doomed baby, he replaced Christopher gently in his crib.

Christopher was still quiet, but no longer peaceful. Agitated, he searched his little world once more for that special puff of air. He would cry in a moment, if allowed.

Julia saw the green L.E.D. glow of another Breath Taker near the crib. She wanted to shiver as its funnel caught a ray of moonlight. Christopher would not be allowed to breathe; to grow. Julia shed the natural terror of imminent death that should have overcome her. She felt unable to spend her last minute of life in the quiet acceptance that would have eased her exit to oblivion. Instead she was furious. Her rage was complete, consuming all other emotion, and much of her dwindling rationale. She could do nothing but die while they snuffed out an innocent, not even flip the bastards the bird.

Sid seemed to sense her anger, or more likely expected it. He rested his chin on her distant shoulder, held his mouth against her ear.

"Julia, Julia," he whispered, his warm lips softly brushing her lobe, "Julia my love, my best student. How could this have come about?"

Because I finally realized that you, your Service, your `machines', and even me are all raving lunatics! She screamed, but the words did not cross the threshold of her mind -- the lethal paralysis had imprisoned her angry retort.

"This infant is evil, Julia. You know that. You read the pre-dossier."

No! Julia screamed, somewhere. `Pre-dossier' my ass, just more sick ravings of the power-mad. She was humiliated by her inability to conjure even a cold stare. How could she have fallen for this bullshit?

"Okay, so he's not evil yet," Sid conceded, "But he will be. I think you have about 30 seconds left, so I'll tell you why he is. And you are."

Thirty seconds of life left. Julia chose not to waste the rest of her life considering either the ranting of a fanatic or reflection of her own misguided life. She let images of Christopher, her savior, her victim, seconds from death himself, pass across her eyes. She would die with goodness in her mind, light in her soul. Still, the fanatic prattled on, unattended:

"The machines know, Julia. They did a scan on this filth as soon as it popped its nasty head out of its poor mother. It reeked with socially destructive political ambition. It was littered with Hitlerian aspirations. That should have been enough, but scans and the psychological profiles of the parents confirmed all. Oh, they're harmless enough on their own, but they would support the monster. Support him!"

Julia no longer had to ignore Sid's demented whispers; her world was a cold gray fog.

"And you, Julia. We knew about you too. Our best agent, I always thought, but the Service knew better. The machines pinpointed the day your evil would emerge," he pressed his mouth tightly against her ear, attempted to force his whispers into her failing mind.

"Why do you think we're here, Julia? I was assigned to remove *you* tonight. Can you believe that? They picked *me*. Well, you're just another missing person now, babe, and the brat is just another Sudden Infant Death Syndrome. And may God have mercy on your souls."

The gray faded to black. Julia had long since left his ugly words behind. The last loose strands of her mind clung to the beauty of her decision until the quiet blackness of death enveloped her.

The End is Clear

When he noticed that his recently gossamer fingers had also taken to trembling, Ralph surmised that it was in reaction to the ten thousand puffs of blue smoke his lungs had ejected over them. Even my own damn fingers have abandoned me, he thought. He smiled foolishly and peered past his rebelling digits to read the two-inch banner spanning his Sunday New York Times. Blood red ink blared to whoever was left to care that the suicide rate had exceeded the combined rate of death by any means, ever. This record apparently included murder, whose rate had also been increasing exponentially for months.

"Duh," Ralph sighed into a fresh cloud of his acrid exhaust, "Tell me something I don't already know." The chances of that were as slim as the newspaper itself had become. The Times' venerable Sunday edition was now less than half an inch thick, folded, and that volume was primarily occupied by advertisements pushing products that were no longer available or desired. The paper's diminished size betrayed without its headline's help the impact of the pandemic suicide rate. Ralph felt that familiar brick form deep in his stomach, again. Over a billion unscheduled deaths in less than a year, and they were his fault.

Ralph dropped the paper neatly onto his kitchen table. He rubbed his thick matted hair, leaving a large oily clump of it erect atop his head. He then examined his hand for anything untoward that may have found its way from his greasy follicles to his estranged fingers. Though there was nothing of note, he absently wiped his hand on the front of his impressively unkempt T-shirt. Ralph had ceased justifying a need to wash a few days after he had buried Margo. His wife of ten years had delayed her personal demise for months, acquiescing repeatedly to Ralph's pleas. Her mortal resolve finally collapsed three weeks ago, after she returned home from a church service to a flock of four people, including the pastor. She never told him, but something about the empty church turned Margo toward death with an inertia that drew from her own definitively rational nature. Her will to die pushed easily past Ralph's failing logic skills. His wife was dead because of him, he reminded himself. Hell, half his family was gone, and the rest prepared to leave. In a silent complaint repeated so chronically that it had become mantra, he wished that he had killed himself before he ever wrote that damn paper. Now he couldn't do it; he had decided to damn himself to the living hell of staying alive. It was the worst punishment he could muster.

Not that anyone would care, he thought. They don't remember who the hell I am, and they'll all be gone soon anyway. Ralph glanced at the paper. Not the New York Times, which would languish unread on the filthy kitchen table indefinitely, but *the paper* – a hand-bound tome whose tattered edge peaked out from under what little news was still fit to print. He kept the treatise, his trumpet, nearby at all times in vain anticipation of the moment he dared forget what he had done.

Ralph had believed that he had made a major discovery a year earlier, and the pride felt good initially. That was when he had hit the big time; an event that mathematicians could rarely add to their curriculum vitae. He was correct then, and it still was an event. But it was an event in the life story of humanity, not Ralph Plasman, PhD. Ralph had, in a beautifully concise proof backed by perfect empirical evidence, offered in his treatise irrefutable proof that there is life after death. And, still unable to shake the thrill that accompanied the first time he typed the thesis, he proved that not only is there an afterlife, but that that extended, perhaps immortal existence is better than corporeal human life and depends in no way on earthly moral behavior.

Ralph's paper initially received the typical cynicism and mocking by his peers that such a thesis generated. But his proofs were tested: first reluctantly, then cynically, then laboriously, by countless minds spanning every scientific, theological, and new age discipline imaginable. With testing, attitudes began to shift, and the news of his discovery spread in a manic wave of information that wetted every corner of the planet. For a few weeks, Ralph enjoyed celebrity outside the scientific community. He appeared with Leno, Dave, Larry King, and even explained his findings to Ted Koppel. He smiled at the thought, and then remembered that he had read each of their obituaries scant weeks after shaking their hands.

"Yeah," he laughed, "That's from when they were still printing obits."

Like his hosts, Ralph's enjoyment of fame was short lived. When the mass media shared his easily translatable and understood proofs to the world, he became a pariah; the guy who both saved everyone and changed everything by voicing an eternally anticipated truth: every living human will transcend to a better state of being after death. Ralph was a god overnight, sewing chaos in biblical proportion and altering societies permanently. By order of his thesis, and through no conscious thought of his own, Ralph dispensed absolution to the good and pardon to the evil while simultaneously making both states morally irrelevant. Two million people gathered in Central Park two weeks after the first CNN report, chewed cyanide together, and dropped to the ground under great banners erected for the occasion. The banners bore only one word: Plasman. The city unceremoniously ('Why bother?" The mayor was heard to ask) buried the empty carcasses where they fell with bulldozers. Just to get rid of the stink.

"Two million," Ralph said into his open refrigerator, "Assholes." He pulled out breakfast: a beer. He had assumed the rational population, the millions who clamored for his crucifixion on a daily basis, would have convinced the death-prone to stay alive. They did not, either by choice or due to their own surrender to Ralph's penultimate easy way out. Ralph had provided everyone an egalitarian solution to all of life's problems, and it included a happy ending. People on the edge of happiness, and there were so, so many, never had a chance. And now, with all the death and misery surrounding the sullen survivors, Ralph had become even less popular. And the death rate escalated unchecked.

The phone rang. Chirped, actually, in that clear electronic tone that had quietly usurped the claxon alarm of the old Bell system decades earlier. Though the chirp was soft, Ralph jerked from the unexpected sound, spilling a dollop of his breakfast. He stared at the beeping debris on the counter beside his sink, not certain under which portion of the chaotic pile of dirty dishes and recyclables awaiting an utterly unnecessary rinse the phone was buried. He paused like a predator, and with the next ring leapt at an empty box of Twinkies. He batted the box aside, startling two feasting cockroaches, and grabbed the phone before its next ring. He turned it on, remembering oddly that he once just had to pick it up, and listened silently.

"Ralphie?" a female voice whispered in his gnarly ear, "That you?" It was Leona, his erstwhile agent. She had come on board, as she would certainly put it, when his fame was still a good thing. Indeed, she was instrumental in helping him achieve much of his current notoriety. Ralph was amazed she still tried to call. He was not amazed, however, that she was still alive. He paused a few more seconds, to calm his racing heart, and spoke.

"Leona. What the hell do you want?"

"Now now, Ralph. I didn't *write* the pape-" Ralph pushed the disconnect button and tossed the phone without emotion into the sink. Its impact on the pile started a chain reaction of tumbling dishes and flying silverware that nearly drowned out the buzz of Leona's redial. Ralph let the phone ring about fifty times. He stood there, three feet away, staring at the evil device, contemplating the true evil at the other end. Finally, unable to resist, and unwilling to toss his phone into the street, Ralph picked it up, wiped some grime off of it with a towel, and turned it on.

"Okay, Ralphie," Leona purred, "I get the hint. Now stay with me this time, I have something important to talk with you about."

"And what could that something possibly be? Want me to go on an apology tour?"

"That's not a bad idea, Ralphie," Leona said thoughtfully, "But that's not it at all. Not yet. Listen, I met this guy –"

"I don't think I want to hear about your mating habits, Leona. I just ate."

"Yeah, yeah, Ralphie," Leona said at a staccato pace to avoid interruption, "Fuck me and all; very funny, very sincere. Now shut up for two seconds and let the evil bitch get her three cents in."

"Fine, bitch. What?"

"Thank you, my love. Listen, I met this guy who's gone over your paper and –"

"That's it? You want to do another damn interview with a pundit? Old news Leona, and you know my answer already, so why do you ask?"

"And why the fuck do you keep interrupting?" she shouted, startling Ralph, "Now shut up and let me finish. I met this guy who has some serious questions to ask you about your paper."

"Like what?"

"You won't believe me. I want him to say."

"Right to me?"

"Right to you."

"Then I guess I'll never know."

"Yes you will," she hissed, "I know you hate me, Ralphie, but this one's important; maybe more important for you than for me. So get yourself cleaned up –"

"I'm dirty?" Ralph asked, absently noting the stench emanating from his armpits.

"Please, Ralphie, this is Leona. Now get yourself cleaned up and meet me at my office in two hours."

"Nope. Maybe I'll clean, but I won't travel."

"It's twenty blocks fer Crissakes!"

"I don't care. I don't want to meet this guy anyway."

"Yes you do," Leona said, releasing an uncharacteristic sigh, "We'll be there in an hour." The line was dead before Ralph had a chance to tell her to go to hell. He shook his head, looked around his apartment, and decided that, though he wasn't going to let Leona and her new buddy in, he would at least use his awareness of her stubbornness as an excuse to take a shower.

In exactly one hour later the doorbell rang. Ralph, clean and dressed in a fresh pair of jeans and cotton shirt he found undisturbed in a guestroom drawer, stared at the door. He did not move toward it, but rather stood in the middle of his living room and waited with his arms folded until the ringing stopped. It eventually did stop, retired by Leona's fist, which rapidly rapped in an incredibly annoying beat. Ralph remained still. Finally Leona turned the knob. The door swung open. About time she remembered I haven't locked that thing in months, Ralph thought. Leona, a tiny, attractive Vietnamese woman of indeterminate age, entered the room with a confused adolescent boy firmly in tow. She set him in front of Ralph, and announced over the lanky young man's bony shoulder, "This is Howie. Howie, in spite of appearances, is a genius."

"Howie." Ralph said.

"Ralph," Howie responded, his glazed blue eyes locked on Ralph's bloodshot set.

"Okay," Leona clapped, "Now that formalities are behind us, tell him, Howie."

"Tell me what?" Ralph asked.

Howie did not hesitate. He stepped toward Ralph and, with some stretching and neck bending, placed his face an inch from Ralph's. A full head taller than Howie, and far more massive than the scrawny young man, Ralph did not feel threatened. But he did feel gravity flowing from the boy, who spoke an instant after he achieved his superior posture.

"Dude," Howie rasped, "You were wrong."

"About what?" Ralph asked.

"The paper, shithead. The treatise on the mutherfucking afterlife. Your conclusion -- you know, the one everybody's been dying over? -- was wrong."

"What the hell are you talking about?" Ralph asked, "Leona, what the hell is he talking about? My conclusions are proven. Who is this kid?"

"This kid is the single soul who held his head above the glory of your discovery long enough to glean its true nature," Leona whispered.

"And what the hell does that mean?" Ralph asked with an unguarded sneer.

"It means that, unlike all the fools who wanted so desperately to believe you, I did the math. All of it."

"Normally," Leona interrupted Ralph's erupting tirade with a manicured hand (where did she find someone to do that? Ralph wondered), "I would dismiss someone making a claim like this way before they got to you. And God knows I have, a hundred times over. But Ralphie,

there's something about what this kid is saying that just
sounds right."

"How the hell would you know? You've never even
read my treatise!"

"Okay, so there's something about the way he's
saying it. Just listen to him Ralphie, and then you decide."

"Fine," Ralph said. He stepped back from Howie and
pointed at the sofa, "Sit."

"Where?" Howie asked.

"On the couch. Over their, under those papers and
blankets and, um, stuff. Just clear a spot and friggin' sit,
okay?" Howie sat. Leona cleared a spot on the other end of
the sofa and carefully sat as well. Ralph grabbed himself a
beer without thinking to make any host-like offers, remained
standing, and said, "Okay, kid, tell me what I did wrong.
You know I won't believe you, because I was right, but
screw it, there's nothing on TV anymore anyway. Entertain
me."

So Howie entertained Ralph. For three hours. First he
described to Ralph the moment of his discovery, when he
read the treatise for the sixth time after retrieving it from his
dead professor's desk drawer at MIT. The first five readings
offered no clue, and had him contemplating suicide himself,
but something – perhaps the thing that compelled the first
four rereads – made him look the paper over a sixth time.
And then, in an empty Cambridge café, he saw the flaw. It
was near the end of the treatise, hidden forty pages into the
proofs. But it was there. Though he had, by default,
unlimited access to MIT's computers, Howie needed a
month to work through the math and eventually piece
together how Ralph's proofs could not be proven. Finally,
because his words were barely denting the great steel doors
guarding Ralph's tattered mind, Howie pulled a laptop from
his backpack and brought up his work. He carefully led
Ralph through everything he had done. After about an hour

of Howie's repetition and Ralph's denials, Ralph finally fell heavily into his barcalounger. Leona handed him her flask.

"Holy shit," Ralph whispered, emptying the flask of the two or three ounces of vodka Leona hadn't yet quaffed, "Holy shit."

The kid was right. Ralph had made a mistake. His irrefutable proof that there is life after death was refuted. And, since that part of his treatise was corrupt, the part about it being a better afterlife had to be tossed out as well. Ralph stared at Howie in silence while he was consumed by sweeping mythological images of where Margo may have really landed after she jumped from the roof, past their open bedroom window. In time Howie shed some of his angry arrogance to squirm nervously.

"What?" Howie asked, "I'm just telling you what I found out, dude."

"Yeah, well, dude," Ralph said, shaking some images of hell and social service in the afterlife loose and stepping on the rest with the mighty weight of his rage, "Why couldn't you tell me this a year ago?"

"Guess I was caught up in it all, too. I never read the paper until Prof offed himself. I thought at first 'Why look at all?' but something about Prof with half his head missing and that stupid smile wrapped around his gun just pushed me to check deeper. I got to admit that, on the surface everything seemed okay. That, mixed with everybody, including a boatload of real smart everybodies, saying you had to be right slowed me down. Sorry, man -- I feel way shitty about that myself."

"So you're telling him that all those people -- what is it now, a billion? -- are dead for real? They had nothing to go to after all?"

"Well, no, Leona," Howie said, "I'm just saying that it's as much of a mystery as it was before."

"But Ralphie only made one mistake. Couldn't he be mostly right, and all those souls are intact?"

"Leona," Ralph sighed, "Go blow up a balloon, then stick a pin in it. The balloon will still be mostly sealed after you do that, what with just one tiny pinhole in it. But tell me honestly it'll stay inflated."

"It would if it were my pin," Leona replied, honestly.

"You're a goddess."

"I'm still alive, aren't I?"

"Leona, have you no shame?"

"Nope, and no shame's exactly what I'll need when we make this public."

"Make this public? Please. Who's that going to help?"

"What do you mean, Ralphie? There're still five billion idiots out there jumping off bridges and stringing their own nooses."

"And they'll believe you why?"

"They won't believe me, Ralphie. They'll believe you."

Ralph lit another cigarette, and held *his* palm toward Leona. "Lady," he said, "And I use the term only because the drama of the moment requires it. Lady, you cannot sincerely think that anyone has any use for my opinion these days, unless of course it's a first-person reaction to slow torture."

"I think you're wrong again, dude," Howie said, "I think those people out there will want to know this thesis of yours is wrong. It'll give them hope."

"Huh?" Leona and Ralph said in symphony.

"Dude. Humans *require* hope. They need to imagine, and not to know, that there is something after they die. It's just wrong when they know it, because that just fucks them up."

"So what you're saying is that if I tell the masses that their afterlife really isn't assured, they'll be delighted by my reverse revelation?"

"Yeah, eventually. First they'll want to kill you, though."

"That'd be something new," Ralph sighed. He took a long drag on his latest cigarette, then looked at it and smiled at his unconscious urge to put it out. Damn, he thought, the survival instinct's already kicking in. He finished the cigarette in silence, carefully mulling over the news that this kid tossed atop the huge pile of shit that was his life. He lit another one, then snuffed it out in the ashtray immediately. Then he looked up. Howie was sitting quietly, arms folded, and unnaturally immobile. He was waiting for a decision, for the god Ralph to choose his next world-rending move. Leona had fallen asleep.

"I know!" Ralph shouted, slamming his fist loudly on the table. Leona started awake with a delightful screech.

"You do?" Howie asked, his tired tone making the rest of his sentence redundant, "About friggin time."

"No, not really. I just needed to make sure Leona's frozen heart was still beating. Or whatever it does."

"It still is, you ungrateful asshole," Leona said sweetly, her middle finger casually raised. Ralph smiled back, realizing after his lips were bent that his gesture was sincere. Wary of treading such emotional turf, he tried to turn his smile into an insipid grin before Leona noticed.

"Fine," Howie said, "Then I guess I still got some waiting to do."

"No," Ralph said, "Because even though I don't know, and never will, I have decided how to deal with this, um, truth that you revealed to me."

"Great!" Leona chirped, "I'll set up something, maybe at the Waldorf if it's available – oh for God's sake, everything's available these days! Shit, I'll just take us right into CNN's studios. They've been abandoned for weeks, but I'll bet the power will still come on."

"You do what you want, you greedy old bitch," Ralph said, somehow with affection, "But I won't be involved in any soul-searching press releases."

"Soul-searching," Howie snorted, "Dude, you'd be the first one to be doing it literally!"

"Shut up Howie," Leona hissed, "This is important. Why the hell not, Ralphie? You've got a world to save, you know."

"Wow, Leona, you are actually making me believe you care about these people."

"Well maybe I just do!"

"Or maybe you're looking to maintain your shrinking client base?"

"Yeah well, there is that, too. I guess."

"Yes there is. At any rate, I have but one response to all these people: fuck 'em. Maybe there was a higher authority that made me, my wife, and every other genius on the planet, miss the obvious error in my proof. Maybe this was God, nature, our own cosmic consciousness, or whatever, culling the herd a bit. Who am I to stop it?"

"You're the shithead who started it!"

"Why Leona. You really do care."

"Hmm," she said quietly, "Maybe I do. That is odd. But it's also totally unimportant. What matters is that you've got some truth to spread, and you're shirking the only responsibility left on the planet that really matters."

"That's deep, Leona, and probably true. But I don't give a shit. Everyone I know is dead, because of me. And they may have all done it for the wrong reasons. Also because of me. Leona, I'm a Catholic."

"So?" Leona asked. Howie was already nodding knowingly, his eyes wide.

"So?" Ralph said, standing so he could pace while he delivered his soliloquy, "So? I'll give you so. Why do you think I'm still breathing? Why do you think I'm still here? I pondered that for a long time myself, and all I could figure was that there is a huge chunk of my psyche, a section of me buried too deep to ever change, but one that will always control my actions. That section told me that if I kill myself,

I would go straight to Hell. That same section, that part of my soul that prevented me from killing myself when everything I knew (until now) told me it was okay to do so, is now telling me, at 105 decibels, that I just sent about a billion people, and Margo, to Hell."

"Ralph," Leona said, becoming visibly agitated, "That's insane."

"Yeah," Howie said, "Especially because if you keep this truth to yourself, you'll be sending a few billion more people to Hell. You really want to do that?"

"Howie, I think after the first few thousand it just didn't matter anymore," Ralph said, silently acknowledging that Margo's suicide at his erroneous hands would have been enough by itself. He continued, "Now it's their choice. And damn them, for real, if they can 't decide to choose life on their own."

"Oh now Ralphie," Leona said, standing and stopping his frenetic pace with her slight body, "That's just not fair. Here's your chance to make a different difference for a change. A decent difference." Ralph allowed himself to bump into Leona. He set her shoulders between his open palms and looked deeply into her eyes. He had never done that before, and was amazed at a depth obscured only by the mist that currently shrouded them. Holy shit, Ralph thought, she really does care.

"Sure wish I did," he said aloud.

"Huh?" Leona breathed, shaken by the unusual embrace.

"Nothing. Listen, it's almost midnight, I'm tired, and I need some time to think about this. Go away for now, and call me again tomorrow morning. Maybe by then I'll have this sorted out."

"Maybe by then another million people will be dead from bad information," Howie said.

"Maybe. But like I said, the scale of it all has escaped me, so I just can't care."

"That's real nice," Howie said, gathering himself to his feet, "Real nice."

"Yeah, yeah. I admire your anger, kid, and I do wish I could still find that kind of feeling myself. Maybe by morning it'll surface. But not now. So – "

"So we should get the fuck out of here?"

"You should. Thanks for the heads-up, Howie. If I ever figure out how it makes me feel you'll be the first to know."

"Yeah yeah yeah. Fuck you too, old man," Howie snatched up his backpack and stormed from Ralph's apartment without another word, or even a glance at Ralph or Leona. Leona stepped in front of Ralph again, and pressed very close to him. Her body felt better to the touch than Ralph would have expected; much softer. He let her put her arms around his waist and draw him in even tighter. He hoped she didn't notice the involuntary (and almost unfamiliar) swelling in his groin.

"Ralphie," Leona whispered, her eyes still misty, "Am I going to see you again?"

"Do you want to?"

"Yes."

"And don't you always get whatever you want?"

"Yes."

"Well, then there is your answer."

"Ralphie," Leona said, touching a warm finger to his lip, "Don't make liars out of both of us." Her voice was soft, sensuous, and shaking.

"Good night, Leona," Ralph said, surprised at his own tenderness. Leona turned and left without further comment. Ralph lit another cigarette.

Dawn was still twenty minutes away, and Ralph decided not to wait for it. Howie's Hope would come with the rising sun, and he had no use for it, or the sun, today. It was time to test his theory. Howie had made an outstanding case against it, and he was probably correct. But Ralph needed to know. It was his right.

His own building off limits for sentimental reasons, Ralph had tritely chosen the Empire State building for his last experiment. It had taken him only a few seconds and a Volkswagen to enter the empty building when the night was still young (this was New York), but it had taken another five hours to figure out how to get the power back on so he could operate the elevators. Ralph didn't want his coda to be a coronary on the stairs, after all. So now he was perched atop the bent iron fence designed to prevent suicides. Gray predawn light unmasked a mural of chalk and paint good-byes covering the wall behind him.

Ralph wasn't going public with anything. Their reaction to his thesis the first time was proof enough of humanity's gullibility. He did not want to embarrass his soul again. So, instead, he decided that it was time to see if Howie was right or, better yet, to cleanse his soul of its guilt, and its catholic conflicts. It was time to know.

"Or not," He said aloud.

Without another word, and with the morning sun's first gentle rays casting an orange glow on the last great building humanity would erect for quite some time, Ralph stepped off the fence.

Repairs

"Tiger!"

"Tiiiigggerrr!" Tasha called to the summer sunset with all the wind her tiny lungs could muster. She waved a piece of bologna high in the air above her head. Out of breath, she slumped to the cold concrete front stoop. She rested her elbows on skinny kid-knees, and sullenly ate the bologna. After carefully nibbling the edge of the lunchmeat, around and around in the tiniest of bites, until the slice was gone, she sighed deeply, smacked the painted concrete beside her so hard it hurt, then tried to focus through her tears.

"Where are you, Tiger?" she mumbled, "You know you're supposed to be here, with me." She dragged herself to her feet, turned and reached up to open the front door. She didn't notice her mother stepping out of sight just before she pulled open the screen door.

Though it was not the first time that Tiger wandered off, he had never been gone from her side for so long. Tasha was confused. Tiger was her beloved cat. He was her only friend, the orange tabby that her mother had allowed her to pick from the cardboard carton in front of the Stop & Shop four years – and half her lifetime – previously. Tasha remembered that she picked well because the big girl offering the kittens cried loudly when she carried her new friend away to the car. Tasha also remembered that she was careful not to look back.

Tasha and Tiger were a virtually inseparable unit, bound from the moment they woke and Tasha gently untangled the groggy cat from her snarled black tresses to the moment she reluctantly fell asleep at night with Tiger purring in her arms. When Tasha became old enough for school, Tiger would escort her to the bus stop each morning, and usually be waiting when she hopped off in the early afternoon. Indeed, there were occasions when Tiger didn't care to wait and joined her on the bus. He made it to school twice, though both times her mother came around to retrieve the errant pet. Tasha did not have a problem with this, though she did wish that her mother would let her keep Tiger in her desk at school during the day. She had even presented a plan to her mother that covered what she was sure were all the bases for the care and feeding of a full grown cat nestled in the cubby beneath her chair. Her mother had smiled, and told her wide-eyed little girl that Tiger didn't need to go to school, and might be happier at home.

"Well," Tasha said as she stood on the concrete porch, "If you're happier at home, then why aren't you here?" She surrendered her vigil for the evening, opened the screen door, and sullenly entered the living room. She carefully pushed the front door closed, her wet brown eyes still peering outside for a glimpse of a returning Tiger before the heavy portal shut the outside away for another night. The door clicked home before she could see anything.

Tasha did not eat dinner. She stared past her hot dog and lima beans two hours beyond the time that the rest of her family had already finished eating and had begun their evening routines. Though she was normally required to remain at the table until she finished all of her dinner, her mother opted this time to let her leave whenever she was ready. Tasha wasn't exercising her usual tenacity by not eating; she was not eating because she was not moving.

Her little body had run out of hope, and steam. Tasha finally realized, after almost two weeks, that her cat was not coming home. Tiger's disappearance had broken her, and she was too new to such damage to know how to make repairs. She didn't even know that she needed repairs. Her mother watched her daughter from the living room, silently allowing the child to remain parked in front of her uneaten dinner without reprisal.

Tasha's epiphany helped, in time, to ease her suffering. She was able, without even knowing the change occurred, to shift her life's focus from her missing cat to the new events and challenges she faced every day. School became important again, as did after-school TV and her expansive menagerie of slightly less responsive stuffed animals. Time was helping to heal the deep wound Tiger had inflicted, and it did so at the amazing rate that only a child could enjoy.

The recovery was not complete, though. Tasha could not look at another cat without becoming weepy. This included cats on TV, in pet stores, and the two cats that still patrolled her family's living room. The presence of a cat would trigger emotions that Tasha did not expect or understand, but hated to endure. Her depression only lasted a few minutes, but time spent briefly grieving did not diminish as the months passed.

By Thanksgiving, her mother was sure that Tasha's happiness was still as hampered by Tiger's absence, as it had been that night after dinner. Indeed, Tasha seemed to be falling into emotional abysses with alarming frequency. In December, when Tasha's mother announced that it was time to write to Santa Claus, her sister and brothers assembled reams of loose leaf littered with lists, descriptions, and even clipped ads from the Sears Catalog. Tasha, however, had scrawled only one sentence on her list:

"Please tell my kitty Tiger how to get home."

Tasha's mother sighed, but was not surprised that her daughter's reality could be so completely corrupted by the removal of a single, ordinary cat. She recognized her hand in the mess, since she had allowed the pet to become far too important in her daughter's life, and then failed to sit down and discuss the possibility and finality of death with her daughter while the time was still ripe. Using the child's age as her excuse and crutch, Tasha's mother had sidestepped a surmountable issue for herself, and allowed a greater ghost than the specter of a dead cat to haunt her child. She watched Tasha's letter to Santa become blurry in her hands, then clear, then splattered with a single tear. It was joined shortly by several more.

"Ordinary?" Tasha's mother said aloud while she wrapped the last of hundreds of presents, each of which she hoped her four children would enjoy until the following Christmas. It had taken weeks, but she suddenly noticed that single word among the thousands that constantly whipped her soul about that cat. She ran the word over her tongue once more as she mechanically attached some cellophane tape to a fold of bright red paper emblazoned with little green snowmen. Then she paused, smiled, quickly hid the wrapped presents in her closet, and reached for the telephone.

Christmas Eve was a melancholy affair for Tasha. Her empty heart was not affected by the joy of trimming the tree her father had retrieved from the forest that morning, or by anticipation of the presents Santa would have delivered by the following dawn. Those annual peaks of childhood euphoria eluded Tasha this year. Her thoughts and emotions were enveloped by Tiger's absence. She prayed to the ceramic Baby Jesus nestled in his plastic crèche by the fireplace. She prayed to Him over and over and over, that Tiger would be under the tree in the morning. She imagined that each piece of tinsel that she carefully draped over the branches of the tree was going to be a toy for her kitty. Yet somewhere, in the back of her mind, she knew that Tiger would never be back. It had been months, and she knew that Tiger had to be dead. Tasha's mind was helplessly buffeted by this whirlpool of hope and despair throughout the evening. Her pain obscured her siblings' excitement, and her reprised grief kept her eyes wide in bed just as late as her anticipation had one year earlier. She did eventually sleep, though her mother could not confirm the easy breath of her drowse until after three in the morning.

Tasha awoke in darkness to the prods and nudges of her older brother. He had been up since four, and couldn't stand the wait anymore. She obliged his whispered demand to join him in a reconnaissance run of the loot in the living room (they weren't allowed to open their presents until Mother and Father were both up). Tasha dragged herself out of bed, followed her brother to her door. The house was bathed in the predawn shadows, but there was enough light for them to make their way to the tree without knocking anything down. Her sister and other brother were already waiting for them in the hall, whispering frantically about the need to get to the living room.

Tasha was last to the presents, and numbly searched for her name among the mountain of wrapped gifts that crowded the darkened tree. She had known that Tiger would not be waiting for her under the tree, but her little throat still tightened when she confirmed his absence. Then her mother emerged from her bedroom, yawning and adjusting the pink felt belt of her bathrobe. Without saying a word to any of the other kids, she leaned down to Tasha's ear.

"Tasha" she said, "Did you hear that noise outside?"

"What noise?" Tasha asked, her heart skipping a beat inexplicably. She did not even wonder how her mother could have heard anything over the din of her ransacking siblings.

"I don't know," her mother said softly, "Maybe you should take a quick look outside to make sure nothing happened. Who knows? Santa's sled could have broken..."

"I don't think so Ma," Tasha said, "but I guess I could look out there if you want me to." She tried to sound disinterested in the chore, but in her soul she knew that an army of elephants couldn't keep her from opening that door. She had no idea why as she ran to the door, reached up and worked the knob. She opened the door, and peered over the sill of the storm door.

"I don't see anything, Ma," she said, "must've been nothing. Maybe the wind."

"Maybe," her mother said, "but you know it's still pretty dark outside. Maybe you should take another look."

"Well okay, if I gotta." Tasha pushed open the storm door, cringed as the cold winter air nipped at her bare feet, then stuck her head through the small space the open door had made. She saw nothing in the predawn gloom. "Nope," she said, "nothing out here at all."

"Are you sure?" her mother, right behind her now, asked, "Did you try looking *down*?"

Tasha did as she was told, peering down, around the door, to the concrete front porch. Something dark was moving on it. Tasha slammed the door shut.

"Ma, you were right, there is something out there, and it's right on the porch!"

"Oh, my! What do you think it is, honey?"

"I don't know. Some animal."

"Some animal? Here, let me turn on the light out there so you can get a better look." She flipped on the outside light, then stepped back so Tasha could peer out the storm door's high window again.

Tasha looked again. This time she could make out the shape of the animal.

"It's a cat, Mom, but it's pretty skinny, and all dirty."

"Does it look familiar at all, Tasha?"

Suddenly Tasha joined the game and whipped open the front door, nearly knocking the greasy cat off the stoop.

"Tiger!" She screamed, "You came home!" She grabbed the cat, which seemed to be entwined in a length of yarn, and hugged it close, crying and rocking.

"Well what do you know, Tasha?" her mother stammered, "I guess Tiger wanted to save himself for Christmas. Stupid cat."

"He's not a stupid cat," Tasha said, scooping the frail bundle into her arms, "He's the smartest cat in the world! He must have been halfway around the world, he was so lost, but he still came back home. On Christmas! What a smart kitty."

"Well, he sure wasn't smart enough to keep himself clean. Bring him inside where it's warm, and we'll clean him up as much as we can. You know we'll have to take him to the vet, too. Just in case."

"Sure Ma, just in case," Tasha said, almost unaware that she was speaking. She brought her best friend back into the house. Her older brother was first to see her, and he pointed at the cat.

"Hey, look, the squirt got a new friend."

"No I didn't," Tasha corrected, "My old, best, friend came home. On Christmas."

"But that's not – Ow!" Tasha's brother was interrupted by a smack from his mother, and then he too joined the game:

"You best take care of him this time, Tasha, so he doesn't run away again."

"Oh, I will," Tasha sighed, noticing finally that there were Christmas presents under the tree, "I will."

And she did. Though his journey had changed Tiger, he once again became her constant companion, and her solution to so many problems.

A Father's Destiny

Carelessly kicking the small rock up the hill, Sydney trudged home. Once more school had not gone well for him. Miss Crawly had caught him napping again, sending him to a far corner past the snickers of generally less innocent classmates. He had not eaten lunch, having lost it to George Parker's ravenous hunger and fourteen-year-old fists. Sydney did not remember the afternoon, as it was lost in anticipation of the final bell. When it had sounded, Sydney carefully left the school yard. He found his kicking rock where he had left it that morning on the roadside. Now he would go home, retire to the same old video games, and hope that his mother was not waiting to pounce on his inactivity. It was a bleak October afternoon, and Sydney was glad for it, because it provided a proper atmosphere for his gray soul.

Sydney was older than his twelve years belied, and he hated that truth, for it marred his entire day, every day. He was trapped in a special prison that allowed him no freedom, no protection from harm. His childhood was an albatross that he bore with grim acceptance. It would end one day, he knew, as it had uncounted times before. But each ending was forgotten as soon as it came, and Sydney was never quite sure a new one would arrive. He hoped, though, hoped with stiff lip and ear bent to any nuance of change in his niche. But nothing changed. All was the same as it was when he was eleven. Not even time changed. Oh, it passed, he knew, and his pants did grow shorter, but all was still the same.

His small Pennsylvania village was still as old, still as grey. His father, his loving, almighty father, was still just as dead, and his mother still as angry. The hill leading to his unpainted house was still as steep as ever, still as long. Perhaps longer, he thought with a sigh, giving the rock a firm kick.

Sydney was small, perhaps five inches shorter than the average height for his age. He dressed impeccably, and not one of his platinum blond hairs was out of place. His green eyes hid securely behind thick wire-rimmed glasses, though he knew he could live as easily without spectacles. His mother, who he rarely saw in the morning, cared even less about his appearance than she did her own. Everything, including his carefully knotted necktie, was Sydney's doing. It set him apart from the children. It reminded him and them that he did not belong. He ignored their children's vicious honesty about his attire, and did not tell them his opinion of their torn knees and gnarled hair. Sydney did not belong, nor did he wish to. He only waited.

Sydney's shoes were not perfect. They were scuffed, worn, old. Like nothing else Sydney used his shoes. Rubber soled, they dutifully and comfortably carried him where he wanted to go, with no complaint, no pain. They were his father's shoes, pulled from the ten cent box at the garage sale his mother held days after the accident. Sydney cherished his shoes.

He loved them almost as much as he did change; at least he thought he did. They were always with him, and easy to fondle. But change was elusive, perhaps absent, and easily forgotten. He caught up to the rock and contemplated it for a moment as it sat still on the dirt. He kicked it softly, allowing it to move only inches. Then he swung his leg with vengeance, and the rock flew through the air, rolling several more feet after landing. Again it stopped, and Sydney frowned. He continued walking to the rock at the same pace, but his gait stiffened as he prepared to send the rock into infinity. He swung his tiny leg and kicked.

The rock did not land. For the first time Sydney lifted his bowed head, to discover the rock's new resting place. Discover it he did, and gasped at what had become of his kicking rock.

It sat in the great palm of a man. Sydney followed the lined palm up a purple sleeve, over a massive shoulder to a dark, smiling visage. Framed in black hair, the man's face was gentle, pleasant, compelling Sydney to feel at ease. The sky blue eyes looked down at Sydney, though they did not smile as the thick lips did. Rather, they absorbed, or held back; Sydney was not sure. He was not able to fathom the depths of those eyes.

It was only then that Sydney noticed the steed that the man was mounted upon. A great silver horse, it stood patiently beneath its master, regarding Sydney with liquid complacence. Though normally fearful of horses, Sydney now felt no need to step back. The man spoke, gently. His soft tones surprised Sydney, as hard speech was the norm in his experience.

"Well kicked, Sydney." His lips hardly moved.

"Thank you," Sydney answered, having sensed no irony. He also did not question the man's knowledge of his name, but felt an urge to question.

"Who are you?" he asked.

"You can call me Merrick, Sydney."

"Why?"

"My other title would only confuse you." Sydney took no offense at this. He had forgotten what offense was.

"Why did you catch my rock, Merrick?" he asked.

"You kicked it to me, didn't you?"

"I did?" The steed grunted and fidgeted a hind leg. The man continued to smile.

"Sydney," Merrick said, "Would you like to ride with me?"

Sydney answered by taking Merrick's offered hand. He was hoisted onto the horse and joined Merrick in the saddle that accommodated both riders. Sydney had ridden before the accident, and knew that he should have been uncomfortable. The saddle should have fit only Merrick, but was made with enough extra leather to hold a passenger of his size. Sydney did not wonder at this. Merrick tapped the steed and it moved, leaving the road at an easy trot.

They pushed into the thick woods that lined the road, passing through the underbrush without a sound. Sydney wrapped his arms around Merrick's waist, merrily clinging to the dark rider, almost shameless in his lack of fear. In time they emerged from the forest, cantering onto a white beach that disappeared in either direction. In front of them was a blue expanse of ocean.

The air was clean and salty. Sydney felt none of the surprise that he should have, and still no fear; as if in a dream. He only relaxed, enjoying the wind in his face as the horse's powerful muscles carried them along the gentle surf. Each stride brought a tremor of joy to Sydney. He had never felt sensation like this before, or at least could remember none. He became lost in the horse's movement, digesting every muscle flex, every breath of the awesome power that transported them. For a moment Sydney wondered where he was being transported to, but dismissed the thought shortly. There was no sense in thinking, he knew. For once the present was not identical with the past and future, and he would live it as he never had before.

The man Merrick was silent at the reins, occasionally turning his head slightly as if to check that his charge was still with him. In time he pulled back and the steed stopped, standing patiently in ankle deep surf. Merrick nudged the horse to dry sand and motioned for Sydney to get off. Sydney bounded from the saddle, anxious for the rest of his adventure to begin.

"What now?" Sydney asked.

"Why Sydney," the man said, "You are slower to become aware this time. I've left you in your time too long, I think."

"Not true, dear Merrick," Sydney said, enjoying the sound of his adult voice, "It takes only as long as it takes me to look myself over." He flexed his muscular arms a few times, as if to become reacquainted with them. Sydney was himself again, standing taller now than Merrick's steed, dressed in black breeches and tunic. At his side swung a saber. A peaked silver helmet concealed his fine blond hair. He felt his new attire with curiosity, saying,

"What, Merrick, must I travel *back* again? Why not ahead, for a change?"

"Sydney, you know the choice is not ours."

"True, but I dislike the past; one must be so careful with it."

"This is a simple job this time, Sydney. If I had the courage I would have done it myself."

"Of course we know that you have no courage, Merrick. That's why I get dragged off on these adventures so often. Now, tell me where we are, and what exactly it is I have to do."

"You're on an island in the Caribbean that hasn't been named yet. In fact, it has only recently been discovered by European man. Unfortunately, it may be doomed to be lost again, along with the expedition that found it."

"Columbus?"

"Right. It seems he has come down with a virus that threatens his life. His crew will not be able to return without him. His benefactors, along with the rest of Europe, will continue to assume that the world is flat."

274 Subspaces

"So?" Sydney smiled a thin-lipped smile, "What does it matter? Men are generally not stupid for too long. One will follow Columbus and the New World will be discovered. We know Columbus wasn't first himself. He was official, that's all." Sydney waved his new sword through the air. It was comfortable, easy to swing, though he dared not use it. The men of these times would slice an amateur like him to ribbons, given the chance.

"That's right, Sydney. Columbus himself doesn't matter, but what he begins does. Spain must have its golden age. The balance of power must shift properly or else history will never be able to spawn us."

"Won't Spain still become powerful?"

"Not after Portugal discovers and claims the New World. The whole hemisphere, in fact, and with sole access to its riches to defend it. England will never colonize. Ultimately Portugal will lose its grip on its colonies, but there will be no United States; just a vast rabble of small countries in endless conflict and upheaval. The inevitable Twentieth Century world wars will not be the same; especially without a United States there to end them. Progress will suffer on many levels. Man will not have matured enough for Einstein's universe, and a world of tiny nations will destroy itself for lack of Superpowers to maintain peace."

"All because of a dying madman who had an insane dream of a round world," Sydney whistled, "You know, I'm in awe once more at how much we two matter. Every time we do one of these little things it saves the world. Where would we be without us?"

Merrick laughed, "Don't get too proud, Sydney. If it wasn't us, it would be someone else. We are here, aren't we? So *someone* must have saved Columbus." Sydney ignored this, hoping that Merrick would drop it. The man did this insight game every time, and it tired Sydney. He was sorry to have started the man. Merrick read him, and continued, "Sorry Sydney, I won't bother you this time."

"Good," Sydney smiled, "But you can bother me with some instructions."

"It's all quite simple," Merrick said, tossing Sydney a small pouch, "You need only to sneak unseen to Columbus's bed and give him a shot of what's in the bag. It's an antibiotic that should sustain his health for a few more voyages."

"That's all, huh? What about the crew that's surrounding him?"

"Make damn sure that they don't see you."

"Right. Which way is it, then?"

"North along the beach, you can't miss the camp. Good luck, Sydney. I'll be back if you're successful. If you're not, well, you'll never know, will you?" Merrick turned his horse and trotted back into the forest.

"Of course I will!" Sydney shouted after him. He sighed and began walking north, wishing that Merrick had at least left him with a bike. It was a short trek, though, as he saw campfires in a few minutes. He moved into the forest.

The camp was crowded with men and the women they had taken with them to ease the journey's passage. All were hunched close to the fires, fearful of the strange lands around them. Sydney did not need to wonder why they were on shore.. He understood that well: too much time in a small, confined place made one wish to be anywhere else. He waited until nightfall, waited until the last of the guards slept, then moved in to rescue history.

It was not difficult to find Columbus's tent. Made of tattered sailcloth, it was the largest lean-to, surrounded by the rest for protection. A sign of loyalty, Sydney thought, usually in this time sick men were left alone for fear of infecting the rest. Inside, Columbus lay in a featherbed, gently washed in candlelight. A woman still knelt over him. Before thinking about it, Sydney moved forward and hit her from behind, hard. She gasped and crumpled to the ground. Columbus was asleep, gratefully. Sydney never did like hitting dying men.

He reached into his pouch for the hypodermic, but froze on hearing a slight rustle behind him. He pulled out his sword and turned, trying to look fearsome enough to avoid a fight. The man at the door held no weapon, and was dressed strangely. The cut of his clothes was right for the time, but the materials were subtly different. Sydney's eyes closed to suspicious slits.

"Who are you?" They both asked at once. They also both recognized the language they shared, and gazed at each other in a silent moment of astonishment.

"Wait till Merrick hears about this," Sydney whispered, almost to himself.

"Merrick?" The tall, grey man said, "Then you must be Sydney."

"You know me?"

"Of course I know you, sir. I was once a student of Sir Merrick's."

"Merrick teaches nothing."

"But he will, after he discovers a need to prolong the Timekeepers."

Sydney would have liked to continue the conversation, but the woman was waking, and he did not want to hit her again. He excused himself for a moment to administer the needle. The gray one did not interfere. Indeed, he seemed to revel in watching, as though he were witnessing his hero, or history itself, at work. They left as soon as the hypo was drained. Once back on the secluded beach, Sydney asked why the gray one was there.

"My people grew unsure of Merrick. The man was very old, and few trusted his ability to read history any more. I see now we should have trusted him."

"Will there be more after you?"

"I wouldn't doubt it, there..." The man never finished his sentence, as he faded away before another word could be spoken. They must have discovered a more efficient mode of transport, Sydney thought, guessing that the return trip happened automatically, after history had been corrected. Nice, he thought.

Sydney continued down the beach to the place where he had left Merrick. He was still there, still mounted, with palpable pride breathing from him. Sydney told him about the gray man.

"Nonsense, Sydney. I will never have need to teach my trade to another. Time may only be traveled once, lest things get to confused, and far too crowded." Both laughed, but Sydney saw that he had struck a nerve in his guide. Perhaps he had learned something he should not have.

"Will this `overcrowding' make me less available for other journeys?" he asked.

"Perhaps," Merrick said, his blue eyes clouded.

"I hate childhood," Sydney sighed.

No more words were spoken. Sydney climbed onto the tailored saddle and wrapped his again tiny arms around Merrick once more. They passed through the thick woods, the great horse silently retracing its steps. Sydney wondered why the man had taken him through the woods at all, since they seemed to have gone nowhere at all.

The horse stopped at the road again, and the man helped Sydney off.

"Thank you, Mr. Merrick," Sydney piped, "But I had wished we could have ridden longer."

"That ride was long enough, Sydney, I assure you," Merrick said. A tear welled in the man's eye. Sydney looked down, ashamed at himself for making the man unhappy.

"Good-bye, Son" Merrick said, spinning the steed in a tight half circle.

"Good-bye Mr. Merrick," Sydney mumbled, not understanding what had been said. The rock landed a few feet in front of him.

Sydney trudged home, kicking his special stone in front of him. It had been a lousy day and he was hungry. He hoped his mother wasn't up yet, so he could watch his cartoons in peace. He let his father's silver sneakers carry him silently home.

The Persistence of Dreams

The Darkness was complete. She was more lost than scared, not sure where she was, or how she could escape. Why escape was necessary, she had no clue. She pried her naked body from the sheet of ice she lay on, feeling the skin on her back rip like paper as she sat up. She did not care; getting out of bed was more important than a little skin. She knew that. She swung her legs over the edge of the bed, relieved that her stressed limbs moved freely. She let her feet fall into the total darkness until they found a surface. She shifted her weight onto cold bare soles, and stood. She extended her arms, hoping to feel her way to safety. Her fingers were level with her waist when they struck hardness. The hardness responded to her touch by breaking the icy silence with a sharp clap of thunder. She cried out as her hand shattered the pane of black glass.

Silver moonlight stabbed through missing shards into the empty room, illuminating the bare floorboards that meekly supported her ivory toes. Nothing else was revealed in the dim light that filtered through jagged glass. She did not care. She was not interested in looking around, only in leaving. She eased her feet over the broken glass that glistened white on the rough wide planks while gingerly avoiding splinters on the loose floorboards. The moon's shattered reflection was her only light. She edged up to the broken pane, felt its jagged hardness, found the frame to which it was mounted. Puzzled, she continued to grope until she was behind the broken mirror that stood, framed in an antique rosewood easel, in the center of her bedroom. When she realized that the mirror was not a window to freedom, the welcome moonlight faded. She cursed herself for solving the mystery, stood still in the total darkness, alone, and waited.

The bedroom was damp. Cold grabbed at her. She felt icy fingers clutch at her, squeezing fear from her frail limbs. She could not even attempt to seek passage from the dark, whose blackness was so complete she could not know in which direction she was searching. She longed to escape the nightmare, to return to the softness of warm satin sheets. The thought brought a smile to her face. Her slightly lightened heart sparked a glow of hope in the distance. A real spark.

In the corner appeared a wire-thin shaft of white light. It was a tiny ray, barely thick enough to be seen, but so anathema to the darkness around her that it was all she saw. It invaded through a pinprick in the wall, near the floor. Fresh morning sunlight filtered through the fist-sized, and rapidly growing, hole. It beckoned, enticing her with the promise of warmth, security. The light streamed, dust filled, through the cracks of a battered, ancient, and quite closed wooden door. The glow energized her soul, prompting her to urge her reluctant limbs toward it. She crossed the frozen chamber in one delighted step. She was glad she did. The wooden door had become obese flesh, and its pulpy mass was beginning to block out the light. She tried the knob, and changed her mind about the exit when the knob tried her. She wanted to recoil, but her legs only fell forward, wrapping around the roaming knob. It shrieked like a girl when it was crushed messily between her thighs. She tumbled feet first through the closed squishy door, but her legs and thin body flowed through it, sensing no contact with the pulsating fat. She slid outside, into the blinding glare of clear blue-skied daylight. She sank ankle deep into soft, caressing red grass. Golden trees with white leaves shaped like giant's hands shaded her from the oval sun. The dirt path led her through a grove of singing pines. The tall trees were already in the third verse of "Que Sera, Sera," so she was too late to lend her own voice to the tune (she only knew the first two verses). She skipped past enchanted squirrels serving tea to giant mosquitoes, and tattered beggars dancing at bonfires. She nodded slyly to a baby shrouded in snakes. She loped through pink pastures, and finally reached the beach.

She heard the ocean breaking violently on massive boulders, but the waves that lapped the vast expanse of yellow sand were tiny. She suppressed anger at always missing the good waves. She felt joy, though, just to be near the sea again. She ached to taste its salt. She stood on the boardwalk, charmed by the distant chords of a calliope's cheerful chatter. A paper railing at her knees prevented her leap to the cherished sand. Beside her a little girl played.

The pony-tailed little blond was carefully removing the arms from her special dolly. When the child tore into the doll's chest with her shark-toothed jaws, crimson plastic blood spurted from the cloth wound. The attack left a messy stain on the weathered boardwalk. She was amazed at the amount of plastic blood that one small dolly could contain, but did admire the way it spread in a perfect circle away from the girl with the nasty visage. Easily turning from the child, she faced a cotton candy vendor laboring at his fibrous craft. The old Italian man in a black striped shirt and no pants noticed her. He refrained from belting out another verse of "Que Sera, Sera" to hand her a tuft of rich pink fluff. As the vendor cackled, she staggered under the sudden burden of the heavy treat. She strained for a moment, still interested in at least one bite of the pink fluffy stuff, but the candy was too heavy. When she stumbled hard against the paper railing, she lost her grip on the cardboard baton topped with a cloud of pink sugar. She dropped the load over the rail, onto the beach.

Citing her need to retrieve the candy, she easily scaled the sturdy rail, and soared from the dizzying heights of the granite precipice to the sand below in just a few backstrokes. She landed on her bare feet, again lusting after the ocean's salty wetness. The beach looked like perfectly stretched golden sable. It tickled her feet for the first few steps. Then it changed. She sensed that change on her fourth step, when the sand grew cold, scaly, and slightly green. She ignored it. Her eyes and mind were focused on the blessed ocean that she knew hid behind the next dune, and she had no interest in the threats of her local surroundings. She was actually surprised when the beach reached up with sandy talons to pull her under and deny her access to the distant crashing surf.

The beach's tenacious grip was hot. Her slender legs felt like burning sacks of cement had been wrapped around them, painfully stalling her progression toward the water. She fought the monster, striking boldly with clenched fists, but the struggle only managed to submerge her hands into angry sand. She continued her struggle, despairing only when her eyes sank below the surface. She waited for loose granules' invasion into her nose and throat, suffocating her. They never attacked. Instead, she breathed normally, though she stood, buried to the top of her head, in her closed grave. The sand had loosened its grip. It was trying to comfort her. She drew increased terror from its warm embrace. Then she suddenly calmed herself, resigned to the absurdity of the moment. She sighed and waited peacefully for the strand to digest her.

She imagined her long platinum hair blowing in the wind on the beach above her. The world would see strange soft grass, and not understand the nature of its roots. She smiled at her fate as a beach potato. Her pleasure faded when a shadow fell over the image of her hair, and she pictured a great hand wrapping itself around her tussled locks. The massive fist tightened, and yanked. She braced herself for pain, but was not prepared for the trip. She was shocked when the painless tug plucked her from the sand in a cloud of dust. She recovered and smiled again. The hand belonged to the good guys.

She swung by her locks in the air for a moment, enjoying the breeze that cooled her crotch. Then she felt the tension on her hair ease, and she settled to the soft sand, facing away from her rescuer. Curious, she turned. The powerful chest of a beautiful man was all she saw at first. She stepped back, taking in the glory of her tall rescuer. He smiled down at her amicably, his clear blue eyes strangely familiar. The rest of him was foreign, though. Greek, maybe. She did not care. He had pulled her from the sand, and would have saved her life if indeed she could have died. That deserved a reward. She moved close to him, and reached her arms up and around his thick neck. She stretched to kiss him, balancing on her big toes. As hers approached, his lips separated. Big time. They became two thin lines of mottled gray skin that bordered two uneven rows of very large, very pointed teeth. She would have rolled her eyes at the forked tongue darting between them if her instant fear of being eaten wasn't already wrestling with her instant anger at such a base betrayal for control of her feelings. Fear won.

She gasped inaudibly, and tried to recoil. Though she felt her body spring back at least a yard instantly, her lips were still closing on the evil mouth. She sighed with despair as the violent face filled her vision, blocking out the blue sky and everything else. When her green eyes nearly touched his torn, red eyes, she felt scaly hands close on her neck. Those hands were enormously strong, but still gentle -- a cold vice carefully not choking, just controlling. When the beast's cold leather lips finally pressed against hers, she felt the blood leave her face, replaced by ice. She shook violently and tried in vain to force out a scream that was trapped in her throat. Then he kissed her, and something changed. His kiss became their kiss. Warmth returned to her mouth. She calmed down, the edges of her world faded from crimson to soft pink. The embrace did not disgust her. She was relieved to discover that she did not hate the creature. They kissed again. The scaled forked tongue excited her, moved her. Perhaps, she thought smugly, she could be happy with this monster.

A distant tolling put fear into the broken eyes of her dead lover. He dropped her, returning to his original pale human form as he scampered away. He was waving from the hard black line of the distant horizon before she realized that his exit had left her floating in the air over the ocean, which roiled a hundred feet below her nicely painted toes. Her realization condemned her to a speedy plunge to the gray water. On the way down she wondered what she ever saw in the damned ocean, anyway. When she landed with a thud, in a seated position, legs splayed before her, on the water, she remembered. She laughed, her heart suddenly giddy. She did not need to swim! She stretched out on the warm, slightly resistant and totally luxurious surface, content. When she rolled over in the soft comfort, she saw the naked back of a man who floated nearby. His raised left arm was reaching above his head, trying to touch the top of a distant bell buoy that bobbed in the waves. The oddly familiar intrusive clang of its bell infuriated her. After the third or fourth try the man with very little muscle definition but quite hairy arms finally landed a spread palm on top of the buoy, sinking it and silencing its alarm. Wait a minute, she thought, its alarm?

She realized her world. The ocean turned to blue satin sheets, the man became Sam, her husband of 20 years, and the buoy, the trigger of it all, became the most dreaded appliance in her home: the alarm clock. Existence was reintroduced. She began a stretch, ending it with a friendly slap on her husband's bare ass.

"Sam, you'd never believe the dream I just had," She said as she rubbed the sleep from her eyes, pushing a strand of sweaty blond hair away from them, "It scared the hell out of me."

"Try me," Sam said, rolling over to face her. He wound up firmly against her, and caused her to fall into a trough with him. The warmth was nice, but she found that the pressure from the waterbed to push Sam against her disconcerting. Normally their connected flesh in the gently buffeting surf of the bed was just fine, but she felt a sudden sweaty anxiety about their latest meeting. She wedged her arm between their naked bodies, trying to appear as nonchalant as possible.

"Um, let me think," she said, and relaxed for a moment, and attempted to remember what had so recently been the most important moments of her life. She shut her eyes, saw only darkness, and whipped them back open again. Though she was inexplicably startled by the darkness, the images that had so recently bedeviled her entire universe were gone. She shook her head, inadvertently rubbing his oily nose with hers. Yuck, she thought behind a warm smile.

"No use," she said at last, "It's gone now. But I tell you, it was really something. Oh well, never mind. It mustn't have been important enough to remember. Oh shit, look at the time. We've got to get to work." She started to roll out of the trough, relieved at the call to duty. This is all so odd, she thought, bed is usually the last place in the world I ever want to leave.

"I was hoping you wouldn't notice," Sam smiled, rubbing her breast. She absently pushed his hand away. He sighed and got up, strolling naked into the bathroom. She watched him leave, admiring his build. She did that every morning, but this time she held a certain fascination with his upper torso that she could not explain. She yawned and studied the ceiling, content once more to lie in bed. She feinted another effort to remember her dream in order to stay in bed another minute before she finally sat up and exerted the extra effort needed daily to swing her bare legs over the high rail of the bed. She lamented the abandonment of her old mattress and box spring. She did not like the waterbed very much anymore. Well, she thought, it was my idea. She cursed her libido, then contemplated what she would have to face at the office that day while she summoned the strength to stand.

After the last stall tactic expired she stood, feeling her feet touch the cold wooden floor. They touched something else as well. A shard of glass.

She swore at the sharp pain and lifted her foot in the air to examine the wound and the errant sliver. The sliver was black.

Like a curtain had suddenly risen before her, she remembered. Her heart went into overdrive. She screamed and scrabbled for the bed. As her fingers touched warm satin sheets the floor became fluid and she fell into darkness; smothered in frigid, liquid wood.

Also by Peter A. Luber:

Works of Fiction:

Oneironauticus

ISBN: 978-0-6151-8290-2

Party Line

ISBN: 978-0-578-03593-2

**Simply Pay Attention
2nd Edition**

ISBN: 978-0-692-54410-5

Published by Sageous

www.ingramcontent.com/pod-product-compliance
Lightning Source LLC
Chambersburg PA
CBHW031002260626
47169CB00002B/657